P9-AQH-028

THE SWAN VILLA

translated from the German by
L E I L A V E N N E W I T Z

THE SWAN VILLA

VILLA

a novel by

MARTIN WALSER

HOLT, RINEHART AND WINSTON   NEW YORK

Library of Congress Cataloging in Publication Data
Walser, Martin, 1927–
The Swan Villa.
Translation of: Das Schwanenhaus.
I. Title.
PT2685.A48S2713   1982   833'.914   81-13410
AACR2
ISBN: 0-03-059372-7

First American Edition

Designer: Joy Chu
Printed in the United States of America
1   2   3   4   5   6   7   8   9   10

ISBN 0-03-059372-7

TRANSLATOR'S ACKNOWLEDGMENT

To my husband William—my gratitude for his share in the work of translating this book

Leila Vennewitz

THE SWAN VILLA

O N E

When Gottlieb Zürn awoke he felt as if he were standing on his head. During the night his head seemed to have become heavier and his body lighter. As long as his head lay with this weight on the pillow there was no prospect of getting onto his feet again. He opened his eyes. He wasn't standing on his head. As soon as he let his eyelids fall, he felt as if he were standing on his head again.

Suddenly he was sitting on the edge of the bed, his feet far below him on the floor. The fear of never being able to get up again had helped him. For yet another day, the threat of being canceled was banished. Gottlieb Zürn has been canceled! Once again, with the aid of these terrifying words, he had made it. School has been canceled, the performance has been canceled. Gottlieb Zürn has not been canceled. This was his magic formula. The push with which he had jerked himself upright was still in effect. By the time Anna's footsteps were approaching the bedroom with increasing firmness, he was already on his feet. Although not a second behind schedule, he would have been embarrassed for her to find him still in bed or sitting on the bed. He didn't want her to stand by the bed wearing the same expression as his mother had when, because he had failed to react to her calls, she suddenly appeared at his bedside—an expression that told him the family was now facing extinction due to a kind of self-inflicted paralysis.

As soon as Anna opened the door he moved as easily as anyone else. But Anna had not come to fetch him. Her expression showed that she had been looking for something for quite a while and was no longer capable of looking quietly in place after place to see if it was there. On her stormy path she kept jerking her head a shade too late in the appropriate direction. After flinging items of underwear about, she rushed out of the room: she was looking for the car key, she said, the spare key wasn't in its proper place either. And during the night Regina had thrown up several times. And again had had a fever of 104. She had notified Dr. Freisleben, and he had asked for a specimen of Regina's urine. What with the antibiotics given to Regina by Dr. Sixt, he thought a relapse was unlikely. He said he would get in touch again with Dr. Sixt.

After Anna had driven off he went across to Regina. Her face was gray, almost mauve. Around her mouth a livid, oval area. Her lips twitched and trembled. Inevitably, if he showed that he was impressed, she would multiply her illness by how impressed he looked. So he restrained himself. Since he showed so little concern, she felt obliged to groan distinctly. As soon as he stroked her, her tone became more passive: unalloyed suffering. Everything she had endured in his absence during the night he was now supposed to acknowledge and appreciate. He stroked her more firmly. That triggered the desired low-pitched weeping. This weeping had almost a narrative melody. Downstairs the telephone rang. She cast her eyes upward, looked resignedly at the ceiling: he had her permission to leave. Most likely a wrong number. No one ever phoned him at eight in the morning. On a Saturday perhaps, when the advertisements appeared, but not on a Wednesday, when he hadn't even handed them in yet. Ten o'clock deadline!

"Rosa, what is it?" he exclaimed. "Nothing special," she said. "I'll be there on Friday." Her voice sounded as if she were trying hard to make it sound bright. She didn't want to alarm him. But, he reasoned, she sanctions his noticing that her voice doesn't sound all that bright this morning. She had just come back from a party, she said, and was now going to bed, later she'd have to go to the university, for a test, so she'd thought it would be all right for once to call her parents at this godforsaken hour.

Was anything wrong?

Why should anything be wrong? That sounded almost annoyed or tragic or cross or reproachful or sarcastic or . . .

So they would be looking forward to Friday—no, wait a minute, he'd be in Stuttgart Friday and Saturday, but he'd be back Saturday evening. As he hung up he heard the overhead garage door rattling and creaking. Anna lugged in two shopping bags and a basket full of groceries. He offered to help put them away. She refused, predictably, remarking that if he did she would never find anything again. The fact that Rosa had phoned at this hour of the day alarmed her too. His fault. He had described the call as being cause for concern. Regina called as piteously as possible for her mother. Anna ran upstairs. He went outside. He signaled to Armin to stay put, no game today. Else lay almost on her back on the Ping-Pong table, flexing and stretching and suddenly rolling herself up in a lightning movement as if to see whether she had caught the gold of the morning sun between her paws. As he passed he thrust his hand into the downy fur of her stomach; she instantly captured it and, respecting the rules, instantly released it again.

He saw that the summer guests had not yet gone down to the lake and that the lakeside path was still deserted, so he went down to the water and swam his medium distance. The water would have been warm enough for his maximum distance, but he lacked the peace of mind to do forty or fifty minutes of steady strokes. Until, with the exclusive listing in his pocket, he had closed the gate of the Leistle villa in Stuttgart behind him, he could only feign peace of mind, and even that required all his willpower.

Julia's breakfast dishes were still on the patio table. There was no sign of Magda's having been there. Hardly had he sat down when he heard Mrs. Schneider calling: "Ellen, tell Daddy please to bring my sunglasses too!" He jumped up and was inside the house before the family from Stuttgart, who had rented the upstairs vacation apartment, appeared around the juniper branches that stuck out untidily at the corner of the house. He didn't yet feel up to talking to strangers. Once they had reached the beach chairs down by the lake and couldn't see into the recessed part of the patio, he went out onto it again.

If only he could speed up the time till Saturday! As always, he would without a moment's thought have given away days and weeks of his life so as to spare himself this drawn-out anticipation of the crucial hour. Hadn't his life thus far consisted mainly of such anticipation? His life was almost too much of a cliff-hanger. Perhaps that was why, since he had become an independent real estate agent, he had lost the urge to gamble at the casino. While he had still been an employee of Dr. Enderle's it had looked as if his passion for roulette might become dangerous. Anna didn't have the slightest desire to gamble, but in the days when he had annual passes for the casinos in Lindau and Constance she had always gone with him. Now he was baffled by his lack of shame in front of her. Always the same old promises, excuses, justifications, remorse, breakdowns.

Anna came downstairs. Regina had at last fallen asleep. Where was the car key, he wanted to know. Anna replied that she had given Regina a Gelonida at eleven, a Gelonida at two, a Valium at three, a Gelonida at six. The main thing was for Regina to get some rest. Maybe they should return entirely to Dr. Sixt? It was really a disgrace that Dr. Cornelius should have lost all interest in Regina since her mother had joined a health plan and she was no longer a private patient. She jumped up from the breakfast table, telephoned Dr. Sixt, and forced him to listen to Regina's condition after nine weeks of antibiotics. From Anna's reactions it was obvious that Dr. Sixt was trying to keep the conversation brief. When she hung up, she was calmer. Dr. Sixt had promised to look in on Regina today. He had also tried to get out of it, she said.

She cleared away the breakfast things. Gottlieb was about to help her but felt at once that, if he removed any dishes, he would be merely pretending to help her; he really didn't feel like it, but at least it would save her a few trips between kitchen and patio—so get busy now. She had already taken everything away. Now he could cut a shred of skin from the tip of his finger as a penance—on crossing the hall into his office he noticed a pair of scissors—but it wouldn't do her much good either. However, schoolboy solutions appealed to him.

He lowered himself into his obligingly yielding, softly contoured desk chair and unfolded the newspaper. Fortunately, what was happening in the world was more important. Yet his eyes slid over all the news items and reports till they reached the advertisements. These were what he enjoyed reading most. Radio and television programs and classified ads were his favorite reading matter. Even in old newspapers. He had no intention of watching the programs or of buying whatever was advertised. He liked to read this kind of information. And today . . . if Anna weren't so completely obsessed with Regina, he would immediately hurry across to read out to her: *283. Private Auction. RESIDUAL HOUSEHOLD CONTENTS of Bansin villa on Tuesday, September 2, in Mitten, commencing 9 a.m.: 1 antique inlaid wardrobe, 1 dk. floral-painted rustic wardrobe, 1 Louis XVI chest, baroque, Lou. XVI & Emp. chairs & occas. tables, 1 Alpine dk. rustic chest, lge. rd. extend. table w. 6 high-b. chs., curv. ft., 4 rd. & 3 obl. Chippendale-style tables, 52 lots silver & silv.pl. objects incl. ov. dishes, bowls, cndl.sticks, cutlery, finest art nouveau, antique rugs incl. Bokhara, Shirvan, Ferraghan, some cert., 1 oil pntg. (David Teniers 1610-1690) unsign., also oil pntgs., etchings, library, porcelain (Berlin), copper, tab. lamps (art nouveau), gray mink coat & many more unspecified items. Can be viewed Monday, Sept. 1 from 2 to 6 p.m. Agent: Jürgen Kant, authorized appraiser & auctioneer, Kempten.*

He would read this to Anna at lunch. Now he had to type his own Saturday ad. After reading it through he tore it up.

While retyping it he realized there was no way he could change the ad. His colleagues and competitors would grin if once again he sang the praises of the two condominium apartments and the mill property with distillery license and its own generating plant located in the future autobahn zone. Let them. A week later it would be replaced with *Unique opportunity,* or: *Dream villa,* or: *Art nouveau jewel on Lake Constance, 19 rooms, every room with different ceiling. Masterpieces of art nouveau stucco work, hall (25 × 40 feet), mahogany paneling, hall window (art nouveau, stained glass), 2 stories high, Wilhelminian construction quality, orig. seat of President of Deutsche Bank, private marina for 30 boats. 4½ acre park, tennis court, lake frontage 220 feet, serious purchasers only. Exclusive listing Gottlieb Zürn (Enderle Real Estate).*

Provided that Mrs. Leistle was to be persuaded. He could handle her sister, Mrs. Bansin. All one had to do was let her talk. For the past few months he had taken her out once a week. She was delighted to escape for two hours from the high-rise building where her relatives had installed her. On each occasion she had recounted to him whatever version of her fate happened to come to mind. Some things remained constant. They may have been the most important ones. That she had lost seven hundred workers in the German Democratic Republic was something she never forgot. She said: "They took seven hundred workers away from us in East Germany." That was always followed by the sentence: "We never recovered from that." Fortunately, she would say, in 1934 she had had the inspiration: "Let's buy some property on Lake Constance!" Otherwise they wouldn't have had anything left after 1945. Needless to say, coming as she did on her father's side from the Danneckers, the Württemberg family of artists, she could only consider a property of distinction. She had known of the bank president's villa before ever coming to Lake Constance. In Dresden people had talked about this villa because the bank president had invited artists from Dresden-Hellerau and Darmstadt to Lake Constance to decorate his home. And now they were taking this away from her. Those ignoramuses. *Ignoramuses*, a term she always used specifically as if they represented a tribe with unmistakable characteristics. To think that her dear boy Eberhard hadn't prevented it, not only that but had brought it about, was responsible for it! True enough, seven hundred workers had been taken away from them in East Germany, but that had happened to other people too, it's always possible to start again, that's her opinion, one can alway start again. After all, he, Mr. Zürn, was the best example. Hadn't he been at the same school, in the same class even, as her dear boy Eberhard, and now where was her dear Eberhard and where was Mr. Zürn? Hadn't the dear boy always brought home excellent reports? Even Mr. Zürn's couldn't have been much better. And now, what was her dear boy doing? An evangelist preacher! Holding up religious tracts as he stood smiling on street corners in Lindau, Wangen, and Ravensburg. If only he had chosen some other area for his discreditable activity. If he had had any decency at all, he would have joined the Foreign Legion, that he would! "Ah me, Mr. Zürn, your mother was better off than I am." While still alive she was privileged to see Dr. Enderle make her boy his partner and successor. Such a cultured person, that Dr. Enderle, a friend of Karl Erb's, no less. Quite frankly, the fact that Dr. Enderle had accepted him, what was it she wanted to say now . . . oh yes, in spite of his Swabian name Dr. Enderle was from the Rhineland, he may well have been the one who discovered Lake Constance for Rhinelanders, but Dr. Enderle hadn't been happy either, an agent such as you don't find anymore, a gentleman, a bon vivant in fact, and not an ignoramus, she had always hoped her dear Eberhard . . . had Mr. Zürn ever run into him? What did he think about it, Jehovah's Witnesses, perhaps there really was a life after death, we must all leave this world much too quickly, wasn't it possible that her dear boy might be on the right track in the end? When all was said and done, she and Mr. Zürn, and even Dr. Enderle, had only been after money while her dear Eberhard was standing on the corner waving religious pamphlets, such a disgrace. In fact dear Eberhard and his wife—who, by the way, had left him and the children and run off with a Berlin speculator, the owner of forty buildings in Berlin and living now in the Caribbean, no one can do better than that, leave all these ignoramuses here behind, her daughter-in-law had been quicker than her to size up the dear boy, but they had both tried to lecture her because in her desperation she had simply *had* to go to the casino, after all if a lady isn't in a position to do that anymore, then, Mr. Zürn, the ignoramuses have triumphed, then she, Mrs. Beatrice Bansin, was ready to give up. . . .

He could have coped with the Bansins, even though Mrs. Bansin disinherited his schoolmate Eberhard, as far as she could, and had him declared legally incompetent. Eberhard, the very soul of good nature, would have given his schoolmate the exclusive listing without hesitation. So would his mother. But when she was about to sign it turned out that she too had been declared incompetent. From the depths of the endless family ramifications had come the decision: legally incompetent, off to the old people's home in Maierhöfen. Now he had to deal with Mrs. Leistle, the youngest sister. But by this time he had such a head start on his competitors that it didn't seem feasible now for Mrs. Leistle to prefer someone else. He had copied plans, designed the prospectus, taken pictures. None of his competitors could come up with a sparkling ad and four-page draft for a prospectus that was almost ready for the printer, plus an advertising campaign.

If he gets this listing, Anna, then even his passion for gambling will have paid off. Mrs. Bansin fondly remembered the beginner and how she used to push and pick up and push her piles of chips past him.

The telephone startled him. It was Mrs. Reinhold. "Yes!" he said, in the brightest, highest tone possible. To produce this rising ye-es he had to sit up straight very quickly. He knew that, if he merely picked up the receiver and said his name, his voice gave people an impression that he didn't altogether like. Mrs. Reinhold exclaimed into the phone—proving to him that he had managed to bring off the bright tone: "You seem to be in fine fettle, Mr. Zürn." "Yes," he exclaimed in the same tone, "a bit too fine, I must admit." She congratulated him. And she knew how he must feel—after all, the most important part of a sense of well-being was that one had oneself to thank for it. "And you know, Mr. Zürn, I really only wanted to give you a tip, but now it seems a bit cheap to discuss matters over the phone, terrible!" She was having some people over tomorrow evening, if he cared to come she would be delighted, then she could tell him about it in person. It concerned the Bansin villa. Perhaps her tip might be of interest to him.

He ran across to Anna, calling out that the exclusive listing for the Swan Villa was now practically in his pocket. It did mean, though, that he'd have to go to the Reinholds' tomorrow evening. He tried to gloss over the fact that Mrs. Reinhold had quite clearly invited him without Anna; he felt that by doing so he had in fact pointed it out. Anna was unsuspecting. She held Mrs. Reinhold in great esteem. Full of admiration, she reported each success the three Reinhold youngsters achieved in school or on the playing field. The oldest Reinhold girl was the top student in Magda's class. Whenever Mrs. Reinhold received a glowing review in the newspaper for her singing, Anna would enthusiastically read out the paeans of praise for the lovely Mrs. Reinhold and her lovely voice. As far as Mrs. Reinhold was concerned, Anna probably didn't exist. The fact that Anna nevertheless always spoke of Mrs. Reinhold with admiration meant, in Gottlieb's eyes, that Anna was superior to Mrs. Reinhold, although in a way that only he would ever perceive. Anna had but one reservation: she didn't like the way Mrs. Reinhold treated her husband. It was really pitiful, she would say, Mrs. Reinhold almost always turned up without him. More often than in real life, her husband was to be seen in the papers in the company of state secretaries from Bonn or Stuttgart or NASA people from Houston, Texas, or business partners from Norwalk, Connecticut, demonstrating the latest developments in his plant (which was part-owned by the Connecticut Americans) for the upcoming satellites. For a time, when the Reinholds had moved here, into the house he had obtained for them, Gottlieb Zürn had been Mrs. Reinhold's tennis partner. For years she had accepted only men as her partners. It was only since she had become friendly with a young male sociologist from the University of Constance that she also played with women partners. Because this sociologist was seen to have the free run of the Reinhold household and because people didn't know what to say about it, they said: Mrs. Reinhold is becoming liberated. The house, situated above the town with an unobstructed view to east, south, and west across the lake, had been bought in her name only.

Dr. Terbohm, who wanted a divorce, had given Gottlieb an exclusive listing on the house because Gottlieb had suggested putting it on the market before the divorce went through so that Dr. Terbohm would know what to expect and what he could offer his wife. Gottlieb had done this because he had heard how terribly thrifty the doctor's wife was. Magda, who was a classmate of one of the Terbohm boys, always had new tales to tell of the inordinate thrift practiced by the Terbohm kids under their mother's influence. On a school outing to Burgundy, the boy had collected all the wine dregs in a bottle at the last bistro and taken them home for his mother to use as cooking wine. If the Terbohm kids wanted a snack between meals, they had to pay their mother cash for the sandwich or the orange. The money for this had to be earned by delivering newspapers, washing cars, or vacation jobs. Magda had been full of pity and admiration in telling them about this family. Gottlieb Zürn had been able to give the doctor some highly appropriate advice. The doctor had mentioned that his wife was still afraid she might starve to death one day. She was, he said, the daughter of a Jena professor of philosophy who had wanted to bring up his family to despise all worldly things.

As a result, Gottlieb Zürn had become Mrs. Reinhold's first acquaintance. The house had turned out to be a good investment; now, ten years later, it was worth more than double, so the Reinholds were among those whom he could face with a clear conscience. If only he had a better idea of the Reinhold marriage! Was she betraying her husband all the time or not at all? Beside her, the huge young sociologist with all that beard and hair looked like a fairy-tale character waiting to be turned back into a prince. Her husband appeared helpless and frail beside her.

One day at the tennis court, while they were watching Mrs. Reinhold play, Gottlieb's colleague and competitor Paul Schatz had remarked to Gottlieb: "There's enough of her to make two Wagner singers." Like everything Paul Schatz said, it sounded very plausible but was totally untrue. Yet somehow it was true. Probably it was perfectly true. The connection with Mrs. Leistle almost certainly came through Mr. Reinhold. The Leistles owned a chemical plant between Göppingen and Plochingen. Perhaps Mr. Reinhold had worked for Leistle before going to America. Perhaps he was even related to Mrs. Leistle. In that case Gottlieb already had two direct lines to his object. No, three: his schoolmate Eberhard, Eberhard's mother (Gottlieb's casino crony) and, via Lissi Reinhold, Mr. Reinhold. This time Paul Schatz didn't have a chance. And if Schatz didn't have a chance, who else was a threat? Kaltammer! Kaltammer wasn't half as great a threat as Schatz.

As soon as Gottlieb Zürn had given Anna the most important news, he hurried back to his office. He was elated. He wanted a smoke. But now he only smoked when he drank. And he never had a drink before supper. He had to impress himself with these feats of willpower. For him it was something of a victory when he ran into Paul Schatz somewhere and saw him merrily smoking away. Schatz would drink a whole bottle of schnapps in one evening. Gottlieb Zürn drank only light wine. When he paraded his own feats of willpower before his mind's eye and compared his increasingly discipline-oriented life with the wild, or at any rate less healthy, life of his colleague and competitor, the depressing thought would occur to him that possibly Paul Schatz wasn't in the least affected by this disorderly or wild or unhealthy life. Since Schatz often talked about his parents, everyone knew that they were nearly ninety and lived in Austria close to the Hungarian border because of their desire to remain as close as possible to their original home, Transylvania, and that, with eating and drinking and laughing, they enjoyed life like any bucolic couple. Schatz himself was married for the fourth time. No one ever heard that he was suffering from anything at all. As for himself, at that moment Gottlieb had the feeling that, unless he made an effort to stay upright, he would plunge headlong instantly and vertically. In thinking of himself he felt only weight, heaviness, meanness. Nonsense, he thought, nonsense. And jumped to his feet.

He called out to Anna that he was going into town to place the ad and that he must really get a haircut too. He'd be back in a couple of hours. Anna asked him not to make so much noise as Regina was asleep. He wheeled his bicycle from the garage through the hall because the raising of the garage door could be heard in every room.

Slowly he rode along beside the lake. He wanted to be completely unaware of himself. These moments were always the most pleasant of all. The morning expanded in the heat. The wind unhurriedly counted the leaves. The lake, a field of glittering furrows. Everything green, green-gold, glittering and dazzling. And everything rustling. And nothing seems to matter. Involuntarily he rang the bicycle bell. The tinkling that dissolved even as it sounded awakened a legion of years. The massive arms of the trees under which he was riding evoked an image from his first catechism: Absalom fleeing on horse-back from the father he had rebelled against, riding under just such trees, the high-flying red hair becoming entangled with the massive branches, the horse galloping on, Absalom hanging by his hair and . . . Gottlieb Zürn almost fell off his bike because the asphalt had been lifted by the tree roots into hard corrugations.

As he handed the ad to Mrs. Sonntag he felt embarrassed. Not much doing these days, he wanted to say, but he couldn't get it out. She might have just accepted Paul Schatz's ad, or J. F. Kaltammer's, ads that were often crammed with big country houses and villas.

Year in, year out, Paul Schatz occupied the top third of the first real estate page. A widish, black-bordered box with the separate ads showing up inside it as narrower boxes. Along the whole width of the upper edge of the surrounding box invariably ran, white on black, the heading: SCHATZ REAL ESTATE. In addition, also white on black, his striking, slanting signature. Next to the signature, an antique seal. On the seal, in a circle, in the venerable script of an old coin: *The Honest Broker*. And beneath the noble white zigzags of the Schatz signature, very small and restrained: *I stand behind every offer with my name.* That was Schatz. And the whole right-hand third of his advertising space he filled with popular advice. He presented himself as a friend of the people. And to do this he bought expensive advertising space every Saturday. He had no qualms about informing the public of warranty decisions made by the Federal High Court, quoting appropriate file numbers. But the public fell for it. By publishing the file number V ZR 22/73 plus the date March 29, 1974, then imparting the information that since that date contracts between parties to real estate deals had been interpreted, as far as the builder's liability for material defects was concerned, in favor of the purchaser, Mr. Schatz was apparently himself convinced that he had performed yet another genuine service to the public at large. Last Saturday's heading: *A good broker offers a whole bouquet of services.* Every Saturday Gottlieb Zürn was annoyed to find that phrases from Schatz advertisements stuck in his head. Every Saturday he compulsively read the Schatz advertisement. Against his will he even read it more than once.

Since he didn't want to confirm to Mrs. Sonntag in so many words that business was slow, he said, trying to assume a slightly ironical tone: *"This advertisement represents only a small part of my total offerings."* Such was the line that regularly appeared in white on black, along the lower edge of the Schatz advertisement. Gottlieb was immediately annoyed with himself. By quoting that man he was capitulating to him. On the other hand, Mrs. Sonntag surely could not imagine that he would occupy any other position vis-à-vis Paul Schatz than that of capitulation. Two condominium apartments in a building in Immenstaad and the ramshackle old mill with distillery license and its own generating plant—that didn't deserve to be called competition. Next week, Mrs. Sonntag . . . She lived only a few minutes away from him, hence his embarrassment over her witnessing his lack of success. Next week . . . No, never mind. She had already skimmed through the ad and, as always, bared her teeth—that was her way of laughing. Apart from her, nothing in this room was at this moment in the sun. The swiftly-bared teeth remained bared, revealing a little of the inner side of her lips. A different red. Between her neck and her blouse or the base of her throat and her blouse or the top of her breasts and her blouse, between her and the blouse was a space that was full of light. Gottlieb couldn't take his eyes away. He felt as if he were lost. Was she looking at him or at his skimpy ad? Were other people beginning to watch him as he tried, like some eleven-year-old, to see something of a woman that he wasn't supposed to see? But he had to see it. What a light, that summer light between her and her white blouse. She stood naked in this light that flowed between her and her clothing. He pulled back his gaze, fished in his pocket. Good-bye, Mrs. Sonntag. Good-bye, Mr. Zürn. The fact that she had a squeaky voice was no consolation.

He was not happy when he was outside again. He had wanted to see more than the top of her breasts. As much as possible, in fact, and for as long as possible. And he was close to fifty. If only he were already sitting under the barber's sheet. Under the barber's sheet he wasn't close to fifty, he was eleven or twelve or fourteen. He believed that a person's age as determined by the year of his birth almost never agreed with his real age. He could remember very clearly that at twenty he hadn't felt in the least like a twenty-year-old. At the time he had felt much older. And now that he was close to fifty he often felt like fourteen or fifteen. By observing himself as well as others he had arrived at the unverifiable conclusion that at some point each person reaches his essential age, which he then retains until he dies. Roughly since reaching the age of forty, according to the calendar, he had been feeling with increasing frequency like someone who had not yet reached fifteen. On meeting someone for the first time he soon found an opportunity to determine that person's age independently of the year of birth. Ever since starting to determine people's ages—his discoveries being totally unverifiable, he obviously couldn't discuss them with anyone—he had noticed that most people were much younger than the calendar forced them to believe.

He had already turned his bicycle around to push it along the sidewalk to Christoph-Strasse when he saw Mrs. Russ turning into the Hofstatt from Christoph-Strasse. He left the sidewalk, swung himself onto his bike, and rode it as if he were driving a car around the fountain and, on the far side of the fountain, turned it like a car into Christoph-Strasse. For years he had been avoiding Mrs. Russ. When he didn't succeed he had to be prepared for a scene or at least some abuse. He had arranged for the sale of a bungalow to her, in good faith that the purchaser would enjoy the advantages of the Section 7b write-off. The vendor had stated as much to him. It had later turned out that, in order to slow down the boom, the legislature had suspended Section 7b from May 1 to November 1, 1973, and it was in that very period that the building permit for this house had been issued. Gottlieb hadn't wanted to shift the blame onto the vendor, Mr. Rilke, who had just gone bankrupt with his handicrafts store, the Treasure Chest. It was his own mistake. The suspended 7b write-off—after all, such things should be at one's fingertips! To be sure, Dr. Russ, who as a dentist was bound to be interested in write-off possibilities, no longer greeted him, but he didn't hurl abuse at him. Mrs. Russ, on the other hand, seemed to be intent on pursuing him throughout her life and his, across streets and squares, with loud calls of "Good morning, Mr. Real Estate Swindler!" Or would she, after eight years, when the forty percent of the 7b write-offs had been used up, cease her persecution? What was particularly awkward was that Mrs.

Russ was a short, dwarfish woman who walked with a cane somewhat too big for her. Everyone must take him for a dreadful fellow. To gyp such an undersized, valiant little woman! Whenever he saw Mrs. Russ he felt like leaving the town, the whole area, forever. If he was given the exclusive listing for the Swan Villa, he could offer Mrs. Russ compensation for the taxes paid on the 60,000 marks of lost write-off. No, never! Bawl out that witch with her cane, that's what he should do. Whenever he saw her and felt a surge of fear and sweating, he would mentally recite the Hamburg Superior Court decision of June 25, 1975: *A broker is not* ipso facto *obligated to verify the statements made to him by his principal. Consequently no liability attaches to him even if he has failed to exclude liability for negligence by including the words "without obligation" in his offer. . . .*

Let Paul Schatz quote *that* text in one of his Saturday ads!

Today Gottlieb Zürn managed to escape undetected from Mrs. Russ. He was already approaching the entrance to his barber's when it occurred to him that he had to go to Mrs. Reinhold's tomorrow. And fresh from the barber he always looked like a figure from a waxworks museum. He cycled back along the promenade. In Dr. Enderle's day there had always been three or four of his colleagues in the garden of the Lazy Bones around noon on Wednesdays. Now usually only Rudi W. Eitel was sitting there, if he happened to be in the country at all. He was there today. Unmistakably rigid. Leaning back. One arm over the back of his chair. Head thrown back. Gaze directed far beyond the strollers on the promenade. And sitting with him, his elbows splayed across the table, Claims-Maier, who now pursued the profession of architect merely as an appraiser and expert and—almost against his will, as he would say—had become a specialist in the mistakes of his colleagues. Rudi W. Eitel was conspicuous by his clothing. Today he was resplendent in russet brown. Plus a mauve shirt. Plus a maize-yellow bow tie with a design of black entrails; from Mexico, at the very least. Plus russet-brown shoes. Plus socks, maize-yellow. Plus a wide-brimmed brown hat. And around his neck a camera. Gottlieb Zürn had the impression that Rudi W. Eitel's mustache had meanwhile been trained in the general direction of Salvador Dali by way of Kaiser Wilhelm II.

At the sight of Eitel staring so ridiculously into the distance and Claims-Maier lolling all over the table, he knew it wasn't worth it, on their account, to park his bike, sit down, waste time. For that, Jarl F. Kaltammer or Paul Schatz would have had to be there too. But he must stop by briefly. Claims-Maier, directing his voice upward to Eitel's head, announced: "Gottlieb Zürn requests an audience, signor." "Have him approach," said Eitel without relaxing his posture. "Did you hear that, Gottlieb? You may approach," Claims-Maier called, then immediately called out to the waitress that Gottlieb would have some of that Bermatinger too. "So early in the day," said Gottlieb. "Well, what's keeping him?" Eitel shouted to Claims-Maier. Not wanting to give Eitel further cause for attracting attention by shouting, Gottlieb propped his bike against the low wall and went over to join them. Rudi W. Eitel did not relax his posture. He held out his hand as if expecting Gottlieb to kiss it. His left eye had a slight squint. Did this account for his expression of disdain and surrealism?

"Gottlieb," he said, in a kind of rasping military tone, "still with the land and property brigade, huh? Master Schatz seems to have done it again in Saturday's paper. Someone like me, straight from La Jolla, might feel like shaking his noodle. But am I shaking my noodle? No, sir. I'm not. Wanna know what I'm shaking? Rudi Weitel is shaking a li'l tree and out fall li'l golden plums. So now ya know what Rudi Weitel is shaking, okay? And wanna know where that li'l tree is at? S'thern California! My Real Estate Inc. is a hit, if ya wanna know. I can't even eat all I wanna throw up when I read that guy's Night School Special! 'Unimpeded lake view,' huh? Jeez, after all these years, 'unimpeded lake view.' Classified ad, huh? Wanna know what *I* feature in my classified ads, huh? CAMEL RACING AT DESERT FESTIVAL! DESERT GOLF CLASSIC! RETURN OF FLYING FISH! LAGUNA BEACH ART FESTIVAL! That's how they pep up real estate in Southern California. Yeah, who d'ya think Frankie Boy calls when he wants to move from Hollywood to Palm Springs? His German pal Rudi! Ya better believe it! Who knows the real safe places in Southern California, no holdups, no shoplifting, no till-tapping! Who's become known for his smashing preventive measures? Rudi Double-U Eetle! For all your security arrangements, please feel free to call Rudi W. Eitel, your real estate agent. 'Unimpeded lake view,' huh? In *his* ads Rudi Weitel has bait of a different kind. San Marino votes seven-to-one Republican. The John Birch Society maintains an office in San Marino. That means an absolute Christian Democratic Union majority forever! Not a black for miles around but, since there's progress: a few Jews and queens, if they can afford to pay the dues. And of course any number of Mexicans to do the work: that's what realtors go for! But 'unimpeded lake view'? His most successful ad had been for a display home in La Jolla, six bedrooms, seven baths, immaculate condition, but now get this: the area where it's located has a higher divorce rate than Hollywood, and that's right there in his ad! He was going to have to close his Agencia Immobiliaria in Las Palmas because the jerks have taken over there too. This continent is for the birds. That's why he decided to become a member of the Brokers' Guild of Southern California! Entrance fee four hundred smackers. So now it's your turn, okay? SEE YOUR REALTOR!"

Rudi W. Eitel could only speak in a loud voice. And as he spoke he made sharp, abrupt, swift gestures, slicing the air with every sentence. When not speaking he immediately went rigid again. He didn't give the impression of hearing what someone else was saying. Gottlieb had last seen him in early February. That was just after Rudi W. Eitel's return from the Canary Islands when he had mixed in as much Spanish with his German as he now did American and had said that from now on he only wanted to live in countries with a Spanish atmosphere. Rudi W. Eitel came from Biberach. As long as Gottlieb had known him, Rudi had remained the same age. According to Gottlieb's formula he was nineteen. Claims-Maier was appreciably younger. Sixteen at the most and, unless forced by disaster, he'd never get beyond that. Rudi W. Eitel phoned once or twice a year. Usually from abroad. He'd say he only wanted to know what the weather was like at Lake Constance. Then he'd immediately go into high gear: his real estate joint was going like wildfire. He was one of the brokers who had been contacted from Washington for offers to ex-President Ford, who wanted to settle in Southern California. But then when one ran into Eitel at the Lazy Bones or the Rex and the waitress came with the bill, he would instantly freeze into complete remoteness and not move again until someone else had paid for his drinks.

Suddenly he said: "Waddya featurin' right now?"

And before Gottlieb could say: Something out of this world . . . the Swan Villa in . . ., Rudi shouted: "Come on, let's have some fun, let us pray."

This was a game they had often played in past years: taking turns reciting the latest Schatz ad, phrase by phrase.

Rudi declaimed: *A good broker offers a whole bouquet of services.* Claims-Maier didn't sit up but lifted his round, sad, white face and said in his most stilted voice *What is the nature of these services?* Whereupon Rudi W. Eitel with a vibrato of graceful amateur charm: *The broker presents you with the rainbow palette of his offers.* All it needed was the Schatz tone of pomposity and solemnity for all three to explode with laughter. Rudi W. Eitel shouted that he could understand Gottfried Zürn, with his law degree, pulling the wool of mock gravity over the public's eyes—*ad majorem professionis gloriam,* Claims-Maier quickly interjected—but not Master Paul the autodidact, and that this very fact was his only feasible motivation: his failure to graduate from high school! Only because of this failure was our Tamerlane from Temesvár forever proclaiming himself Moses and brandishing the tablets of the law. Waddya say, comrades? We're agreed, he wows us, okay? Claims-Maier: "Tamerlane is wrong, Hindenburg is right, he's Hindenburg from Budweis, his first name's Paul too." Gottlieb said: "If we want to be accurate, he's a Hindenburg who sees himself as a Bismarck." "Right," shouted Rudi, "right, *the honest broker!*"

"The bill, please miss," called Gottlieb. "He can pay the bill all right but he can't leave," shouted Rudi W. Eitel. Or had Gottlieb also become a jerk like Master Paul or that genius of opportunism Jarl F. Kaltammer who, paraphrasing Kennedy, had switched to JFK Real Estate. . . . Gottlieb saw that he wasn't going to get away that quickly. But of course he had missed going to the barber. In order not to waste his time entirely, he brought up the subject of the Swan Villa. What value, very roughly, would Claims-Maier put on such-and-such a house? Claims-Maier refused to be told anything about the Swan Villa. Good God, if he didn't know that house, he wouldn't be worth a row of pins. Well now, the Swan Villa . . . "Shut your trap, Helmut," shouted Eitel. "Don't pretend, just to show off your vast knowledge as an appraiser, that you've ever heard of a Swan Villa! Listen, I'll beat your brains out if you try to put anything over on our cosy little circle. We're all buddies so we don't mind letting our pants down when we're together! Young Gottlieb here is only putting you on, there's no such thing as a Swan Villa, and if there were, who wouldn't get it? Young Gottlieb here. Because our super-colleague Schatz would get it."

"Kaltammer would get it," Claims-Maier exclaimed in a voice that reminded Gottlieb of kids playing soldiers. Had they forgotten that friend Kaltammer hadn't always, eyes glazed, torso rigid, bullied an odious partner around the ballroom floor in dance competitions because—even ten short years ago—he had foamed at the mouth demanding the abolition not only of ballroom dancing but of society itself?! Had they deliberately forgotten those leaflets, the products of his masturbatory activities with university kids in Constance, which claimed that brokers were vampires, that architects and realtors were mere lackeys aiding the monopolist-capitalists to optimize their ground rents?! Those ground rents were in turn the real reason behind the petrification of home construction, which was treated as a commodity! And that's why the ideology of land ownership was to blame for an economy that set values on real estate and parceled it into lots, which was why they were calling for the abolition of private ownership of that means of production known as land. In any case, according to Marx plus Kaltammer, land ownership had nothing to do with the true process of production. Thus the salvation of mankind required the lighting of only *one* more fire: the one in which all land registry records were to be burned. . . .

Claims-Maier, when he started on the subject of Kaltammer—and for him not to start on that subject was impossible—could not contain himself. They had been at the university together and later shared an office. According to Claims-Maier, the only ideas Kaltammer had developed were those that couldn't be put into practice without Louis XIV. An out-of-out theoretician, even at the university he'd skipped Structural Materials I and II as being beneath his dignity. You know the story about Frank Lloyd Wright receiving a wire from a client, "Roof leaking, rain has already damaged grand piano," and Wright wiring back: "Move piano." That's Kaltammer for you, the same aesthetic arrogance. The only thing that surprised him, Maier, was that he wasn't embarrassed! A few short years ago, architects had been the lackeys aiding the monopolist-capitalists and the realtors had been vampires, now he's the smoothest operator in the business, running the ideal combination of brokerage, building supervision, sales, and administration. Gottlieb said that perhaps Kaltammer did feel embarrassed, how was one to know? "Right," Rudi W. Eitel shouted, "let's think big of Jarl F. Kaltammer, ballroom dancing is his penance! Just look at him as he rips off a paso doble, rapes a tango, wields that spindly blonde from the travel agency in a rumba as if she were a sword, and all with that blank, uneven pale face and yellow hair, yellow-haired and pale, but with Latin American ambitions to the core, a dancer of the revolution through and through. . . ."

"Just a moment, just a moment," shouted Claims-Maier, "Weitel doesn't know what he's talking about!" Ever since Kaltammer's student period—"Period!" whinnied Rudi, splaying his fingers and turning his gaze heavenward like a madonna—since the end of that period Kaltammer had had himself driven every Friday in his Deuxchevaux gas-cheater to Constance, where a private plane waited to fly him to Burgundy, no less! Aristocracy, aristocracy, all the way! Every weekend, aristocracy! Burgundian aristocracy! Two princesses! Not one princess, but two! No less! For him Kaltammer was a count! With his shot-silk raincoat! Count Kaltammer. And he took the liberty of adding: Kaltammer *Aspergillus niger!* After the mold that routinely developed in the buildings Kaltammer had on his conscience. Since employing a qualified engineer and a commerce graduate in his office, Count Kaltammer had been causing less damage. But in a Deuxchevaux to a private plane! And why? Count Kaltammer had to pay for the gas to the aircraft himself. And Count Kaltammer was parsimonious to an extent of which even the paucity of his facial expressions gave no hint. Could anyone but Kaltammer laugh and curse, be cheerful and angry, with one and the same face? Even at dance competitions there was one face for every dance, and the uncanny thing was: it was always appropriate!

Gottlieb had finished his third glass. He should have phoned home long ago. But these pricks of conscience gradually faded. He noticed that he was smoking but didn't want to notice it. Because other people had sat down around them, the trio had gone indoors. They waved away the menu. At some point Rudi W. Eitel switched off. He had fallen silent; instead of staring obliquely up he was now staring obliquely down, under the table. Claims-Maier said: "I know what that means: he's staring at Caesar's feet. From now on you won't get through to him anymore. Whether we stay or leave makes no difference just so long as we pay for his drinks. That's how Vercingetorix sat. When all was lost, he rode out from Alesia and, in full panoply, wearing his plumed helmet, seated himself at Caesar's feet. Caesar had ordered his ceremonial chair and dais to be set on the rampart. Vercingetorix immediately realized that the maximum surrender was going to be demanded of him. And he was much handsomer than this Caesar. Caesar wanted to look at him. By allowing their eyes to meet, Vercingetorix was expected to concede that he was nothing while Caesar was everything. Vercingetorix did not look at Caesar. He did not want to give Caesar the satisfaction of allowing their eyes to meet. He sat down on the dais on which Caesar's feet were resting and stared at Caesar's feet. He withheld from the conqueror the acknowledgment of the conquered. And what is a conquest worth if the conquered refuses to acknowledge it! Caesar could feel that, by refusing to let their eyes meet, his enemy demonstrated how little he felt defeated. When all was said and done, Caesar had only managed to conquer the Celts with the aid of the Germanic horsemen. It was not the Romans but the Teutons who had conquered the Celts. That's why Vercingetorix stared at his feet. Caesar never forgot that. Five years later he had Vercingetorix beheaded precisely at his, Caesar's, feet. In his last moments Vercingetorix stared at Caesar's feet once more. I'm sure Rudi is seeing Caesar's feet."

"Let's go."

First Gottlieb had to pay the entire bill. Then he had to accompany Maier to the Rex. If he didn't, Claims-Maier would be offended. In that case Gottlieb would have wasted several hours, paid eighty-two marks, and offended someone who spent his time running around town influencing people. He was also a source of tips. Gottlieb couldn't remember ever having received a tip from Claims-Maier, but there was no question that it could happen at any time. One doesn't offend someone like that. At the Rex, Claims-Maier immediately draped himself over the table again, an effect which because he was short didn't entirely come off. But he pushed his elbows as far across the table as he could. Once again Gottlieb asked Helmut what kind of a value he would put on the Swan Villa. Claims-Maier was an acknowledged authority on evaluating the intrinsic worth of buildings. After a mason's apprenticeship he had worked his way up to becoming an architect but, after the partnership with Kaltammer hadn't worked out, he had ceased to venture into the construction field and restricted himself to delivering expert opinions on construction damage and related problems.

"I'll tell you, Gottlieb, because it's you and because during the last fifteen years you've worked against me less than any other adult in this town! I'm not saying you've never worked against me. 'Never' would be asking too much, obviously. But the little, the very little you did work against Helmut Maier, that you managed to do, Gottlieb, better than anyone else in town. Kaltammer, who will always maintain his leadership in the local 'get-Maier' group, has proved that it is possible for someone to become a lion in the construction field even if he's incapable of designing a roof gutter that doesn't cause damage. There's one thing he can't do: damage himself. No matter what he does or says, it doesn't damage him. Back to the subject, Gottlieb. I predict that it'll be Mr. Kaltammer who makes off with the Swan Villa. Not you. Not Schatz. A snooty, top-drawer Swabian family isn't going to be impressed by some Mr. Three Percent from the Balkans, but Jarl Count Kaltammer—*Aspergillus niger* of the shot silk, he'll get the Swan Villa. No matter what you do, Gottlieb. That's the law. The system. The simple fact is that properties of that size are handled at the Kaltammer level. This is a Kaltammer society. This society produces Kaltammers the way Kaltammer's buildings produce *Aspergillus niger*. And just as Kaltammer's buildings are destroyed by Kaltammer's *Aspergillus niger*, so this society is destroyed by Kaltammers. But just so you won't have asked in vain: a detailed estimate is irrelevant in view of the villa's historic associations, but you can suggest to the Leistle lady that she ask 2.5 million marks, negotiable, that'll make her feel good. She should be able to get 1.8 to two million for the hundred thousand cubic feet of historic space, built in 1905. As a building, one can't fault it. As to its usefulness, its feudal design makes it problematic. A connoisseur's piece. Nice if you could get it. Here's to you, Gottlieb. I always say: other people talk about their illnesses, I talk about Kaltammer. But let me tell you: I have never, at any time or any place, said *why* I have to talk about him. What he did to me is something only I know. I doubt whether he knows."

When Claims-Maier paused for a second, Gottlieb said over his shoulder: "Mario, the bill please." He paid for both. Claims-Maier protested. Put his hand in his pocket and pulled

out some bills, saying he would never enter this place again if
he wasn't allowed to pay. "Gottlieb," he said, in his agitation
wiping the sweat from his forehead with the crumpled bills,
"Gottlieb, my friend, I implore you, don't do that! If you pay
now, you'll be working against me." Gottlieb relented.
"Ecco," Claims-Maier called out, "two more of the same!"
Now Gottlieb protested that it was after three, that they'd been
waiting for him at home for hours. Claims-Maier indicated
that he would hold this premature departure against Gottlieb
forever. Gottlieb sat down again. Neither said anything. It was
a silent battle. Then Gottlieb stood up, put his hand on
Claims-Maier's shoulder, and said: "Helmut, I simply must."
Helmut reacted like Else when she wasn't stroked firmly
enough: he lifted his shoulder toward the hand. It was like a
plea uttered with tear-filled eyes. Gottlieb realized that he'd
have to be in a rage to be able to part from Claims-Maier.

"Rudi is gradually turning into nothing but a con man,
wouldn't you agree?" said Claims-Maier. "I feel sorry for
him, really I do. He and I and you, all the others don't matter
anyway. And now one of us three is a con man. One a
boozer." He pointed to himself. "And one"—pointing to
Gottlieb—"a child." Gottlieb made a circular movement with
his index finger against his temple, then placed his hand on
Claims-Maier's head. How old was Gottlieb now? "Close to
fifty," said Gottlieb. He didn't look it. "Take care, Helmut,"
said Gottlieb, and walked so slowly that Claims-Maier could
have called after him. If he didn't call, he had only himself to
blame for staying behind alone. He didn't call. Gottlieb didn't
look around, otherwise he would have gone back. He didn't
like himself for being able to desert him. But if he stayed with
him, he'd be one of them. One with Claims-Maier and Rudi

W. Eitel. He had been shocked when Claims-Maier said that
Eitel, he, and Gottlieb belonged together. If he hadn't said
that, Gottlieb might have stayed.

He pushed his bike to where the footpath started and
cycling was forbidden, slowly swung himself onto the saddle
and, in spite of buzzing thoughts, in spite of the urge to ride
without touching the handlebars, rode home with both hands
firmly gripping them. It occurred to him that he had already
been surprised twice at meeting Claims-Maier, believing him
to have died of cancer of the liver. So Claims-Maier considered
Rudi a con man. Gottlieb also wondered, of course, whether
Rudi's stories weren't exaggerated. But since he somehow
visualized all Rudi's stories as they were told, he also believed
what Rudi was saying. In any case, it required an effort to
doubt what Rudi said. He couldn't attempt to do that until he
had left Rudi. To doubt in Rudi's presence what Rudi said
would have been impossible. Rudi is a hidalgo, he thought,
without knowing what he meant by that. When Gottlieb
reached out for the Japanese camera hanging around Rudi's
neck, Rudi had shouted: "Don't, you'll burn your fingers!"
And when Gottlieb had looked at him with raised eyebrows:
"Let me tell you, it's hot! But then it only costs two hundred
and ninety."

Now Gottlieb Zürn wished he could have taken back everything he had said on the terrace of the Lazy Bones. That was
no way to talk about Paul Schatz. Paul Schatz had done more
than anyone else for the good reputation of the realtor's
profession. It was madness to make fun of Paul Schatz in a
public place. He was bound to hear about it. If at least
Gottlieb's thoughts had matched the careless words he had
spoken under the influence of Rudi and Claims-Maier. It was

always other people who determined how and what was discussed. He would never have minded making a few snide remarks about Paul Schatz. But not such a display of mockery. And two tables away a pensioner with a mottled bald head had been studying a hiking map. With a rubber-tipped cane beside his chair. Looking as if all he was good for was the shakes. And studying a hiking map! A spy. Of course a spy.

Gottlieb knew such notions were unfounded. Still, he was scared. But then Paul Schatz's friend-of-the-people pose in the ads *was* ridiculous. *Generally speaking, the execution of the notarized sales agreement does not entail an immediate transfer of title in the land registry.* The public always falls for this legal jargon. Paul Schatz is the very image of a broker, of the reliable broker, in the Lake Constance area. There is not the least whiff of commercialism about him. Yet he pulls off the biggest and best deals of any realtor in the triangle of Zürich, Stuttgart, and Munich. No ads had better layouts than his. Little works of art, they were. Well, could anyone doubt that Paul Schatz was an artist? Hadn't there been an exhibition of his paintings this summer at the Cavazzen House in Lindau? And one person who didn't go to see it was Gottlieb Zürn. Because he was foolish enough to imagine himself a competitor of a man who barely deigned to notice him. How could he ever have allowed himself to be roped into such lousy behavior by Rudi, that somewhat questionable idler! Rudi W. Eitel, although he came from Biberach, led an extraterritorial existence. Immune.

It was time for Gottlieb to come up with a sensible assessment of Paul Schatz. He could feel his reluctance to do so. Why must he of all people have a competitor who was superior to him in every respect! Since Paul Schatz was now also heading a citizens' initiative for an autobahn routing well away from the lakeshore, there was no possible stand that could be taken against him. There's a man for you! Concerns himself about the right things. And all the things he concerns himself about! He writes articles for the newspaper when the Federal Railway, even though electrically powered, fails to cover the section through the Black Forest between Offenburg and Constance as fast as it should or could, but doesn't because it . . . Gottlieb had already forgotten the convincing arguments put forward by Schatz the train traveler. Schatz takes up his pen against environmentally destructive river-straightenings and in favor of the restoration of old buildings. And you live your own little life, selfish, ugly, petty! An ugly, selfish little child, trying sixty times an hour to adapt out of sheer fear, weakness, the desire to please. A child . . . he had hardly been able to control himself when Claims-Maier uttered that word. Perhaps Claims-Maier would forget his discovery again. If Gottlieb had contradicted him there would have been an argument, and in Claims-Maier's alcoholic orations Gottlieb would have appeared ever after as "Gottlieb the child." Paul Schatz's example shows: nothing pays off as well as boldness.

Gottlieb made up his mind finally to be bold. Most of the people he knew were bolder than he was. Anna had once said that it was never possible to find out what he was thinking but only what he thought others wanted to hear; even toward the children he was never anything but tactical. That was already having disastrous effects; the children had unconsciously adopted his attitude and were already thoroughly warped. His decision finally to be bold was enough to put him in a kind of panic, sure as he was that *his* boldness would have a different outcome from Paul Schatz's: a fearful fiasco. Or a kind of destruction. To be bold . . . a person must be able to afford that. Some time or other, yes. The urge was there all right, but the idea of finally wanting to be bold made everyone around him instantly seem like adults. And he . . . he should have tried to change Claims-Maier's mind about calling him a child without letting him notice it. He was close to fifty. And mustn't tell a soul that what he really wanted to call most people was "adults." They would think he was trying to make himself younger than he was. That wasn't it at all. Oh well, maybe two to four years. But certainly not five. He hoped Claims-Maier would forget what he had noted, or rather noticed.

At home he managed to enter his office unseen by going through the garden. The house was filled with pounding and rattling sounds from the piano. Julia and Czerny. Then, when she switched to more airy Bach inventions, he could hear the hurrying rise and fall of Magda's violin from upstairs. If they were both devoting themselves so passionately to their practicing, Regina must be awake. He lay back with delicious heaviness in his desk chair. Was there anything more artificial, more insulting, than activity? Else came in through the window, sat herself down on the windowsill, regarded herself with complete aplomb for a moment in the pane of the open window, settled herself into a position of ambush, and peered into the shrubbery. A cat is always doing something. And when it is doing nothing, it is doing that.

Suddenly Anna stood beside him. He had heard the sound of the piano abruptly cascading into the room but had been incapable of reacting. Anna was . . . well now, was she as outraged, as beside herself, as she made out? Simply not to turn up for lunch! He was worse than a child. And as for Regina, he couldn't care less how she was, could he! He said: "Eitel and Claims-Maier . . ." That did it! With those two, of all people! He asked her to postpone the sermon. How was Regina? Dr. Freisleben had phoned. In his and Dr. Sixt's opinion, the urine analysis did not account for the symptoms as described by Anna. He had wanted to see Regina, so Anna had taken her there. In the waiting room Regina had suddenly started to cry. Anna asked: "Is the pain so bad?" Anna couldn't help crying too. Everyone in the waiting room stared at the mother crying with her child. When Regina sees her mother crying too, she laughs and asks why her mother is crying. "Because of you," says Anna. That makes her laugh even harder. "She's just like you," said Anna. Dr. Freisleben examined her. He and Dr. Sixt were of the opinion that a dermatologist should be consulted about the red blobs. But first she had gone to see Dr. Sixt. After all, he had been treating Regina the longest. Now he says it no longer has anything to do with her kidneys, that's to say, nothing to do with him. More likely with her ovaries, Regina was fairly big for her age. In that case he would act only in a consulting capacity, merely to help the child. The way things had gone so far was typical of the present system. No doctor felt responsible for the case. Personally he believed that she was suffering from a herpes that had not fully developed. Sensitivity to palpation indicated merely hyperesthesia, not kidney trouble. So back to the dermatologist, Dr. Landwehr, who had said last Friday: Maybe a tick bite. He had meanwhile talked to the neurologist, Dr. Niebergall, who, on Dr. Landwehr's advice, had tested Regina's reflexes on Monday and pronounced them normal. So he was no farther ahead. Dr. Freisleben, who is now insisting that he has merely taken over this case from Dr. Cornelius, suggests consulting another neurologist since he apparently didn't entirely trust the one consulted by Dr. Landwehr. He suggests Dr. Finkenbein. For tonight he has prescribed Dolviran and Neurobion.

Gottlieb went upstairs with Anna. In passing, he said hello to Julia. Magda's door was closed. Regina lay inert. When she spoke, she hardly moved her lips. She obviously wasn't well. But she was still able to demonstrate that she wasn't well. Or was he merely imputing this for the sake of his own peace of mind? If only one knew why one thought something.

"Now for our sitz bath," said Anna. For twenty minutes she had to massage Regina's external private parts with cold water. That was supposed to draw the inflammation downward. Her cousin Leonhard had recommended this when Magda had had that bad throat infection. Gottlieb had no desire to watch the procedure. He could tell how seriously Anna took her battle against Regina's illness by the fact that she hadn't offered him anything to eat. That had never happened before. Else, noticing that he was unable to get down to work, jumped from the windowsill onto his desk, and from there, after first patting out a resting place with her two splayed front paws, settled down on his lap. The warm, soft weight of fur caused his private parts to react. The tendency of these parts toward bizarre reactions was nothing new to him. Alcohol, of course, might also be partly to blame.

If only it were already Saturday. Stuttgart, Parler-Strasse, Mrs. Hortense Leistle. Maier considered 1.8 or two million possible. If it were 1.8, twice three percent would mean

108,000. Even if he had to knock off two percent one way or the other, it still meant 72,000. Yet that in turn seemed almost too little. But why shouldn't somebody be found who would pay two million! Then, if he let himself be taken down two percent, he would still get 80,000. That was a respectable amount, a figure that pleased him. The prospect of 80,000 marks got him started. Paul Schatz was famous for never allowing any bargaining over the commission. It was said that he had more than once demanded twice 3.33 percent. And got it! All the same, Paul Schatz wasn't considered in the least greedy. And Gottlieb, who usually managed to wangle a commission from one side only—from the vendor or the purchaser, depending on whether it was a seller's or buyer's market—felt constrained to regard himself as greedy. And so he was. He could tell that from the dizzy giddiness that came over him at the thought: 80,000.

The prospect of large sums awoke the memory of his parents. He always earned money under the eyes of his mother. Perhaps the same thing happened to Paul Schatz. Now, when he wanted to think of his mother, he remembered Paul Schatz. Sometimes he was afraid that, whenever he wanted to think of his mother, he would have to think of Paul Schatz. The more strenuously he resisted this, the more indissoluble the connection between his mother and Paul Schatz might become. But why, for God's sake?! His mother had never been greedy. Her lifelong inability to do anything but earn money to the point of exhaustion was due to her never having had any money because his father had had no talent for earning it; had been ill too, and, before he was fifty, dead. All her life she had had to work off the debts that had accumulated as a result of his father's hopeless business practices. She had barely managed to keep her inmost being free for God. Everything else was put to the service of earning money. She earned money just as someone who has fallen into the water makes swimming movements. Her children would have been in outright physical danger if bankruptcy had thrown the family out of the house. Could he imagine his mother other than poring over figures? Always doing mental arithmetic. Memorizing promissory-note due dates, deducting interest on debts from potential revenue, adding up creditors' accounts: that's how she had sat, her hands lying on the table, sometimes scratching each other or busy with each other like two little animals left to themselves. When his mother counted, she moved her lips as if she were praying. But it was figures that moved those lips. Her eyes were smaller than nature intended. A gaze made ever narrower by the exertion of all her inner forces. The large, wide-open eyes she had in the two photos taken at the time of her marriage at twenty-five, when she moved from Wigratsweiler down to the lake: those eyes he had never seen! He could only remember that critical or suffering contraction of her eyes. His mother was *not* greedy. He was. Collecting money gave him satisfaction. The realtor's commission invariably destroyed the relationship between himself and his client. With the commission, everything he had done was destroyed. His activity had become transformed into mere money. My nihilism, he thought, and the idea pleased him.

One day, when he had enough money, he would probably think differently about money. But what is enough? No more debts. But that would be sheer stupidity. That much he had learned from his mother. Nevertheless, with his unsteady income he often felt like a man driving a motorboat with a hole in the bottom who has to drive fast to make the front half of the boat, where the hole is, rise and stay out of the water. The moment he slackened speed, he would sink. He called that his analogy boat. If all went well, his life would at some point consist only of the money he earned during his lifetime but hadn't yet spent. His poems were the only thing he could protect from that relationship to money which destroyed all that was real and meaningful. Since almost every day he spent a few minutes—sometimes even a few hours—writing poems or tinkering with earlier ones, he frequently found himself thinking of how he could exploit them. But he was shocked each time such a thought came to him. For the fact that his poems couldn't be exploited was their most important quality. And without a trace of humor his next thought was: apart from the fact that they are quite unsalable. But even if they *were* salable, once sold they would be worthless, destroyed, even if they had previously had a value or a meaning. They were not good poems. Even so, he couldn't persuade himself that they were bad poems. They're certainly not good. That, too, he told himself without a trace of humor. Even in the outermost reaches of his soul he allowed no dissenting opinion to this judgment to survive. They're not good. But not bad either. They were his poems. That's all there was to it. There was nothing he would rather regard himself as than a poet. But he knew he mustn't tell that to anyone.

He immediately saw himself surrounded by adults, i.e., experts looking down on him with severity and concern. He lay in his tipped-back armchair and looked up at them. If he told them he was a poet, they would certainly want to see his poems so they could tell him whether he was a good poet or a bad one. If they told him he was a bad poet, he would be unhappy. He was also inclined to hope that one was a poet regardless of whether one was a good poet or a bad one. That's all there was to it. His poems were closer to him than those of real poets. Didn't everyone have to make his own poems?

The thing that bothered him most about contemporary poets was that they kept nothing back. Each wanted to outdo the other in confessing. What interested him was what one could keep to oneself by writing it down. That was probably because of his shyness or cowardice or insincerity or immaturity. There he was, back again with Anna's criticism. Anna maintained that one never knew with him whether he meant what he said or whether, in saying something, he was hiding what he meant. That's how perceptive Anna was. In his poems he tried to express the idea that, in saying something, he was always trying to hide something. If he could manage, in saying something, to express what he was hiding, he would have expressed why he wished to write poems. Other people build their toy railways up to the very walls of the rec room, or collect rocks until the glass cabinets are all full, or hunch over their stamp collections: he wrote poems, that's all there was to it. True, it was a favorite pastime that had to be kept to oneself. There was no club for that. His favorite pastime would tolerate no witnesses. Not even in his own family. Nor did it need any witnesses. The tone of exaltation was his favorite tone. But only as long as he was alone with that tone.

If he *were* a poet—in the eyes of others too—that in itself was for him a contradiction, "poet in the eyes of others too"— he would resume his father's name. Before taking his law degree he had assumed his mother's name and so acquired a guilty conscience about his dead father. At the time he had held an emotional nocturnal conversation with his father, who had already been dead for thirteen years. Mon très cher père, he had begun à la Mozart, and had talked until he was convinced that his father was now agreeable to one of his sons taking their mother's name. He couldn't allow himself an easy win because every attempt of his father's to obtain a bit of security and permanence for himself or his children was immediately answered by the world around him with annihilating blows. That one of his two surviving children should wish to divest himself of his name was a kind of continuation of all that had happened to this father during his lifetime. But precisely because it was a continuation, Gottlieb had compelled his father to agree. World War I, prisoner of war, illness, bankruptcy, and death before he was fifty: didn't this sequence of miseries flare up in a kind of wild or poetic brilliance if the last son but one now even obliterated the name? It must be possible to disappear. Like his father. The manner of his life and death was for him the essence of poetry. In the figure of his father he had built up for himself an example of a man able to consent to a hopeless disappearance.

While rotting away with open wounds as he approached death, his father had still remained day by day aware of his financial ruin as it advanced with parallel swiftness. He witnessed his own complete annihilation. It was said that he neither cursed nor screamed. He had been more like a soft breath. But so he always had. Several people said he had always been a quiet man. In spite of all that Gottlieb had picked up about his father, he had retained the impression that his father had somehow been quiet and fragrant. Although he could still recall that his father, as he rotted away, had given off a sweetish, repulsive smell, the picture that stayed with him was of his father's life having somehow been quiet and fragrant. Precisely because of its painful course and foul-smelling end, perhaps. A worthy butcher had told Gottlieb's mother more than once that her husband was a *Batsche*. The *a* was pronounced as in "wall" or "ball." *Batsche*, that's what people in Mitten called a shapeless, worn-out house slipper. Once, because of his interest in Paul Schatz, Gottlieb Zürn had been reading a book about Transylvanian Saxons and Banat Germans and had run across the expression *Batschker*, the term used by those people for a knitted slipper-sock. So that was what his father had looked like to someone who despised him. When he thought of his father he always had to think of the temperamental butcher's term of abuse. He could still remember the butcher's way of swaggering in, a toothpick in the corner of his mouth and one corner of his apron stuffed into the apron string tied around his stomach, presumably to keep it from getting in the way of his pedaling, as he always came by bicycle to the tavern run by Gottlieb's mother.

Ever since he had read this, there had been an indissoluble link between his father and Paul Schatz by way of *Batsche* and *Batschker*. What he envied Paul Schatz for was not his real estate company in Vaduz, Liechtenstein, his two nineteen-unit apartment buildings in St. Gallen, his high-rises in Chur, but that his parents were still alive, that here, many hundreds of miles away, through their son's remarks being passed around, one's picture of them was as clear as if they had been the Roman couple in the Latin primer; in other words, that whatever Paul Schatz did was done as his proud and happy parents looked on: that was what Gottlieb Zürn found enviable. By contrast, what could he have shown off to his parents? His house! Yessir, his house! If the practice of his profession netted him a house like that, then . . .then . . . The term "real estate agent" wouldn't have sounded good to his mother's ears. She would have screwed up her eyes as if obliged to look into a painful light, and her right hand would have scratched the back of her left even harder. "Real estate agent": to her mind that would have been almost as bad as "poet." There was nobody from whom he would have had to hide his poetry secret more carefully than from her. To that extent his mother was positively a guarantor of his poetic status, a status that depended above all on secrecy. As long as he told no one, he was free to cultivate his self-image as a poet. But he couldn't believe in it any more than someone who says of himself: I am handsome! There are statements, it seems, that one must hear from others. He hoped that many people possessed something equally secret, something that for them was the most important thing in the world. Probably everyone was in truth a poet. Least of all those poor people who must strive night and day for recognition as poets.

Inside the house the battle was still going on between Julia's pounding and Magda's bowing. Magda and Julia made music like prisoners banging spasmodically and hopelessly with both fists on indestructible doors. Their music-making sounded to him like cries for help. Did they intend to become musicians? Probably. What else could justify their flinging themselves with such abandon into this time-consuming activity at the expense of their homework? Surely they were taking a chance. But it was up to Anna, wasn't it, to look after that. That was her department. He had to think about the Swan Villa. He was tempted to drive over again right away. He felt a craving to enter the hall and see all those blue swans on the soaring stained-glass window swimming toward him through the narrow winding water as if propelled by light. On the left of the winding waterway, a naked youth; on the right, a naked girl; he in an even more bilious green than she. Both as far apart as the picture permitted. Which explains why they look yearningly at each other across the whole picture of reed, swan, and water. The youth stretching out arms and hands to such an extreme that it would seem he must break or at least dislocate them. The girl grasping her head with both hands in sheer agony. And above the tall glass triptych the fascination extended even higher. A glass semicircle in which everything came together to form a complete image of longing. Swans, water lilies, water, and an evening sky lavishing golden fires. And he hadn't tried to photograph that yet. For the planned prospectus.

There was also the tall oblong carved relief outside, on the right of the entrance, that he still had to photograph. Not so much for the swan peering out from the carved tendrils as for the inscription encircling this swan relief in extravagant lettering: *Hic habitet felicitas, nil mali intret*. If he planned to use this motto as a heading for the prospectus, he would have to furnish proof that the words existed on the building, otherwise he would be no more than a poor imitator of Claims-Maier. There was never a Claims-Maier expert opinion without a formidable Latin quotation. A Latin saying in the construction and real estate field, that was Claims-Maier for you! This urge to quote betrayed the self-educated man. He felt a close kinship with Claims-Maier but hoped he was better at hiding what they had in common. He crossed out the motto from his text. Now the heading. On one of his slips of paper he found:

Unique Art Nouveau Dream Jewel on Lake Constance. Kaltammer would have put that down without hesitation. He recalled the first sentence of a Paul Schatz text: *Verily, this is THE offer of the decade!* In its unscrupulous exaggeration it was a Kaltammer phrase, but the benevolent, archaic "verily" turned it into a Schatz phrase. He typed:

This property has no equal anywhere. With Kaltammer, every second bungalow that had as much as one rattling sash window became *a luxury Engl. style country house.* And at least once every season he could offer *by far one of the most beautiful estates in the whole of southern Germany.* The thought of such sentences paralyzed him. He couldn't compete with that. In a kind of defiance he wrote over his first sentence the heading *Art Nouveau Lakeside Villa.* He found the word *house* demeaning to this villa. Perhaps he should take a picture of the northeast turret by itself. At least of its two upper floors, supported by two jutting cornices, with their perpendicular oval windows surrounded by molded tendrils. And the painting along the staircase wall leading up from the hall to the gallery! A naked woman standing on a swan as it races along, preparing to take off. She is apparently causing it to race along—race upward, in fact, since the swan is racing up from the hall into the gallery overhead—by means of a thin white wand connecting her hands to the swan's neck. The woman and her swan race along on dark green, foaming, wind-whipped water. A photo album ought to be put together to document this house. He had to force himself to turn to the sober marshaling of facts.

19 rooms, 13 baths, 6,690 sq. ft. floor space, hall, dining room, gun room, billiard room, music room, blue drawing

room, bar, sauna, utility area, tennis court, marina for 35
boats, mature woodland area, murals, ornamental ceilings in
almost every room . . .

And what about the lamps! And the wallpaper! Gold
herringbone design on maroon background! Would he manage to capture the colors of that stupendous hall window in a
photograph? In green water, blue swans, and the closer the
swans were—the lower down in the picture—the paler they
became. The closest swan, the lowest, almost white.

And Eberhard Bansin hands out "Awake!" pamphlets at
the Ravensburg railway station. And his mother would rather
have spent her last months betting on "00" and "even" than
be in an old people's home. And if Dionys, the former gar-
dener, who was still allowed to occupy the coachman's house,
hadn't been a drinker whom it was easy to bribe with two
bottles of Müller-Thurgau, Gottlieb would have had no idea
how to gain access to the jewel. Close though he had been to
obtaining the listing, the two trusteeships had moved him far
away again.

He had already been called three times to supper. Now Julia
flung open the door and said in a shrill voice of mock anger:
"Gottlieb, aren't you coming?" And over her shoulder she
called out that Gottlieb—she was the only one of the girls who
called him that, and more and more often—was sitting there,
staring into space and keeping his family waiting. Then, on
the terrace, they were only three. Regina's fever was creeping
up to 102 again, said Anna, and Magda was still in the kitchen
and, as usual, fixing something for herself. For a while there
was silence, then Anna said: "If she doesn't come now, I
refuse to eat any more." She stopped, turned away from the
table, but outward, toward the garden rather than the open

door through which Magda had to come. "Please go on with your supper," said Gottlieb, afraid he would have to join Anna's hunger strike. He was hungry. "If *she* can stay away from the table, so can I," said Anna into the evening greenery. Julia said: "Bull." Gottlieb nodded. Julia—probably to divert the tension that had so swiftly arisen—said that Stefan Schatz had just pulled off another tremendous stunt. When no one reacted, she said to her father: "I thought you were always so interested in him?" In the latest issue of the school paper he had called the principal a gift-wrap democrat because the principal had refused to set up a complaint barrel in the school yard, as Stefan Schatz had demanded in the previous issue. They remembered, didn't they? Anna didn't remember and had no wish to be reminded now of anything so trivial. Stefan Schatz, Julia said, now addressing only her father, had persuaded the almshouse winery to let him have an old barrel that he was going to set up in the school yard so that any student could pin slips and sheets of paper to it, to publicize whatever was bugging them. Stefan Schatz had said that, as the one most deeply concerned with the school paper, he had discovered that it was always the same guys writing in the paper, and they were writing more to please themselves than for the sake of a general cause. So a medium had to be found in which everyone could exert public criticism, even if they weren't the least bit interested in literature.

The principal had refused permission to set up the complaint barrel because, he said, Stefan's article showed that he wasn't interested in critical cooperation but only in confrontation and that Stefan demonstrated this by his incessant personal attacks. After all, the Education Act for Baden-Württemberg was not his—the principal's—test paper. Now in the latest issue Stefan was hitting back. If the principal refused this tiny first step toward democracy, he would look for another spot in town—but this time one hundred percent public—for his complaint barrel, possibly with the aid of a citizens' initiative; then the whole town could take note of the students' complaints and criticisms on the ferry dock or on the Hofstatt. "I know you admire him," said Julia. Personally she didn't care for the way he was carrying on now, although, when it came to the genuineness of the principal's democracy, she felt Stefan might have something there. But it was just another stunt, she said. Gottlieb Zürn felt that, for Anna's sake, he must allow the subject to peter out by not responding.

Scarcely had Julia stopped speaking when Anna jumped up and said she couldn't stand it another second. At that moment Magda emerged from the kitchen, carrying her plate with both hands and, as if oblivious, sat down in her chair. Gottlieb knew that Anna expected him to say something reproachful, vengeful, to Magda. So he did. He chose his phrases to include the comment that the same thing happened every day. That, of course, gave Magda a chance quietly to point out that, for the very same reason, she couldn't see why anyone should get worked up over her preparing her own meal. Anna was about to protest. Gottlieb asked her to refrain. The main thing was that they should sit at the *same* table, he said, even if they weren't eating the same food. This vegetarian business, said Anna, was something Magda, now that she was approaching her final exams, could no longer afford. The brain needed . . . "Please, please!" said Gottlieb.

The telephone rang. Julia ran to it. From the dialect she used it immediately became apparent who she was talking to. It had often exasperated him that everyone in this family always adjusted promptly and totally to the person calling. If a North German phoned, each member of the family was in instant command of the North German intonation. With Anna he had the impression that in her instinctive instantaneous adjustment she went far beyond mere inflections. How dare she reproach him with insincerity! With her one could detect not only the various regions but even the individual character of the callers. Her voice would be pertly bright or somberly gentle, depending on the other person. When she used the almost unadulterated local dialect, Wigratsweiler was on the phone. These conversations were always the shortest.

Julia was soon back, looking pleased and excited: her cousin, the Wigratsweiler Julia, hadn't been home for two days. If she should show up here, Agnes asked to be told immediately. Notify the police, Gottlieb thought. This news was obviously the first comforting thing Anna had heard today. "Poor Agnes," she said. "Why didn't you call me to the phone?" Obviously Anna would have liked to exchange a grievance or two with Agnes, if only because at the moment, since none of her own had run away, she was in spite of everything somewhat better off than Agnes in Wigratsweiler. Mothers are people too, thought Gottlieb, an idea that pleased him. Julia thought it was neat that her namesake cousin should have disappeared. How did Magda feel about it? Magda shrugged one shoulder. Only now did she place the soup plate on the table and begin to spoon up its brimming contents—a whitish-gray mushy substance, obviously cold. At the same time she ate an apple. Gottlieb thought: She sits among us like a prisoner. "Poor Agnes," Anna said again in that blend of sympathy and complacency.

Regina appeared in the doorway and ran around her

mother toward Magda, clung to her and said it was a herpes. But Anna was already up and dragging her back into the house. Regina's appearance had been enough to animate Magda's expression momentarily. Now she resumed eating her mush. The bell rang. Julia ran to the door. Magda carried on with her eating. Julia came back disappointed. Just Antje. She had brought Regina's homework. After a few minutes Anna became uneasy. What were they thinking of, homework! Regina couldn't do any homework! She dashed upstairs. Almost immediately she could be heard abruptly sending Antje away. When she returned she said Antje had been prancing around beside Regina's bed, humming with half-closed eyes: "I'm the best, I'm the best"! Mr. Gerber had told her today, in front of the whole class, that they could consider themselves lucky to have Antje Jensen, that she contributed greatly to the class. And because Regina hadn't witnessed this triumph, Antje had come to the house to act it out for her.

Magda rose, picked up her empty plate, and left. "Magda," called Gottlieb, "can't you stay even for a second?" "What for?" she said. He wanted to say: Because. But she gave him such a look that he could say nothing. Her long thin neck no longer seemed capable of supporting that heavy face. "Come on now," he said. She said she had to work. On what? An essay. What about? Madame Bovary. "Still Madame Bovary," he said in a lower tone. "Yes," she said, and left. Even before the summer vacation her excuse for not staying with the family had always been: an essay. Madame Bovary. Even around Easter, when they went skiing and wanted her to join them on the slopes, she had said: "Madame Bovary." At first he had thought she was being conscientious.

At that moment Mrs. Schneider came through the garden

from the lake and, instead of passing them and heading straight for the upstairs apartment, deliberately started a conversation with the Zürns. She had been down to the lake again thinking that Ellen, whom she had sent down to bring back the sunglasses she had left on the beach chair and who had returned without them, simply hadn't looked properly. But to tell the truth, now that she'd been down there herself she hadn't found the sunglasses either. She was sure that the Zürns, since they had children themselves, would understand that her question to Ellen as to whether the girl had reported that the sunglasses weren't down there without looking properly was not entirely fanciful. Gottlieb said that Mrs. Schneider's question must be called realistic, even if in the case of such a well-brought-up girl as Ellen the normally appropriate and necessary question might for once not be necessary. But why not necessary? Because Mrs. Schneider invariably asked this question, a question that might be just a shade too severe. So the question was only superfluous because it was always asked. In cases where it was not asked, it wasn't superfluous either, but absolutely essential. Right?

Although, said Mrs. Schneider, he had phrased this more from a legal point of view, as a mother she must agree with him. Mr. Schneider and Ellen appeared around the elderberry bush to find out what was keeping their mommy. Mrs. Schneider said the sunglasses really weren't down there. "I told you so," said Ellen. Mr. Schneider said: "They can't have vanished from the face of the earth, so let's have another look while it's still light."

Mrs. Schneider and Ellen stared at Mr. Schneider. They failed to see why they should all three go down to the lake again. Mother and daughter knew the sunglasses weren't there. For a moment there was silence. Above each of the three heads of the Schneider family a swarm of mosquitoes was seething in the evening light. The heavy air suddenly carried the sound of bells up from the lake, where there certainly weren't any churches. The roses immediately looked as if they were surprised. And the hollyhocks, Gottlieb wanted to cry out: Look, the hollyhocks are turning their blossoms to listen, like deer turning their ears. But he took care not to. "Come along," said Mr. Schneider. "Ellen, didn't you hear what Daddy"—she said the word differently from that morning—"just said?" But since still no one made a move, and perhaps would never again have made a move, Mr. Schneider sprang between mother and daughter, seized them both by the hand and, talking loudly about the sunglasses, swept them down to the lake.

Gottlieb began to carry in the dishes. He thought with admiration of Mr. Schneider. The way he had sprung forward. The way he had seized their hands. The way he had acted. Gottlieb couldn't remember ever having seized a hand like that. He wished he could have had his hand, too, seized by Mr. Schneider so that he could go down to the lake with them to take frantic part in the search for an undiscoverable pair of sunglasses. But that was out of the question. Quite out of the question. One family looks for the sunglasses, the other carries in the dishes. Indoors he didn't merely set down the dishes, he even stacked them in the dishwasher. Although he didn't feel like it, he wanted to help Anna.

T W O

Anna, who had made up a bed for herself in Regina's room, came storming in. She has an appointment at Dr. Finkenbein's for the EEG but she also has to take a sample of Regina's morning urine to Dr. Freisleben. However, since she can't very well stop there with the car she would appreciate it if Gottlieb would drop her off at Dr. Freisleben's and drive on with Regina to Dr. Finkenbein, or would he rather take the urine. . . . No, no, he would take Regina for her EEG. The night had been terrible, said Anna. Her appearance confirmed it. Regina looked as if ghosts had been buffeting her face all night. What had yesterday been grayish-mauve shadows around her eyes now seemed to have taken on actual color from which her red eyes looked out.

As Anna got out of the car she said she would follow him to Dr. Finkenbein's and bring along the referral. On the neurologist's waiting-room door was a notice saying: *October 1—Don't forget to bring your medical card!* Apart from himself and Regina, the waiting room was occupied by an old couple drained of all color. *He* said to *her* in a low voice: "I'm going to say that you're not yourself. That you felt faint." She looked straight ahead as if she hadn't heard. After a long time she said: "Felt faint." She said it as if deeply disappointed by her husband, as if she had expected much more. He, stubbornly: "I'm not going to say you collapsed." No reaction from her. He, almost desperate: "What d'you want me to say?" Then a woman with a hearing aid comes in, sits down in the almost empty room right next to the couple, as if she belonged to them, and looks Gottlieb boldly in the eye. The receptionist leads Regina away. Gottlieb is not to go in with her. When she comes back with Regina she asks for the referral. Gottlieb says his wife will be bringing it any moment. The receptionist says he can't take the child away until the referral is there. She actually holds Regina by the hand. Up to that moment it had looked protective. Then the door opens, Anna comes in with the referral, the receptionist lets go of Regina, they can leave. Regina tells them excitedly how her brain waves were measured.

At home he hurries into his office. He must phone some clients. He would like to be able to present Mrs. Leistle on Saturday with a few impressive interested parties, to make it easier for her to give him the exclusive listing. Qualified, of course. Vendors, especially women, always believe they have to employ as many brokers as possible. It is almost impossible to make them see that, with many brokers working on their property, none of them will take a genuine interest on their behalf.

First he called his cousin, Franz Horn, who handled the properties of the firm that employed him. Only six months ago

Gottlieb had found an industrial site in Markdorf for the firm. Of his 22,000-mark commission, he had remitted 2,200 marks to his cousin who, as Gottlieb expected, had returned the money, so he had ten dozen bottles of Hagnauer delivered to his home; those had been accepted. The secretary put him through. Gottlieb said: "Is that you, Franz?" Franz said: "Oh Gottlieb, it's you!" Yes, it was, said Gottlieb. How was Franz, and Hilde, was Hilde well too, was she still singing, you don't say, more than ever, and one knew nothing about it, life was so hectic one hardly got out anymore, and the kids, my God, almost through high school, but that's how it is, kids grow up, isn't that the truth, we don't get any younger either, do we?

Was Thiele happy with the Markdorf site? By this time he'd easily have to pay 10,000 more for it. Now Gottlieb really had something that Thiele had been looking for for quite a while, really something quite special. Built in '05. Nowhere else in the world was there a house under such trees, with such a marina, on such a lake, not to mention the tennis court, what he'd call a chance in a lifetime. If Franz and Gottlieb wanted to do the right thing, they should get rid of their own little houses right away and buy that property. Never again would they have such an opportunity. And why don't they? God, Franz, damn it all! Why not? He doesn't know. He really doesn't know. A forced sale, Franz! That Mrs. Bansin, Franz must have heard of her, she's blown it all, she and her son; Eberhard, the dear boy, used to go to school with Gottlieb, that's how he managed to get his hands on this fantastic buy.

So, to repeat, mother and son have blown it all. She gambled, had a losing streak. Now young Bansin is a Jehovah's Witness standing on the Marien-Platz not far from

them in Ravensburg, a basset hound beside him, Franz must
have seen him, yes, right, that's young Bansin, the one with
the funny-looking dog. That's what happens when a person's
on the skids. They used to have their factories in the East, of
course, a thousand workers, somewhere around that, and
without their factories they can't exist. Produced looms, in
Chemnitz. My God, that's something Thiele should be told! A
man who has built up Chemnitz Dentures over here has a
right to be first in line when a house decorated mainly by
Dresden artists comes on the market. Something of such
unique historical interest naturally attracts buyers and con-
noisseurs. Gottlieb believes one should be able to get it for 1.9.
Then there would be the renovations. After all, the owners
haven't done a thing for thirty years. A new roof, a new
heating system, a new coat of paint, the marina has suffered
the most, but with 400,000 a person could do a lot. Then he'd
have something he can sell at the drop of a hat for twice the
price. But if Gottlieb knows Arthur Thiele, he'd never sell it!
Crazy about boats and tennis the way he is! Even the bathrooms, and their fixtures! Huge rooms, Franz! Thiele has only
to see it, and he'll buy! Which means that Franz and Gottlieb
would have reaped a nice reward for themselves.

Franz Horn groaned. "Oh Gottlieb," he said. This couldn't
have come at a worse time. Since all the profits from the
dentures couldn't be reinvested in dentures, and since the
denture production—which, though flourishing, was rather
specialized—had made diversification seem advisable, a plant
for a new production was being built on the Markdorf property. For Gottlieb's ears alone: windsurfing boards. Since they
knew all about plastics and Thiele was crazy about water, this
seemed an obvious step. But it meant a terrible strain on

capital resources. They were simply overextending themselves. That was his opinion. Thiele always went head over heels—perhaps even on principle—way beyond what Franz Horn deemed feasible. And now on top of that a commitment of over two million, just for a place to live, that was entirely out of the question, especially right now. In five years, when they had reached their first goal of selling thirty thousand surfboards a year, they could talk about it. . . .

"Franz, for God's sake," Gottlieb interrupted his cousin, who was known in the family as a pettifogging pessimist. Why couldn't Franz just toss the idea to Thiele, just for fun? After all, Gottlieb knew only from Franz and no one else that Arthur Thiele was looking for something of the kind and was the right man for it. "True, true enough," exclaimed Franz Horn, every day Thiele was cursing his exposed-concrete, flat-roofed view bungalow, although by now a lot of shrubs and trees had grown up around it. Every day Thiele quoted some bioconstruction apostle who conducted tests on students in wood or concrete cells to prove how concrete and plastics are damaging to both mind and soul. It was pathetic to hear that giant of a man shout: I'm suffocating, I'm suffocating in this concrete box!

"There you are then!" exclaimed Gottlieb. "And now he has a chance to get out! He'd be 500,000 marks ahead simply by renting out thirty to forty berths in the marina, anyone would pay ten years' rent in advance just to get in. But Thiele will keep the marina for himself, he'll declare it an experimental area for the development of his surfboards and he'll finance the cost by write-offs, that's Thiele for you, am I right?"

"It'd be just like him," said Franz. "But more than 1.5 is

out of the question, Gottlieb, I swear it. Even 1.5 is madness. Every mark beyond that, a crime. In Markdorf we're creating a hundred and twenty new jobs, Gottlieb!"

Franz would toss the idea to Thiele, then they'd see. At the moment Thiele was in Norway, in Bergen, to negotiate with one of the leading European jaw surgeons. Also to do a bit of fishing on the side since he was so crazy about water. Thiele would be back Monday. Franz would put him in the picture right away, although he was afraid that, once Thiele saw the rooms and bathrooms described by Gottlieb, all that vitality and enthusiasm of his would make him think only of the parties he could throw there, and he'd simply grab it. What Thiele had in mind at present was something between Neuschwanstein and Karinhall. He had already bought his second Breker sculpture. Of course Franz would tell Thiele everything he had heard from Gottlieb. Though Thiele wasn't a day younger than Franz, Thiele had now become the young prince, the hothead, while Franz was the elder statesman. So Franz, in describing the property to Mr. Thiele with every possible reservation, would not come into conflict with his loyalty toward his cousin. The more he warned Mr. Thiele, the more impetuous Thiele became. That made sense to Gottlieb. He asked Franz to warn Mr. Thiele in no uncertain terms and to say hello to Hilde and the kids.

Gottlieb then proceeded to take out Baptist Rauh's file, although he knew everything about this client by heart, from his phone number down to the most recent business deal. Like his mother, he could have got along almost without writing anything down, his memory, like his mother's, particularly where figures were concerned, apparently being of unlimited capacity. Baptist Rauh was at the studio, he was told. Mrs.

Rauh was so curt that Gottlieb couldn't take it for mere moodiness. Most likely she had gradually come to hate him because he kept on inciting her husband to buy more property in the Lake Constance area. During the last fifteen years he had put Mr. Rauh in the way of five properties, the first one while he was still in Dr. Enderle's employ. Mrs. Rauh, who was born in Hamburg, had not the slightest interest in her husband's part of the country. He came from Hergensweiler. She wanted to make him a true denizen of Hamburg. But— and this was worse—she could not, or would not, look at figures. Otherwise she would have been aware that the five properties, which together had cost 160,400 marks, were by this time worth 750 or 800,000. Mrs. Rauh had never put in an appearance at any of the viewings or the closing of any of the deals, which were always followed by quite lively parties. A model for furs and hats, she was much in demand in Hamburg and Berlin.

Whenever Gottlieb saw him, Baptist Rauh looked as if he needed a vacation. As a composer and lyricist he was probably at the mercy of even more bookings than his wife. Mr. Rauh liked to say that, as soon as he retired from Hamburg and built a house on one of his properties here, he wouldn't touch another cigarette. He would lead a different kind of life, become a different kind of person, write a different kind of music. He always seemed to see himself on the brink of this change. He seemed to be slaving away in Hamburg and elsewhere just to be able to return to his native region. Lately it had quite often been he who had called Gottlieb and asked whether Gottlieb didn't have a farmhouse for him or some old, overgrown house by the lake. Best of all, a farmhouse by the lake. He had lost all desire to build his own house, although during the last twenty years nothing had attracted him more than building, than being present at the excavation, when the foundations are poured, the walls rise. Now he suddenly lacked all feeling, all desire, for that. Something old, best of all an old farmhouse with plenty of superfluous buildings, in a remote situation, such was the vision now pursuing him.

Gottlieb thanked Mrs. Rauh very much and told her he would take the liberty, if he might, of phoning again in the afternoon. He tried to invest the two sentences with an almost magical, quite irresistible warmth. But the cold "Just as you please" at the Hamburg end of the line made him doubt the potency of his warmth.

He tipped back his contoured chair and lay motionless. To his horror, as it were, he realized he was glad not to have reached Baptist Rauh. This happened to him quite often, his being glad when someone he phoned wasn't in. He lay with his eyes closed and saw, as if passing before him in lights on a tall building, the continuously repeated words: Happiness is when I phone someone and he's not in. Outside, the Schneiders, apparently on their way back from the tennis court, were just going down to the water. Mrs. Schneider said to Mr. Schneider: "One should never try to return balls like that."

In a voice which immediately betrayed that her strength was already overtaxed and that at the moment she could tolerate nothing but obedience, Anna called the family to lunch. Today he carried his cup of coffee over to his office. He had to demonstrate to himself and his family that he had no time to waste. He frequently had to test himself to see whether he was in danger of becoming lazy. When he observed others he saw that they were either working or doing nothing, resting, taking it easy. This distinction was unknown to him. He was always in danger not only of doing nothing but of never doing anything again, which was why he had constantly to force himself to do something. He took pains not to allow that innermost, profoundest mood to surface, a mood that was bound to lead to the confession that he never did any work and never wanted to do any work and was always just pretending to be working. The fact that he worked almost continuously was due solely to his fear of that terrible inclination to do nothing.

Tonight he must ask Mrs. Reinhold some questions about Mrs. Leistle, then tomorrow he could adjust his text and his advertisement to the impression of her character that Mrs. Reinhold was going to give him.

At four o'clock he phoned Baptist Rauh. He didn't want to reproach himself, he said, for not having told Mr. Rauh of this opportunity. Mr. Rauh's properties could be sold today for 800, maybe 900,000 marks. For 1.6 or 1.7 it might—he emphasized *it might*—be possible to acquire this wonderful example of art nouveau, with all its marvelous appurtenances: the turret, whose circular stories—the two top ones, at least— were embraced rather than encircled by stone garlands; the harmonious main entrance surmounted by a gable resembling the hood of a Gothic madonna . . . he mustn't get carried away, he didn't want to perturb Mr. Rauh. That he was calling at all could only be justified by his own perturbation. Ever since seeing the Swan Villa he had been trying to prove to himself that he couldn't buy this exquisite specimen. But each time it was demonstrated, with increasing clarity, how impossible it was for him to buy the house himself, the more he was tempted to buy, buy, buy. All he was doing now was letting Mr. Rauh share in his own perplexity and perturbation. As one native son of the area to another. "Tell me yourself, Mr. Rauh, did I have any right to keep this from you?" In a low, weak voice Baptist Rauh said: "No, Mr. Zürn. Thank you." Gottlieb could hear Mr. Rauh drawing several times on his cigarette. "But how," Mr. Rauh went on to say, "how?" "That's just it," said Gottlieb Zürn. "Of course, the marina could easily fetch 300 or 400,000 from a yacht club, but wouldn't that mean selling the nose off your face?" He would be more inclined to advise letting the tennis court go to one of the hotels for 80,000. So if Mr. Rauh could lay his hands on 700,000, he would advise him to buy.

Mr. Rauh softly repeated the figure. A strong emotion seemed to take hold of his voice. He had to see the house. He didn't know how he could lay his hands on 700,000 but he simply had to see the house with the madonna hood over the entrance and the turret with its stone garlands and all the rest of it. And right by the lake? With a marina like that? Yes, and walls two foot thick! He would never sell it! Mr. Zürn, what can you be thinking of, sell the marina?! The marina was the one thing that would manage to persuade his wife to come with him. She was crazy about sailing, just crazy! "That would clinch it," said Gottlieb. "My God, Mr. Zürn," said Baptist Rauh, "that'll clinch it! At last! If Bruni goes for it, I'll be more than twice as strong." "She must see the house and the marina," said Gottlieb. "We'll be there," said Mr. Rauh.

Now Gottlieb had to put on the brakes, describe the situation, the premature but justified nature of his call because he wanted to put one of his best clients in the picture before the crowds started coming. Mr. Rauh will talk to his wife, Gottlieb will talk to Mrs. Leistle, next week Gottlieb will phone again. Why wait so long? says Mr. Rauh in alarm, why not on

Saturday when Mr. Zürn would be back from Stuttgart? Gottlieb said he also wanted to be able to get Mr. Rauh some concrete offers for his properties in Hochbuch, Motzach, Taubenberg, Rehlings, and Hoyerberg; that would take time, till Wednesday at the very least. "Wait a moment!" Mr. Rauh exclaimed. Couldn't Mr. Zürn at least tell him by the weekend whether he and Bruni could fly to Zürich and drive over, whether or not it would be a good idea just to take a look at the place?

"All right, we'll talk on Sunday!"

Baptist Rauh—never changes. When that fellow gets all fired up it takes more effort to keep him away from a property than it does to get others to look at it.

Anna came in to tell him that Dr. Freisleben was now advising that Regina be taken tomorrow to the children's ward of the hospital. The EEG hadn't turned up anything, but the child's condition was such that a thorough examination in the hospital should not be postponed any longer. Gottlieb was all in favor. He would immediately phone Mrs. Ortwein, who came Fridays to do his correspondence, and ask her if she could come Monday or Tuesday. Mrs. Ortwein, who at the best of times could speak only in a complaining, dragging, offended, slightly protesting voice, said this didn't suit her at all. No doubt she wanted to get the most out of the change in routine; nothing material, but Gottlieb was supposed to apologize profusely and kowtow to her. Everyone seems intent at all times to get as much as possible out of everything. Gottlieb said: "Forget about it, Mrs. Ortwein, come tomorrow." "Yes, but would that really be all right?" In that case his wife would just have to take Regina to the hospital by herself.

No, no, she didn't want that either, in that case she'd call her sister in Freiburg to ask her to come one day earlier or later. "But I can't have you do that!" said Gottlieb. Nonsense, she could always try. She told him to hang up, she'd phone him right back. She phoned right back. It was fine. Her sister would merely have to change the date for her car inspection. So she'd be there on Monday. In the end it seemed to have given her unalloyed pleasure to have switched everything around. Never had her dragging voice shown so much animation. Probably he had always misjudged Mrs. Ortwein besides misinterpreting her tone of voice. Isn't it funny that one thinks one has an uncomplicated relationship with a person to whom one gives money while with a person from whom one receives money one no longer has, for that very reason, any relationship at all? If everything, especially logic, he thought, were to be based on this experience . . .

Anna came in carrying a bunch of roses whose red deepened in color toward the center. She held out the flowers to him. Mrs. Reinhold only admired bouquets consisting of flowers of the same sort, but under no circumstances must these flowers be of the same shade, said Anna. For details of that kind she had a memory as inexhaustible as was his for details about his clients. He drew Anna to him. She held the bouquet at arm's length to protect the roses. He went upstairs, put on his lemon-yellow trousers, the shirt of palest pink, and his tropical-weight jacket, brandy-colored with fine black checks. Since, as always on such occasions, he was ready much too early and didn't want Anna to notice how excited he was, he stayed in his room, unable to settle to anything.

As often as he tried to visualize Mrs. Leistle, he always ended up with an impossibly respectable female image, straight from the hairdresser, suit sheathing her like armor, ruby brooch, cream silk blouse with tie collar. To top it all, a tiny pillbox of a hat with a scrap of veiling. And in an angular way, lean. And what else? Incipient mustache? Yes. Even if he were to endow her with another score of details, he simply could not see her. Her face, her eyes . . . ? He was urgently in need of a few more details so that when he emerged at the Parler-Strasse house from a light hallway into an even lighter living room, he wouldn't have to cope with surprises as well. He wished he could stay in his room and not have to tell anyone why he didn't want to come out. He knows why he doesn't want to come out. But his reasons are so ridiculous, so shameful, that he could only confess to them under torture. Not that he didn't long to get out. Desperately. But under different conditions. Certainly not if he had to show up at Mrs. Reinhold's. Face Mrs. Reinhold's guests. Each one of them good, clever, fragrant, reserved, attractive, unapproachable. Gottlieb felt an urge to sit down on his Kirman rug. For a moment he imagined he could crawl away into the dense thicket of his rug. Or at least crawl around on it. But even that he had to deny himself. It was time to leave.

There on the gravel driveway stood the black-and-white Monteverdi Safari, shining immaculately as ever. This was the plush conveyance in which the young sociologist drove Mrs. Reinhold to do her shopping, play tennis, go sailing. This oversize vehicle, which was equally suited for being chauffeured in state as for use on prairie or desert, appeared to be reserved for drives with the young sociologist. When he was on his own he drove his little Renault, looking ludicrously cramped and squeezed in it. He was a giant of a fellow. A Saint Bernard. When he and Mrs. Reinhold, who also tended to be larger than life, were seated in the Monteverdi Safari, everything looked just right. Anna couldn't understand why Mrs. Reinhold would drive a car which, wherever it was parked, immediately broadcast the fact that Mrs. Reinhold was not far off. Anna would have understood if Mrs. Reinhold had concealed herself and the sociologist. Anna doesn't think in liberated terms.

Worse than being the first guest and arriving too early was to have to approach the group of those who had already arrived and were busily chatting away as a clique, and then having to decide with whom and in which order to shake hands. Mrs. Reinhold accepted the flowers, recognized the concept as her own, was touched. Because this time he actually was the first, he couldn't simply embark on the subject of Mrs. Leistle and give the impression that this was the only reason for his arriving so early. Mrs. Reinhold could have brought up the subject, but she sent him straight out onto the terrace. He never did manage to utter his excuses for his overpunctuality. She had promptly called out: "Giselher, a vase!" And where was Dr. Reinhold? Judith, that was the name of the daughter who was always top of Magda's class, that much he knew. Benjamin was the one who was always competing with Stefan Schatz for first place in Julia's class; he was also junior regional champion in some kind of fencing. But which? And the youngest girl was called. . . ? Was she in America? Anna had told him everything, but he hadn't paid proper attention. Once again he had failed to realize the necessity. And there was really nothing simpler—let alone cheaper—if one wanted to please people than to remember a few facts about their children. If now he could have asked whether the daughter, whose name he didn't remember, in

America, in the city he had forgotten, was still as happy living with the family that Mrs. Reinhold had somewhere said something about, something Anna had picked up and reported and that he had already forgotten while he was still listening, the evening would probably have been his. If only he would grasp the fact—and behave accordingly—that there is always necessity.

As soon as Mrs. Reinhold announced that all the guests were there, the little group strolled out onto the terrace and were waited on by Giselher and the Italian maid, who was addressed as Anna. Giselher wasn't even wearing a tie. In his case it was not noticeable because his beard turned his curly head into a curly ball. Dr. Terbohm and his young wife had still been laughing with Kaltammer when they shook hands with Gottlieb. Kaltammer had been even more surprised to see Gottlieb than Gottlieb had been to see Kaltammer. Kaltammer, in a petroleum-colored silk suit, was there with a Baroness Reitmor, who, compared to him, looked particularly healthy. In Gottlieb's scale of ages, Kaltammer was a freak. Gottlieb considered him an infant old man. There was no intermediate age into which he would have better fitted. The second Mrs. Terbohm still looked exactly as she had twelve years ago when she married the doctor. But even then, though she had been much younger, she had looked as if she were twenty-nine. Now perhaps she had just reached that age. So at the moment she was in perfect harmony with herself. She radiated without even trying. There is nothing I cannot love, that was what she radiated. Gottlieb looked across to Mrs. Reinhold as loyally as possible and at once had to admit— although a moment before he had considered this impossible—that she could hold her own. The verdigris green of her

pure silk was so transparent that, as far as one could see, there
was nothing under her dress but herself, yet that in turn was so
submerged in greenish twilight that there wasn't as much to
see as one thought one was about to be allowed to see. All
evening, Gottlieb Zürn could not keep his eyes from constantly
feeling their way up and down Mrs. Reinhold's ample figure,
his eyes simply refusing to be told by him that there was no
more to be seen even at the hundredth glance than at the first.
And, because in order to rid himself of his fear and tension, he
quickly had a lot to drink, and because, when he had had a
few drinks, he could never keep something of immediate
importance to him entirely to himself, he abruptly took over
the conversation and recounted—without knowing what
motivated him—that this summer they had had a couple
from Mönchengladbach in one of their vacation apartments,
and that the husband, a physicist, had spent seventeen con-
secutive days behind binoculars mounted on a stand, observing men and women, but probably more likely women than
men, on the boats passing by. As soon as the physicist spotted
something worthwhile, he had photographed it with the aid of
an enormous telephoto lens. One Saturday evening, when one
of those motor cruisers had anchored about eighty yards
offshore, the man from Mönchengladbach had not come back
into the house until after dark, no matter how shrilly his wife
had shouted her "Heinrisch" from the upstairs window. And
by seven o'clock on Sunday morning he was back at his post.
Spent all day Sunday watching the practically naked young
couple idling on deck. How slowly, for instance, they had
rubbed each other's skin with suntan oil. So slowly, in fact,
that it was impossible to take one's eyes off it. In the afternoon
the young man had started to give himself a shower. Half lying

down. On the prow. She had handed him the shower. Kneeling. Then he handed her back the shower. Then she soaped him, rubbing the soap in even more slowly than the oil in the morning. Then massaging with a brush. Still the woman doing it to the man. Then showering again. Not the man showering himself but she him. All of him, in fact. Then he showering her. With the same ritual slowness and thoroughness. Finally the young man out on the lake had slowly taken the binoculars from her outstretched hand and looked through them. The man from Mönchengladbach had caught their attention. Then he'd handed the binoculars back to the girl, got up, cleared the deck, raised the anchor, and slowly moved off. He, Gottlieb Zürn, would like to know the kind of faces made by two people observing each other through binoculars of equal strength! That's how he finished his story.

Well, if Mr. Zürn hadn't mentioned that this voyeur was a physicist from Mönchengladbach, Lissi Reinhold exclaimed, she would have thought he was talking about a boy of fifteen. "You should say twelve," said Dr. Terbohm in a martyred voice. "But you seem to have kept the observer quite nicely under observation too," said Mrs. Reinhold. Gottlieb Zürn blushed. He frequently told stories of this kind in order to find out how others judged what he did or would like to do. Mrs. Reinhold found it delightful that Gottlieb Zürn blushed. He had the feeling that his blushing had intensified as soon as Mrs. Reinhold noticed it too. He was acutely aware that his face was fiery red. Crimson, probably. Crimson to purple. Like, under certain circumstances, the head of his sex organ, he thought, couldn't help thinking.

Before being stared at became totally unbearable, the baroness said: "It's the sunset." That was a marvelous sentence.

They all looked out toward the west where the sun had just slipped down behind the purple forest fur of the Bodanrück, leaving behind a glowing spectacle. Mrs. Reinhold said: "Isn't it nice when someone can still blush even though he's no longer twenty but . . ." Since Gottlieb believed she was hesitating, he felt obliged to say: ". . . close to fifty." Oh yes, she exclaimed, he had said that when they first met, ten years ago. "And," said Gottlieb, "it's truer now than ever." The youngest-looking, of course, was always Kaltammer, said Mrs. Reinhold. Didn't the others also think that Kaltammer looked spookily young? Gottlieb thought there was no better way of expressing it. It was a mystery to her why Kaltammer had given up dancing. Kaltammer said: "But unfortunately I no longer blush." Everyone laughed. Gottlieb felt condemned. Not fifteen, twelve! No one had defended the physicist from Mönchengladbach. Giselher remarked that Erikson had said that the great handicap of the industrial nations was that they produced few adults. Lissi wanted that restricted to men. Her husband—whom, by the way, she had to excuse for the moment, this evening for the first time he was playing against his chess computer at the sixth level, it seemed to be taking some time, unfortunately that was keeping Judith away too— her husband had asked her the other day, when they were talking about Jarl, what kind of a name that was, and sheer intuition made her say: from the Lower Rhine. Kaltammer has uncannily large, lashless eyes. When he moves them, he visibly shunts them from here to there. One has the feeling that wherever his gaze stops it strikes with a distinct little cymbal beat. It goes "ding." Looking at Giselher: ding. From him to the baroness, to Mrs. Reinhold: ding, ding. His gaze never roams. It jerks from target to target. "Lower Rhine is not quite correct," he said. He had his Norwegian grandmother on his mother's side to thank for his first given name. Prima ballerina in Copenhagen, married to the German military attaché, accompanied him to Warsaw, Madrid, and so on. Sheer homesickness made her see to it, throughout her life, that the family was given Nordic names. In Norway, Jarl was some sort of term for a chieftain. Every valley had its Jarl. In English it was Earl, something like a count. Gottlieb admired Claims-Maier's perspicacity. He had sensed that. "Earl Kaltammer!" shouted Mrs. Reinhold and Giselher simultaneously. He had never been a Jarl, he had always only been called that, said Kaltammer more solemnly than was necessary. Then he stopped and, with raised eyebrows, gave Mrs. Reinhold a look of extreme willingness. His yellow hair—Rudi was right, it was yellow—cut equally short all over, closely fitting his head, shone in the evening light. "Isn't it funny," said Mrs. Reinhold, "now I suddenly see the blond of your hair quite differently. Your blond has nothing in common with Giselher's Berlin blond." Kaltammer's was more genuine. And far and away more genuine than her own Hedelfingen blond. Jarl's blond was, in the best sense of the word, penetrating.

And she went right on to tell them what had happened to her in Boston fifteen or more years ago on account of her really quite insignificant blond coloring because, of course, she had not been a Norwegian but one of those terrible Germans. Jewish taxi drivers, Jewish furriers, Jewish dentists . . . oh my Lord! And since she had Jewish friends on several continents she need hardly emphasize that in describing these antiblond pogroms she wasn't motivated by anti-Semitic feelings. She had lived with her husband in Boston for two and a half years.

In Brookline. Every house a brownstone poem from the nine-teenth century, humming, rhyming, warming. And seventy percent Jewish. That's why her husband had wanted to live there, of course. Because of the children. Where Jews are in the majority you always find the best schools. And Jewish kids are the most ambitious, which could do one's own kids nothing but good. And so it did. But one time Judith had caught her finger in the Chevy's electric window—they hadn't been used to those in Germany, of course!—so off to the hospital with her on Sunday, Judith right onto a stretcher, she herself holding the little head, but when the doctor lifted off the nail tears had gushed from her eyes, and he of the handsome black locks and Rubinstein head had said: "Stop that! When your people gassed our kids *you* didn't blubber." But that made her bawl even harder. And what their German shepherd didn't have to suffer! It's all private roads there. And, believe it or not: people had still been so sensitive that Lissi actually had to send the dog back to Germany.

By this time the baroness had lost all track of what Mrs. Reinhold was talking about. Everybody explained it to her. Hitler had loved German shepherd dogs, that was why the Jewish neighbors in Brookline had asked if she would kindly spare them the sight of this German shepherd. "Oh, I see," said the baroness. And what had happened to the dog? It was a tragedy, said Mrs. Reinhold. The poor dog had been sent to her mother's in Garmisch. A year later it was dead. Pined, wasted away, never recovered. "Le pauvre chien," the baron-ess said, in such a protesting crescendo that "chien" struck the highest and strongest note. Gottlieb admired the tact that had prompted her to express her sympathy for the German dog in

French. Kaltammer said: "N'en parlons plus." After that there was silence for a moment. Only Kaltammer shunted his gaze.

Dr. Terbohm cleared his throat and asked what Mrs. Reinhold's dog had been called. Tristan. Everyone nodded as if, after what they had heard, it couldn't have been called anything else. He had once had a Yorkshire terrier, the doctor said, called Winston. Then he told them what had happened to him in Passau with Winston. He said he was telling them this although Barbi, when he told this story, always said to him in front of everybody: "You don't know what impression you give when you tell that story." "Yes," said Barbi, five times as loud as he, "he doesn't know, but go ahead, by all means, tell them your Winston porn." He told it. Gottlieb couldn't listen to Dr. Terbohm because he had to stare at Barbi. Her breasts reached from both sides far into the low-cut opening of her riotously flowered gown. No question, this evening there was no place with a greater pull. But Mrs. Reinhold and Dr. Terbohm had already threatened anyone looking there with the curse of eternal puberty. Yet everyone was sure to have watched Barbi on a surfboard. There she wore, held in place by strings, four equally tiny triangles, two above and two below. Golden, light red, or pale green. A few days ago Gottlieb had watched her in rough weather showing two husky Orientals how to windsurf. They couldn't stay on their boards for even a second, while she had had no problem whatever. She kept stopping beside one or the other as each was constantly climbing out of the water. To do so, she simply let the sail flutter in one hand. The board stopped immediately, and board and sail under her hand seemed like a horse waiting for its rider to remount. Then, pull back the sail, the wind grabs it, she leans way back, with her hair dragging in the water she zooms off.

Mrs. Reinhold screamed. And everyone else was laughing. Fortunately they laughed so loud that one more or less made no difference. Giselher laughed the most mightily. If Saint Bernards could laugh, they would laugh like that. Giselher's laugh was not only terribly loud but also terribly slow. It was the slowness that was so shattering. Suddenly Mrs. Reinhold started to scream again, but in a distinctly higher tone than the first time. She pointed at the middle between Giselher's straddling legs. The seam of his jeans had parted just where it shouldn't. At that point, wrapped in yellow, so much had bulged out that he surely must have felt it as a relief. The fact that Mrs. Reinhold was a trained singer could be heard even when she screamed. Barbi said that, after this success, she would never again say anything against her husband's Winston porn. The fact was, she was straitlaced, she had been aware of that ever since marrying this gynecologist. Giselher called: "Anna! A napkin!" Anna brought one. For today he was hors de combat, he said, after stuffing the napkin into his belt in such a way that it hung well down over the damage.

"Il faut célébrer les faux baptêmes," said Kaltammer, raising his glass to Giselher. Dr. Terbohm's story had reminded him, he said, that he had once had an employee, in fact almost a partner—those in the business, like Mr. Zürn, would probably know whom he meant—this man who for a short time had been almost a partner of his, who had meanwhile become one of his most vigilant enemies—really, he persecuted him the way Nero did the Christians—this outstanding Kaltammer persecutor, then, had had such a genius for compassion that he had regularly liberated the dogs of the neighborhood from their sexual plight by masturbating them. So, just as in Dr. Terbohm's terrier story, one might ask whether the liberator hadn't also been doing himself a favor. Gottlieb Zürn saw Kaltammer distinctly shunt his gaze onto him. Obviously this was the moment for him to say his piece again. He could add spice to the story by mentioning the name. A situation that suited him down to the ground. He was in a position to fulfill a clear expectation. He liked nothing better. Without the slightest hesitation he interjected the missing element into Kaltammer's story: Claims-Maier. In this situation he would have sacrificed even the name of his mother or father. Even his own. To be able to do what someone else desired deprived him of all willpower. It wasn't self-denial that made him comply so readily. It actually gave him satisfaction. Was it selflessness?

The success of this story, including the unmasking of Claims-Maier, would have been moderate without the appearance of Dr. Reinhold. But the entry of Dr. Reinhold and Judith, who was growing up tempestuously in her mother's image, was accompanied by the black Labrador bitch Wunni. And Wunni immediately found her way to Giselher and, once there, insisted on putting her nose under the napkin. And Dr. Terbohm, quick as a flash: "Aha, another damage claim inspection!" That triggered a gust of laughter spiced with shock. Barbi said, punching Dr. Terbohm in the ribs hard enough to make him squeal: "You've sure got some nerve!" in the thickest local dialect. Kaltammer assumed a look of pained surprise. For a girl whom one could only think of as a cosmopolite to speak this gruesome dialect! All dialects were embarrassing, the local one was painful. Barbi said, again in dialect: "Oh, cool it!" Kaltammer had closed his ears at the very first tone. Kaltammer said softly—which meant: I'm saying it softly but I have to say it—that he found the local dialect and the local population equally hard to take. The fact that there were a few individuals—with his long torso he bowed deeply in Barbi's direction—who had triumphed over all the horrors of such origins was as exciting as anything else that went against all probability. The average local mentality. That smug uncouthness, that constant display of respectability . . . Dr. Terbohm drew Barbi to him and said: "By marriage you're a Westphalian!" . . . and despite all the appreciation of everything provincial shown in recent years, surely one must admit that it was the newcomers to the area who were responsible for anything that really functioned properly. Giselher, a Berliner himself, didn't wish to deny that but, since he did research in Constance on provincial conditions, he was in a position to prove that political-historical circumstances were responsible for the pugnacious backwardness of the local population.

Mrs. Reinhold, now that her husband and oldest daughter had joined the circle, was seated closer to Gottlieb and whispered: "That would be a topic for *him*." Gottlieb merely nodded. He didn't know what she was talking about. If *he* were there, Kaltammer wouldn't have dared to run down the dialect like that. And even lower, quite archly: "If *he* had come, I couldn't have dared invite Jarl, could I?" Gottlieb nodded without knowing what she meant. But he began to have an inkling. Who could she be speaking about like that if not *him*?! "Have you seen *his* exhibition?" Now he was sure of it. *"He"* was Paul Schatz. Was she making fun of Gottlieb? Raising her voice she announced to the whole circle that, being a native of Hedelfingen, she could understand anyone who found dialects painful, but she had been waiting all evening for someone to mention the exhibition at the Cavazzen House! She took it for granted that no one, apart from her husband, had missed it. Kaltammer stood up somewhat abruptly, saying that the baroness and he should have left an hour ago. But he didn't want it to look as if he were sneaking off so as to avoid commenting on his colleague's paintings, which he found brilliant; he dared to say this also in the name of the baroness who, as they knew, wanted to become a painter or already was one. "Julienne, qu'est-ce que tu aimes plus, être ou naître?" "Naître," she said. "Bien sûr," he said. It was too bad this man should waste *his* herculean yet delicate imagination on such a terrible occupation as that of real estate agent. On the other hand, what would have happened to this profession if *he* hadn't been there. It was due mainly to the influence of this man that it was possible to minimize one's horror at being a realtor. But perhaps he, Kaltammer, was talking out of turn now that he had retired to the more contemplative-custodial pursuit of dealing in Burgundian châteaux. What was being built hereabouts could be neither lived in nor sold without harm to the soul. The fact was that since the eighteenth century nothing had been built. The bourgeoisie had never learned how to build. Hence the realtor was not solely to blame for having to deal in nothing but ghastliness. So, long may *he* live! "We hope *he* will return safely from Vienna!"

During these pronouncements Gottlieb had begun to feel hot under the collar. Escape forward, he thought, and said: "Anyone who heard *his* oration at the grave of Dr. Enderle, or one of *his* speeches concerning the autobahn, or has read one of *his* articles in which he lashes out at the Federal Railway, or the farmers or the environmental authorities, the school board, the outboard-motor industry, the Lake Constance Water Board, the Chamber of Architects, the associations of hunters, sports fishermen et cetera et cetera et cetera, knows that *he* is not only a highly gifted painter but also a veritable wordsmith. Hardly had the name of their present hostess been mentioned in conversation with *him* when *he* had instantly and unerringly coined the phrase: There's enough of her to make two Wagner singers." So he, Gottlieb Zürn, would drink to *him*.

The sound of conversation was torn by a silence, then Lissi Reinhold called out: "Let's hope he only meant the voice!" Then she burst out laughing in all the fullness of her well-trained voice, and the laughter was so worth listening to that no one had to say anything for a while. No one joined in her laughter. Gottlieb felt he should say something. Kaltammer and his Julienne now left. He steered her out. At the last moment he turned around, bowed, smiled once more at everyone present, then acted out how he had to tear himself away from each person; with South American élan he turned on his heel, waved back over his head, and they were gone. The applause must have reached his ears.

In the silence left behind, Mrs. Reinhold asked whether Gottlieb felt as Kaltammer did about being a real estate agent. Gottlieb said that being a real estate agent made him happy because the job consisted of nothing more than the person performing it. Kaltammer had always hated the occupation. Gottlieb Zürn reminded them that, during the year of student unrest, Kaltammer had helped Constance students compose and distribute leaflets calling for the abolition of the real estate profession. The German Socialist party had done the same thing, Giselher remarked casually.

"Which German Socialist party?" Gottlieb shot back.

"That of the 1973 party convention in Hanover," said Giselher.

"Exactly," said Gottlieb, "but that doesn't even exist anymore. You can't very well say that the German Socialist party has anything against the real estate profession. . . ."

" 'Had,' I said," mumbled Giselher.

"My God, had or didn't have," Gottlieb shouted rather than exclaimed, "but no longer *has*, whereas the gentleman who has just taken his leave on *one* foot, like the Hoofèd One in person, is still, *still*, preaching contempt for the very profession that has brought him millions. Whereas the German Socialist party, my callow young sociologist, and you can put this in your pipe and smoke it—the German Socialist party, jointly with the Free Democratic party (and all honor to them for it) has initiated a revision of the real estate code that will put an end to the casuistic accumulation of regulations dreamed up over decades by what were often less than enlightened courts. The occupation restrictions that followed Hanover have been left behind, while the dandies of the cultural revolution are still celebrating victories in the silken lap of an applauding bourgeoisie, flattered by a rootless sociology because they despise roots while still cultivating an 'environmentalist' image of themselves."

Well, fortunately he felt that such aspersions had long ceased to apply to himself, said Giselher with a smirk. "That's up to you!" shouted Gottlieb. A shame that the gentleman who sees fit to call himself an agent for Burgundian châteaux but who probably makes ninety-five percent of his millions in sales as a contractor for high-rise concrete silos that he then sells room by tiny room to German and Swiss citizens whom he despises for their limited outlook, whose dialects cause his ears intense pain—a shame, a great shame, that his cynical tirade against the profession was allowed to go unchallenged! Gottlieb Zürn, himself a real estate agent, was hardly in a position to challenge him, but one would have been justified in expecting this from a sociologist who might by this time have come to his senses. . . .

"End of debate!" Mrs. Reinhold's voice rang out. "Although," she went on in her normal voice, "I happen to know that *he* would agree with you. You practically spoke in *his* name. Are you aware of that? *He*, of course, wouldn't have shouted, obviously. *He* never shouts." "Lissi, forgive me," said Dr. Reinhold in his soft voice, "since I wasn't in on the beginning, just tell me quickly who *he* is?" "How typical of my husband!" cried Lissi Reinhold. "I know for a fact that you were here when *he* was first spoken of this evening. It so happens that today the first mention of *him* came incredibly late." Nevertheless, said Dr. Reinhold, he still didn't know who *he* was, would she please forgive her stupid husband.

"It is unforgivable not to know at once that it is *he* who is being spoken about when *he* is being spoken about." She was sure Mr. Zürn wouldn't be offended if she now let it be known that she hadn't invited Kaltammer until *he* had declined. *He* had suddenly had to fly to Vienna. To see a specialist. An urgent examination that she hoped wouldn't reveal anything serious. In her opinion there was no one at the present time with *his* command of the old masters' technique. The winter lakeshore near Langenargen, pallid, vague, and suddenly that only slightly outsize female breast, flesh-colored and firm, on the cold beach. Or the primevally overgrown mouth of the River Argen in a somber, thundery light, and precisely in the crucial area where the water is no longer river and not yet lake that naked female leg emerges, rising at an angle but not fully extended and wearing a shoe, again that strident color of human flesh in otherwise pure Nature. Or that little sky and water picture, shining with an unearthly light, in which that human tongue sets the tone, floating in the water, so red, so graceful, and this time not terrible at all, as if it belonged there and was enjoying it, as if it was enjoying everything. But her favorite had been the hollyhock picture. The hollyhock with the three tall stems. The blossoms ranging from pale pink to purple. And looking out of the topmost blossom, *his* own face. "Paul Schatz," Gottlieb quickly whispered to Dr. Reinhold.

For the last time Anna brought something to eat. After the salmon with mustard sauce, which Jarl F. Kaltammer claimed to be almost as good as the Gravet salmon he had marinated himself, after the green figs wrapped in Parma ham and the assortment of cheeses, there was now a mousse. This was consumed as slowly as possible, and there was some further discussion of *his* pictures. Suddenly Dr. Reinhold had disappeared. He left even more inconspicuously than he had arrived. Judith leaned back, stretched, and said: "Giselher, are you staying the night?" Her stretching startled Gottlieb. He said he had stayed two hours longer than he had meant to. "So have we," said Dr. Terbohm. "You can say that again," said Barbi; she was already on her feet and, although Gottlieb had no idea why, put her hand down the front of her dress. Now only the wife of Dr. Cornelius remained seated. She said that this time she was suffering more than usual from jet lag. Mrs. Reinhold intoned the coda. How nice to have seen each other again. But she hoped it wouldn't be so long till the next time. In any case they wouldn't be going away for a while.

They'd be in touch. "Must've been quite an evening," said Judith. Mrs. Reinhold said it was irresponsible of Judith to still be up seeing that the day after tomorrow she was making her first public appearance in Constance with the Lake Constance Symphony Orchestra. "Anything to get rid of me," Judith could be heard to say as they left.

He parked the car outside. Without turning on a light he crept into the house. As soon as he was in bed, Anna whispered: "You're late." She went on to ask what it had been like. He said that Dr. Cornelius and his wife were back from America. And what did Dr. Cornelius say about Regina's illness? Oh, said Gottlieb, it had been practically impossible to talk to him. Because of the jet lag. "Excuses," she said, and turned over. It was too warm in the room. Stifling. He crept to the balcony door, opened it wide. Back in bed, he felt unable to relax. He lay as if made of something completely brittle. On his left side something was contracting. He could do nothing about it. Anna could have released him. But for that she would have to admit to his being there. It really was exasperating, how little notice she took of him. He thought that at all times he would welcome something sexual. It didn't have to be anything special. Just something to acknowledge the fact that he shared the room with a woman. After all, as long as Anna was in the room this fact couldn't be disregarded for a second. And what couldn't this fact lead to! And that this fact was so rarely and, so to speak, sporadically responded to, gave rise to the kind of pain that results from privation. Watch out now! You're guiding your thoughts in one direction only until you're ruthless enough to fall upon poor Anna. You're trying to work yourself up to enforcing your conjugal rights, admit it. To practicing the *manus* marriage of ancient Rome, is that it? As he was leaving the party he had touched Lissi. Somewhere on her hip. He had encountered a string. What was she wearing that belonged to this string encircling the bare skin of her hips? Why hadn't she mentioned Mrs. Leistle? Why had she talked like that about Schatz? Why had she addressed those first remarks only to him? Had she wanted to humiliate him?

Far away in the distance he heard thunder. It was reassuring to think that his tense, wakeful condition might also be caused by the weather. So all he had to do was wait till the thunderstorm arrived and discharged itself, till the rain came down, then everything in him would be released too. Mrs. Reinhold will probably call up sometime during the day, apologize profusely, and then supply him with the necessary tips for negotiating with Mrs. Leistle.

He fell asleep. Dreamed. He was walking with Paul Schatz up a mountain path. To the left of the path the meadow fell steeply away, to the right rose an embankment with hazel bushes. Autumn. They trudged slowly uphill as if each wanted to make it easier for the other. But the other should not gain the impression that anyone doubted his ability to step out more briskly. This peaceful ascent was brought to an end by Gottlieb Zürn when he suddenly ceased walking but continued to advance without moving his feet. His feet firmly together, he jerked his way uphill. By sheer willpower. Because he wanted to amaze Paul Schatz. And when he saw that Paul Schatz was amazed, he stopped. Jerking himself forward by sheer concentration and at the same time smiling had been so exhausting that he was afraid his breath might fail him at any moment. They slowly walked a few steps side by side, then with a gentle push Gottlieb took off and hovered ahead of Paul Schatz: he would have liked to reach out to him and lift him up in the air beside him. To hover with Paul Schatz and to know that he, Gottlieb Zürn, was responsible for this hovering together, that would have been the ultimate. But in order to maintain the concentration necessary for this hovering, he had to hold his breath—the slightest breathing would instantly result in a fall—and in order to hold his breath he had to keep his arms pressed tightly against his body, which meant he couldn't reach out his hand to Paul Schatz. When he could no longer stay up in the air, he just barely managed a landing beside Paul Schatz that looked as if it had been deliberate.

He awoke, and lay rigid with breathlessness. Even when he was awake it took him a few moments to be able to breathe again. At first he dared inhale only tiny amounts of air. A deep breath, he felt, would still be beyond his strength. The thunderstorm was already close. He ought to get up, get some fresh air. But where to find it? The air he breathed in had no effect. This ineffectual breathing discouraged him. He had to find Mrs. Reinhold worth loving before he could hope for any relief. But then she would be the first to call anyone neurotic who forced himself to want to love someone in whose presence every second became one of horror. Her nature tends to extremes. The person she cannot maltreat she adores. From those whom she maltreats she expects adoration. She is mood exemplified. She would look her most attractive with a harmonica, looking naïvely coy across it into the camera. On the other hand, nothing would suit Anna less than a harmonica. And anyway, looking into the camera would be unthinkable for Anna. Anna is the opposite of an extrovert. The moment anyone so much as enters the house, she is no longer herself.

As long as the vacation apartments are occupied, she won't go near the piano. But in fall, in winter, then she'll sit down at it, then it's as if in the middle of the forest the ground opened up into a chasm and, from depths existing nowhere else, music came streaming out. Really, sometimes it annoyed him that she should be so like Else, who also disappears the moment strangers arrive.

Maybe Dr. Reinhold is something like Anna. He hasn't said a word. His wife always talks across him, past him. The baroness asked him how his game against the computer turned out. The computer had signaled: "I lose." Would Lissi tell him that Gottlieb, as he left, had put his hand on her hip as if inadvertently? He couldn't help himself. I'd rather die than not put my hand there, he had thought. But his hand was already there. And he had even risked her being aware that his touch had been deliberate. She hadn't slapped his hand. Although he had encountered that intriguing little string against her skin, he had removed his hand at once. Didn't Dr. Reinhold mind one's touching his wife a bit? So many things one doesn't know! Perhaps she had thought it was Giselher's hand. Of course! He had touched her body in order to convey to her an illusion of irresistibility. She must help him to obtain the most important, the finest listing of his career. No other agent had as much right to this listing as he. He was no construction czar, building concrete silos! He had no administrative office in Vaduz for apartment houses and second homes. He had two vacation apartments in his own house and a single-family cottage in Immenstaad. That was his nest egg. He was still only a broker. He produced nothing. That humbled him and made him proud. Those Kaltammers, Schatzes, and cohorts with their offices in Liechtenstein and

Switzerland! By this time they could all be living off the interest. But they carry on. Put up wicked buildings and give themselves airs! There should be a law! No, there shouldn't at all. Money is what they are after. More and more money. Money is the best defense against death. Because figures are what count. Because the figures with which time is reckoned are wrongly conceived. One needs counterfigures. Time passes! Bull! It accumulates. Every second that allegedly passes by means one more second in the world. But the feeling that time passes has prevailed. Thinking in terms of loss dominates. That explains the need for money. Profit. More and more. Money is the positive factor. Perhaps because it is younger. As a concept. So far it is the most universal one. Anarchists like Kaltammer rake in money, are fantastically avaricious. Schatz the faultless big shot surrenders not one tenth of one percent to any widow. And is renowned for his community spirit, benevolence, and so on. To have made enough money to last ten lifetimes would probably give one the feeling of looking through an open door onto a plain of boundless freedom. Money would mean living without stop-watch and whip. Money would provide a sense of immortality. If he had ten times as much money as he presumably needed for the rest of his life he would automatically feel his life expanding into the future. To be without money is to be cut off. And how totally exhausting to be without money! Even a little money means one doesn't have to try quite so hard to be a good person. One can let oneself go. One is in a way immune. What nonsense he had talked at the Reinholds'! Kaltammer never says anything off his own bat. He has to be asked for a comment. He has no need to impress. Everyone knows how much floor space is taken up by his offices in the Ritter Building.

And furthermore, Gottlieb had babbled on about his daughter Julia too, how, in order to close the zipper of her jeans, she had to lie on the floor, grab the zipper tab with a pair of pliers and, lying on her back, holding her breath and drawing in her stomach, pull up the zipper. Last Sunday, when the family had been about to leave for Birnau Church for the concert, she had torn off the tab of her zipper, there was no way of closing her pants, she had refused to put on another pair—there was never more than one pair she considered fit to wear—so an argument had flared up that had ended by ruining the evening for the whole family. "That's why, Mrs. Reinhold, we were unable to hear your concert on Sunday. Within half an hour we were all so mad at each other it was hopeless." None of this was true. He could only pray that Judith wouldn't tell the story in school. Julia would turn to ice from hurt feelings if she ever heard of this calumny. But he had to talk like that. He needed money, was dependent on Mrs. Reinhold, so had to find an excuse for having missed last Sunday when she was singing in Birnau. Now he was begging Julia's forgiveness. It wouldn't really matter, Julia, if you were to lie flat on the floor and pull up your zipper with pliers and break off the zipper tab and so cause a quarrel and prevent the family from going to the concert. Julia, forgive your father who, as you may have noticed, has a hard time being one. The yellow-haired millionaire-anarchist in his olive-green silk suit doesn't need to resort to such mental acrobatics.

The heavy pressure under Gottlieb's breastbone now seemed to be boiling up. Where his left arm lay across his body, he felt a pain. A heavy bar of pain. Gottlieb raised his arms behind his head. That made it feel lighter. For a few minutes. By now the thunderstorm had arrived. Above the house and garden. A flash of lightning coincided with the crash of a violent thunderclap. And already the rain was lashing down. It seemed to be actually hammering against the house. But Gottlieb Zürn's left side still would not relax. Outside, more was to come. Already he could hear the next thunderstorm approaching from a distance. Again it took some time for it to arrive, for the rain to come beating down. Five times during that night the thunderstorm came. Five times it poured. Gottlieb lay there wide awake, counting the times. Not that he was worried about the constriction on his left side. He was familiar with that. He did not think of it as an illness. Rather as something personal, distinctive. The longer he dwelled on the evening at the Reinholds', the more often he went over all the words, both his own and those of the others, the more rigid he grew.

He replaced the words he had spoken with new ones. He improved them, found no satisfaction in any version. He had shouted not only at Giselher but also at Lissi Reinhold. He'd been making such an uproar that she'd had to silence him. And there wasn't the slightest doubt that Kaltammer would hear from Lissi every word Gottlieb yelled after Kaltammer's departure. With her singing talent she would probably even parody the volume. No matter how hard he tried to reshape the evening, it was beyond salvaging. He knew from experience that for at least another two weeks he would recall those phrases—his own and those of the others—with pain. After two weeks the evening would gradually fade, and with it the pain. But worse than what had been said was what had been unsaid! What a lot one has to keep to oneself. And that applies to others as well. He must assume that the others had put on just as much of an act. How odd. They think of you as you do of them, if not in even worse terms. But that's outrageous. Absolutely. It's not possible. It's not possible that they should think of him as he thought of them. That would be intolerable. It is the illusion that others do not think of one as one thinks of them that keeps human relations alive. But then he doesn't think badly at all of the others! Whatever he had yelled out about Kaltammer he could at any time replace with the opposite. Could he? Yes, now he could. After having said what he said. But one must be able to say it first. When asked whether one shares Kaltammer's low opinion of the real estate profession, one *must* smilingly counter, as Dr. Enderle did in ticklish situations, with the question: Ask me another! Then everyone laughs and the conversation moves on to the subject of seal hunts, whale hunts, ruthless Soviets, inscrutable Japanese, color slides . . . How simple that would be if . . . if . . .

He would have liked to get out of bed now if it weren't for his fear of waking Anna. Apparently Mr. Schatz now wanted to conquer that tiny minority of mankind who were not yet prepared to kneel in admiration before him—the handsomest, strongest, greatest, most virile, most rational of beings—by projecting a cancerous disease onto the wide screen of publicity: so now he is not only the healthiest of men but also the sickest! Gottlieb felt justified in believing that Paul Schatz had been so far ahead of him in every aspect of life that the same seniority might well be maintained where death was concerned. Try as you may, your pity is never going to be uppermost, Gottlieb thought. His favorite music of the moment, the *Eroica*, came to his mind. Someone dies before you do. Bliss and terror. Wasn't he fulfilling the law by triumphing over Schatz through death? Wasn't he now almost a pro? No, he was not. When Kaltammer said he only hoped Schatz would return from Vienna a healthy man, he had been genuinely moved. Such people are true human beings. How wrong again, how absurd, prejudiced, tendentious, touchy, malicious had been your earlier thought that the rich could more easily afford to be human, didn't have to work so hard at it, and so on. Look at Kaltammer! He has empathy. He *is* a human being. You aren't yet. Not by a long shot. . . .

But, despite all his attempts at self-criticism, he couldn't help feeling better now. He really felt well. Perhaps, too, because there was no more thunder in the air and the early morning light was shining into the room and a softly pattering rain was blurring everything.

T H R E E

By following the signs they found the hospital. A concrete castle that might have been dropped into the forest from another star. Some of it was painted green, to match the forest no doubt. Throughout the time they spent with him, the doctor smoked as if he were facing execution in half an hour. That had a relaxing effect on Gottlieb Zürn. He felt on a par with the doctor. First they had to deliver Regina to the children's ward, where the concrete walls were gaily decorated with children's artwork. Then Anna was asked to tell the doctor all about it. She reported. Her tone, because it was so restrained, so palpably subdued, was alarmingly serious. Anna's voice seemed to be drumming. Softly and urgently. He must say that if he had been the doctor he would have immediately dashed down to the children's ward to do something about this child.

During the night of June 13 to 14, cramplike stomach pains. The next morning, blood and mucus in her urine. A few days later, violent bladder pains. June 20, examined by Dr. Sixt, urologist. X-rays. Two tiny white spots show up in the bladder. Pyelogram with full anesthetic. The doctor had suspected foreign bodies. Apart from a bladder inflammation he found nothing. He prescribed fifty tablets of Eusaprim. July 20, seen again by Dr. Sixt. Urine still not right. Dr. Sixt: "We want to cure the condition, not merely alleviate it." A further fifty Eusaprim prescribed. July 22, a raised red spot the size of a silver dollar on her back. Itching. Treated with herbal compress. Spreads. During the night following the third day of renewed Eusaprim treatment, vomiting, headache. July 24, temperature of 102, further vomiting. Dr. Cornelius, the pediatrician, diagnoses intestinal flu, prescribes Perenterol. When asked whether the spot, which had meanwhile grown larger, could be due to the Eusaprim, he said no. The spot was due to an insect bite. From July 28, no more fever. Itching now all round the waist; there was a general sensitivity of the skin to the touch. During the night of August 10 to 11, diffuse attacks of pain. Dr. Cornelius thinks it is an inflammation of the nerves, prescribes Baycillin and Neurobion. The spot, now larger still, turns pale in the middle but fiery red at the edge. In the night of August 11 to 12, further spasms of pain. Because Dr. Cornelius is going on vacation he refers the case to Dr. Freisleben. In the days following the twelfth, considerable improvement. Sensitivity of the skin remains. On August 24, in the evening, headache. Because of the red swellings, Dr. Freisleben, the pediatrician, refers the case to a dermatologist, Dr. Landwehr. August 25, Dr. Landwehr examines the red spot and says it's a tick bite. Takes out a book and shows them a picture of a red spot very similar to the one on their daughter's back. Dr. Landwehr thinks it might be meningitis.

Referral to Dr. Niebergall, the neurologist. August 28, he tests her reflexes, everything normal. Dr. Freisleben takes a blood count the same day. Normal. Pains increase. Dr. Niebergall prescribes Gelonide. Back from his vacation, Dr. Cornelius cannot or will not become involved in the case again. On August 28 the child starts vomiting again, just as she did during the first week in June. August 30, they succeed in bringing Dr. Sixt the urologist back onto the case. Dr. Freisleben, while emphasizing that he is merely acting on behalf of Dr. Cornelius, prescribes Peremesin and Cibalen. August 31, Dr. Finkenbein, the neurologist recommended by Dr. Freisleben, orders an EEG. Normal. Dr. Freisleben and Dr. Sixt decide to send the child to the hospital. At the moment the child is miserable but is out of pain, and the vomiting has stopped, too.

The doctor had made some notes. He asked only one question, and that, Gottlieb felt, was because he wanted to replace Anna's use of the word *blobs* with *blebs*. Were the red blebs still visible? No, said Anna, they had been gone since the morning of August 27. Gottlieb didn't think Anna had even noticed the offer to say *blebs* instead of *blobs*. She was completely absorbed; besides, his tone meant more to her than his words.

They went downstairs again, tried to create lasting goodwill among the nurses and to persuade the two other children—a Greek girl who had almost completely recovered, and a girl from Ailingen who had been in a serious accident—to be nice to Regina. Theano, the Greek girl, whose father was just leaving as they came in, wanted to chase them out again immediately. Regina was the first to understand why. Since Theano's father had left, she didn't want Regina's father *and* mother to be there, especially since Regina herself had hardly been there an hour. "Go, go!" she screamed, stamping her legs in her bed, "go 'way!" Regina asked her parents to leave. It was clear that they would help Regina most by leaving at once.

On the highway Gottlieb turned east instead of west. He wanted to take Anna to Mitten, to the Swan Villa. "Do you remember how on our wedding day we deserted all our relatives for an hour and Eberhard invited us for coffee in the winter garden and how Mrs. Bansin never took her sharp eyes off us? What a relief it was to get back into the familiar atmosphere of our relatives! We told them that Mrs. Bansin had spent the whole time trying to find out whether her dear Eberhard's development had been slower than Gottlieb's. Apparently she was alarmed to find that a former classmate of her son's was getting married while her son still preferred to play the field."

He always felt slightly giddy on plunging into the shadow of the tall trees. Those houses standing among such trees on green cushions by the lake! All those Tuscan villas! And Wilhelminian mansions! And the trees had been brought there by the original owners from wherever they had made their money, from Sumatra, Kenya, Canada, the Caucasus.

He parked the car well away from the gate. One never knew. The side gate was open. He hoped Dionys was there. There had been no answer when he phoned. Dionys's wife never answered the phone, Gottlieb knew that. And Lydia, their daughter, was in Vancouver. The last time he'd seen him, Dionys had said Lydia was going to have her mother come and live with her there. Gottlieb had known Dionys

Dummler for donkey's years. For the greater part of his life, Dionys had been a cooper at a wine merchant's in Mitten. And had that lovely, pale wife who spoke High German and the equally lovely daughter who also spoke High German. Mother and daughter had always walked through the village as if the weather were bad and they were strangers here or felt insulted. After suffering a spinal injury in the cellars, Dionys had taken on the job of caretaker at the Bansins'. Now he walked bent over like someone inspecting his toes or standing in front of some barbaric judge.

Gottlieb waited so that the Swan Villa could have its impact on Anna again. Today the gable over the main entrance with its wistful curves and the northeast turret with its upper stories garlanded by liana reliefs made Gottlieb think of a woman and a man standing side by side. The door to the utilities area was open. They walked through to the hall. Part of an enormous spider web had detached itself from the ceiling and hung like a soiled and spectral flag for several feet across the staircase next to the naked woman nudging the swan on its upward journey with her white wand. Anna switched her gaze from the dramatically motionless spiderweb flag and looked straight ahead again to the south window, where, separated by winding stream, reeds, and ever-whitening swans, the naked couple stood with their infectious yearning. Gottlieb read aloud the text that ran along the upper arc of the window in contorted lettering, the text he had deciphered more than twenty years ago when Eberhard Bansin had brought him to the Swan Villa for the first time: *nu brâht im aber sîn friunt der swan/ eine kleine gefüege seitiez./ sîns kleinoetes er dâ liez./ ein swert, ein horn, ein vingerlîn./hin fuor Loherangrîn./wel wir dem maere reht tuon,/ sô was er Parzivâles suon:* Now his friend the swan brought him/ a handy little boat./ He left his treasures there,/ a sword, a horn, a little ring./ Lohengrin went off in the boat./ If we read the legend aright,/ he was Parsifal's son.

At the time, he discovered that Eberhard himself had never spelled out the inscription. Eberhard was interested only in chemistry and in his basement lab carried out experiments that he had to repeat at school. Several of the professors used to hold discussions with him in front of the students, who were proud of Eberhard although they understood nothing of his wild scribblings on the blackboard. Eberhard was the genius. He was the first of any of them to have his face covered with pimples, and they lasted the longest; in fact they are still there as he stands at the corner of Ravensburger-Strasse waving the *Watchtower* and asking people who are about to feed his noble basset please to refrain since he has to keep the animal in shape for international dog shows.

Gottlieb heard Dionys Dummler's voice, coming from the billiard room. Looking in he saw Dionys, pursued by a brindled swan, retreating backward toward the door. At any moment the infuriated swan would thrust its hard beak into Dionys's face, helplessly exposed because of his bent back. It was a fully-grown creature but had the same light brown patches as cygnets still swimming in their mother's wake or even riding on her back. Gottlieb shouted: "Dionys, over here!" Dionys reached out behind him; Gottlieb took his hand, pulled him out of the room, and closed the door a split second before the hissing, rampant fury reached Dionys.

"Jus' look at that stupid ol' bastard!" said Dionys. Although he had lived in the area for thirty or forty years, his speech still betrayed his Bavarian origins. "Without you he'd've pinched my earring!" said Dionys with a grin. The tiny gold ring showed up more clearly now that Dionys walked doubled over. To think that now in his old age he had to be an animal keeper! Mrs. Leistle was much too good-natured. Imagine allowing the SPCA to leave the beasts here just because the construction going on makes them short of space. And he had all the bother! That holy terror there had been driven off by its parents because it hadn't lost its brown patches, though it had long since reached the size when it should've turned white. Actually it was now an adult that had remained a child. That's what was so dangerous. It was already so vicious that it couldn't get along with anybody. Dionys had tried giving it a young dabchick, also sent along by the SPCA, to look after, to give it something to do. The swan would have killed it instantly if Dionys hadn't intervened with a stick. Dionys had also tried sick ducks that didn't even move: the swan showed the same fury toward everything. "An animal like that should be put out of its misery," said Dionys.

Gottlieb tried to introduce Anna, but Dionys wouldn't hear of it. As if he didn't know Anna! Surely Gottlieb couldn't have forgotten? Hadn't Lydia taken piano lessons from Professor Eisele, just like Anna, but Lydia didn't have it in her to play, her mother just forced her into it. The trouble was, she had to try out on the child everything she considered refined, till it became too much for Lydia, and that's why she was now in Vancouver. But she was having her mother go over. Nothing would stop her. And her mother was going. Day after tomorrow. She was leaving the dog behind. Lydia had written, her mother yes, but not the dog. Not a word about him, her father. But he would never have gone. All the money in the world wouldn't make him go to Vancouver. He'd get by all right here. He was only worried about Bubi. He'd never been able to get along with dogs. Last night Bubi had run away again. And wasn't back yet. Anna asked what kind it was. A spaniel, said Dionys. "Yes, they're like that," said Anna. "We had one too. Remember, Gottlieb, how the night after President Kennedy was assassinated Flori ran away for the first time and then kept on doing it?" Once again Gottlieb marveled at Anna's memory. Actually it was more than a memory: it was a complete inability to forget anything.

He handed Dionys the plastic bag containing the two bottles. "Why, Gottlieb!" protested Dionys. "Gottlieb, Gottlieb, what are you up to again! You didn't have to do that, y'know!" What did Anna say to that! But that's how Gottlieb was! Always had been. He still remembered how, in the days when he, Dionys, had been a cooper at Zanolari's, Gottlieb, who was just a little squirt at the time, used to clean out each barrel for five pfennigs. And what a fine job he did! Beautiful! You'd have a hard time finding anyone else to do them that clean. Those huge barrels. For five pfennigs, Anna! And today he has a university degree and can make as much money as he likes. And he's right! He'd be a fool to do anything else! Dionys hung the bag with the bottles on the door handle, listened for a moment, and said: "Let's go—as soon as that fellow's alone he behaves himself." He took a bottle of beer out of a pocket of his blue smock, opened it and, with dreadful contortions, drank it at one go. Because it required such an effort to twist himself into a position where he could drink, he apparently drank all there was once he had got himself into the right position.

What else was new, Gottlieb asked. Next Tuesday the

auction, said Dionys. In the Blue Drawing Room. The key was at the courthouse. On Wednesday Mrs. Leistle herself was coming. Gottlieb said he'd like to be around when Mrs. Leistle came. He'd be seeing her tomorrow in Stuttgart, to make all the arrangements. Was she meeting anyone here? Yes, a Mr. Schatz, her secretary had told him.

A Mr. Schatz! Gottlieb cried. That was really a joke, seeing that tomorrow he was going to pick up the contract in Stuttgart. And Schatz was a colleague, or rather a competitor. Why would she still want to see him, said Gottlieb. And anyway he was sick! He was in Vienna!

He twisted this way and that. He could have burst into tears. "Jesus!" he said. And again: "Jesus!" And to Anna: "So tomorrow comes the crunch!" He arranged with Dionys that he would be around when Mrs. Leistle met Schatz here. One can't be too careful. And anyway, as soon as Gottlieb had the contract, Dionys would have earned himself an extra month's wages. Not another word! And now could they make a quick tour of the house before leaving? As long as they liked! But not on the ground floor. That was full of animals. Hedgehogs on a polished wooden floor! Seagulls on marble! He shook his head. He'd be going down into the basement to feed some rabbits.

Gottlieb drew Anna to his side and, pressing her closely to him as if to enlist her aid against Schatz, walked with her up the broad staircase and through the various rooms with their painted walls and ceilings full of stucco leaves and tendrils. "Don't worry," he said. "This time I'll show him what's what. Don't worry." He drew her into the room with the fresco of the naked Leda beside the swan as it stood gazing up at her with outstretched neck. Although Leda was pulling the swan toward her, she was looking not at the swan as it pressed against her left side, but toward the ground on the right where two eggs had just cracked open and four children were tumbling out. "The birth of Helen," said Gottlieb. Actually he meant to add that he had looked it up in the encyclopedia. He placed himself so close to Anna that he was touching her slightly. He wanted to mobilize her. Against Schatz. For himself. The sunshine reached Leda's feet and the four children, casting a glow on the bit of meadow from which Leda had picked a flower. One step beyond the figure of Leda as she stood there so powerfully and so lightly, the border of reeds hinted at a shoreline. If Anna was responding to the moment as he was, she should add a little pressure to their tiny shoulder contact. Then he in turn could seek her closeness a little more overtly. Then it would be her turn. Then his again. Not a stick of furniture left in the room. But beside the tiled stove, a stove bench. "Anna, a stove bench." Without any reaction from Anna he pretended that, by shifting his weight from one leg to the other like Leda in the picture, he was unconsciously coming closer to her. But Anna did not react. "Don't worry," he said, placing his arm around her and drawing her to him. Pointing to the least interesting part of the painting, to the four newly hatched infants, she said: "Just as many as we have."

He dropped his arm. For her to draw him closer, as Leda drew the swan that was snuggling up to her, was more than he could expect since she was looking only at the children. True, Leda was also looking only at the children. But even so she was still drawing the swan closer to her. With both hands. He turned away, not knowing what to do with his annoyance, took a few impatient steps, stood in front of a closet door and, to give a belated meaning to his steps, was obliged to open the door. He feigned an interest in the interior of this built-in closet. To his surprise there was another door in the back of the closet. Just like in Regina's Narnia story, he thought, opened the door, and found himself on the bottom step of a tiny spiral staircase. He climbed up inside it and was one floor higher, again in a closet, pushed open the door and was in the room with the red wallpaper with its slanting rows of six ammonite shells, and between each row a naked woman, draped with jeweled necklaces, her head placed in front of the sixth shell, the shell's spiral a kind of pagan halo. He no longer felt like showing Anna this room.

On their return home, a piece of paper stuck to the front door caught their eye: a note frum Julia to say she had taken Armin to the dog-training center. They found Magdalena lying on the sofa, motionless, staring at the ceiling. On the back of the sofa, as if a part of its decoration, crouched Else. Because the cat was crouching above her, Magda somehow looked pathetic. She did not react when her parents entered the room. For her not to be playing the violin if Julia wasn't playing the piano was nothing new. Gottlieb sometimes had the impression that Magda only played to prevent Julia getting farther ahead on the piano than she was on the violin.

Anna at once sat down beside Magda and asked her if she wasn't feeling well. "Why shouldn't I be feeling well?" she said tonelessly. Had she had lunch? She had, Julia hadn't. Why was she lying there like that? Just because. If there was nothing the matter with her she could just as easily sit up! "What for?" asked Magda. Anna glanced at Gottlieb. Gottlieb said: "Why don't you go out for a breath of fresh air?" Magda said: "What for?" *Cui bono*, thought Gottlieb. Hadn't she been reacting quite often recently with that question?

"Oh, let her be," said Gottlieb in a pacifying voice. But Anna couldn't stand Magda lying there staring at the ceiling: perhaps she wasn't feeling well. Magda ignored them. Normally she never had a moment to spare, and now she was lying there like that, Anna said almost in despair. "Come on, Magda, do get up. Go and wash your hair." "What for?" said Magda. "Because you haven't washed it for three weeks, and today is Friday." Magda ignored her. "My God, I'll go crazy in this house!" Anna cried, got up, and went into the kitchen. Gottlieb called out, less consoling than exulting, that one didn't go crazy that quickly. She'd be surprised how long it took before she went crazy.

He went across to his office, sat down in his armchair, tipped it back, and looked at the dog roses that hung in through the open window, as if they were giraffes, and inquisitive. Tomorrow Judith Reinhold was giving her first concert. His kids had to be pushed like wheelbarrows; if he stopped for an instant, they stayed right where they were. Other people's kids pulled with a will. They practically dragged their parents along with them. Perhaps he just felt this way because he had hoped . . . what had he hoped? Probably something magical, nonsensical, redeeming. Probably he just wanted to lie back in his chair and wait until the last of the summer guests had departed, and then for a whole winter count money. He didn't want to gasp for air in deafening industrial plants. He didn't want his kids to gasp for air in plants like that either. That was all he knew. Would ever know. Not for him. That's all there is to it. He was irritated by those wasps. The wasps are invading the house. Hey there, defender! He jumped up, killed the wasps, tossed them out. Now it was quiet.

Outside Mrs. Constabler was coming around the corner. As long as the family had been spending their vacations here, her husband would come for weekends from construction sites where, as he had told Anna, a person could only communicate by yelling. Mrs. Constabler called out very slowly: "Isolde, I'm off to do some shopping." Isolde called back: "Ye-a-ah." Mrs. Constabler called out even more slowly: "No mischief now!" And Isolde called back in the same way: "Ohh-kaay!" That wonderful harmony of the Constabler family from Solingen. What an imperturbable woman! That fantastic slowness! And Isolde, replying for herself and her three brothers, the perfect echo! What an afternoon. The action was taking place on the bit of lake seen between the oak branches. A light swell struck by the rays of the sun. And each striking ray bursts into sparkles. And those sparkling fountains, while new rays constantly produce new sparkling fountains, move with the light waves before a light wind to the northeast. And this isn't a passionate day? Magda! One ought to climb up into the tops of the oak trees, build a hut there, surrounded by rustlings. Or stand in the light like Leda, her hands touching the swan, her eyes on the children. But surely not that stretched-out, corpselike rigidity on a cold sofa! Or was she right? He should have been on his guard long ago. The fact that Lissi Reinhold hadn't phoned proved how little he had been on his guard last night. His tape hadn't registered a single phone call. Should he phone her? Weren't you going to give me a tip, Mrs. Reinhold, about Mrs. Leistle, the president's villa? You see, my train leaves at 6:19 P.M., my appointment is tomorrow morning at nine. . . .

But if she didn't call him, he couldn't call her. Once again he found himself running through his words that night and replacing them with better ones. That crack about the two Wagner singers had probably been his worst mistake. A backfire if ever there was one. How she had laughed! She might have thought he was quoting the remark because he considered it an insult. But if he had believed he could implicate Paul Schatz with that remark he must himself have thought that it referred to the size of her body, not of her voice. And that made him the one guilty of the insult! He had uttered those words. Before witnesses. Those words wouldn't have existed, would never exist, if they hadn't been uttered. And he had uttered them. And that ghastly laughter which Lissi was forced to burst into had proved how appalling those words were for her. And he was still thinking of a tip! And patronage! Most likely, instead of calling him, she had phoned Stuttgart and said: Hortense, you can forget about this Mr. Zürn. The only person who deserves this listing is *he*, give it to *him*, when *he*, with God's help, returns a healthy man from Vienna.

Luckily, when it's a matter of business, rich people are very down-to-earth. That would be in his favor. Let Mrs. Leistle investigate who was the better agent for that house. Armin was whimpering outside. He let him in. Armin immediately went on his knees and lay down as flat as possible. He did this when he was afraid. Probably he had run away from Julia at the training center and was now scared of retribution. Just like me, thought Gottlieb. You have me, but whom do I have? he thought. It was something Ludwig had once said to him, Ludwig whom he no longer had either. He had risen so far in the banking world that he had inevitably lost sight of Gottlieb. Gottlieb soothed Armin, promised to defend him against Julia's wrath, and went out with him onto the terrace, where

Anna had set the table. Else was still crouching above Magda's head. While they were having coffee, Julia came in, flushed and almost in tears of rage and disappointment because Armin had simply run away from her while they were still on the way to the training center. Just because a passing motorbike had backfired. And she had been practicing all summer to cure Armin of being gun-shy! What a dumb, stupid, cowardly, impossible dog! "He'll never be a real dog!" she cried. Armin lay flatter and flatter. Only his eyes were turned up. A look of misery. Gottlieb tried to arbitrate. After all, Armin had had a difficult childhood. Sent to the shelter, months behind bars. Probably he had had some experience with a bang that he hadn't yet overcome. "Bull," said Julia. She demanded that Armin finally come to terms with his childhood. She was constantly being disgraced by this infantile creature! Gottlieb came up with his standard phrase: "But then he's the most beautiful dog in the world." Julia lay down crossly beside Armin but gradually submitted to the nuzzling attempts at reconciliation offered by the beautiful infantile creature. A blissful couple.

Anna, on the other hand, wanted to know what was going to happen with Magda. Since the door was open, Magda could hear what was being said about her. If she was of any mind to listen at all. Julia said Magda had told her she was going to drop out of school. "And why?" asked Anna. "Why don't you ask her?" said Julia. "Does she know what she wants to do?" asked Gottlieb. Yes, work for a tax consultant or a lawyer, said Julia. Gottlieb called into the room: "Is that true?" No answer. Was it true, he asked again. Anna said that if Magda wanted to leave school before graduating, at least they would have to discuss it. From inside came an apathetic "what for." Gottlieb jumped up. And because he had jumped up he had to speak louder than necessary. And because he was already shouting he felt he had to raise his voice even more; he couldn't shout loud enough to be heard by this thick-eared daughter of his. She could, he shouted, treat anybody she pleased like that, but not him. At least she should have said what her grievance was before behaving like this. Why, for God's sake, why! But by now he was no longer even interested in her reasons. And what was more—would she kindly make a note of this?—once and for all! Enough-enough-enough! After all, there were other problems in the world besides kids. He wasn't here in the world just for fun either. Stupidly enough he had always thought that in a family, yes, he'd been arrogant enough to believe that in his family things were different from so-called reality. His mistake! Obviously it was the same here as everywhere else. Everyone went as far as they thought they could. Everyone did whatever they liked. Good enough. Fine. Let's introduce the principle of reality into this family. Magda could credit herself with having accomplished that. But what this meant for her personally was something she was going to find out.

He had been walking up and down in the room in front of Magda, faster and faster, until he had achieved so much momentum that it was enough to take him to the door of his office and inside. He slammed the door, then sat down in his armchair, quivering and trembling. From weakness. That morning, when they found the doctor was already smoking as they entered, he had noted with satisfaction: The weaker one smokes. Now he noted: The weaker one shouts. Through the open window he could hear Julia trying to convince Armin it wasn't he who was being shouted at. If at least Mrs. Reinhold would phone. Hadn't she called him the day before yesterday especially to give him a tip? Then she had felt impelled to invite him. Then for the entire evening she doesn't get around to doing what she has invited him for. So surely she must now call at any moment and say: Forgive me for . . . Must she? No "must" about it. Her husband's company, of which he probably owned one third, had a turnover of 100 million marks, yet had no more than two hundred employees. Originally the firm had been called Shulmann & Frost, now it was called Reinhold Enterprises. And if a person who worked there was asked what he or anyone else was doing there, all one was told was that one mustn't be told. The Americans, one was told, NASA! In order not to feel like a Russian spy, one stopped asking. No, Mrs. Reinhold didn't need to call him. He needed to sit at the telephone like a cat at a mousehole. And that's what he was doing.

When it was time to pack his things and get a ride to the station with Anna, there had still been no call. Okay then, no tip, no patronage. As he got out of the car, he asked Anna to try to talk to Magda. Also to give his love to Regina. And to Rosa, who had said she'd be arriving today. He walked quickly away from Anna because he was afraid it would depress her to see how weak he was at the moment of departure. And he was going to the front. He was marching off. Tomorrow the battle. Since he will almost certainly return as a kind of conqueror over Kaltammer and his associates, it's better for their eyes not to meet until the moment of his arrival home.

As he walked toward the railway station he felt better, freer, stronger with every step. Anyone who thought he was finished was very much mistaken. By the time he reached the station steps he felt buoyed up with the spirit of enterprise. Go right on lying there, Magda, I'll be back to raise you up. Tomorrow afternoon. Magda hadn't given the slightest indication as to whether she had even noticed that he had walked right past her as he left his office. She had stared up at the ceiling. He mustn't let himself be impressed by that. One quick glance, and immediately look away. It was terrible, the way she lay there. Unimaginable, what she might be thinking, second by second, nothing in her field of vision but the plain white ceiling. He wished he could have seen whether her eyelids were still moving, but he couldn't look that long. Tomorrow, Magda. Hold everything please, till tomorrow. When he would be back. Then.

A glance at the clock. He had plenty of time. There was never any appointment for which he did not arrive much too early. Never in his life had he arrived too late for anything. It was simply unthinkable. He was immediately aware that statements of that kind were typical of him. Something always came rushing out that he immediately had to curb, take back, retract. How was a person supposed to amount to anything? Be anything? At the ticket counter an old woman was buying a ticket for her husband standing mutely beside her, and the young ticket agent used a huge pair of scissors to cut off one-third of the ticket before handing it to her. Gottlieb thought: What an uncouth society we are.

He traveled first class. He still felt out of place in first class, but his clients traveled first class and would have lost all confidence in him if in walking by they had happened to see him in second class. If I were a dentist I'd travel second class, he thought.

In Singen, as he changed trains, he found himself caught up in hordes of eleven- to thirteen-year-olds, girls and boys, who poured down the stairs, pushed their way up on the other side, flooded the train, without realizing, without even thinking, that they were in a railway station. They were coming back from an outing. All of them excited. All of them talking, yelling, all the time, all at the same time. One sweeping along the other. The result was an immense, high-pitched, hammering sound, a universal soprano of hundreds of children's voices, a climax that knew no end. Gottlieb let himself be borne along. To stay in this swarm, forever, that would be the thing. But he had to tear himself away from this blissful yelling and sit down in a compartment where two businessmen were talking about a third who was simply no longer equal to the demands made on him. Apparently this inadequate person worked for one of the businessmen in Switzerland. The latter, his boss, was saying as Gottlieb Zürn came in: " 'There's nothing wrong with the scenery,' I told him dryly, 'but where are the customers?' " They both laughed. The boss went on: " 'Let me cheer you up a bit,' I say to him. 'It doesn't mean you have to go round the bend—look, I'm not going round the bend!' " Even louder laughter. "I'm not going round the bend!" he repeated, to feed the laughter again. Gottlieb unfolded his newspaper and listened: "I haven't run my own business for twenty-four years for nothing. I've simply reached the point where I'm ready to pack up, frankly, ready to pack up. . . ."

The air in Stuttgart was scarcely fit to breathe. He carried his suitcase to the Hotel Unger, then, following a street map, walked on toward Parler-Strasse. Uphill. He found the house but walked quickly past it on the other side of the street. Red sandstone, bossed blocks, easy to find again. Not much to be seen anyway on account of the wall, the trees, the steeply rising grounds. Tomorrow morning, shortly before nine, he'll turn up here again, on foot, ring the bell, and hand the maid his card. There's no reason at all to believe that a black card with raised gilt lettering such as Kaltammer carries is of any advantage. A Mrs. Hortense Leistle, no matter what impression she may want to give of herself, has no time for a black card with gilt lettering. There are some things that can be relied upon in Stuttgart. He will only have to meet Mrs. Leistle's eye to discover whether, although she rejects black cards, she is in other respects an insensitive silken dragon. Perhaps she was a real charmer, one word would lead to another, one could talk freely to her, after two hours they would be in agreement and, after the austere but delicious tea, drink a glass or two of Hohenloher.

Down in the city again he wandered around for a while along the streets between station and hotel, studying the store windows, comparing prices as if his sole purpose in coming here were to go on a shopping spree the next day. No sooner was he in bed than he realized the night might become a problem. If only he had drunk a bottle of red wine. Tightwad. Intending to make sixty to ninety thou tomorrow and not even allowing himself a bottle of red wine. But it wasn't penny-pinching. He simply hadn't done what he wanted to do. It was a familiar situation. In restaurants he often ordered a dish he didn't want while knowing quite well which one he did want.

He would like to know who was in charge inside him, how such decisions were made. All right, no wine. All right, stay awake. Better to appear on the battlefield tomorrow suffering from lack of sleep. Battlefield. A wonder they hadn't thought up a more hypocritical expression!

He phoned Anna. Any word from Mrs. Reinhold? No. Mm-hmm. And Regina? No more vomiting. She had been quite calm, but very subdued. What was that supposed to mean, subdued? Anna often used words in such a way that one had to assume she did so both consciously and unconsciously at the same time. There was no point in asking. Rosa had arrived. But not alone. He was called Max. A cameraman. She couldn't say much about him yet. As soon as the voice of that Max fellow could be heard at the front door—he spoke rather loudly and with a strong Bavarian accent—Magdalena had jumped up and gone behind the house and, after Rosa and this Max fellow had gone out on the terrace, crept up to her room. Rosa wasn't too well, she could see that at once. She hadn't been able to talk to her yet. If Mrs. Reinhold should call, would Anna please let him know immediately? And how was he? He?! What did she expect?! Fine, of course! Couldn't be better. He had a nice room, a wonderful bed, what more could he want.

Then he lay down again. He was pretty sure it was his remark about the two Wagner singers that had ruined everything for him. He could thank Mr. Schatz for that. No, himself. He found himself repeating in his mind every word that had been spoken on the terrace. Including those he had already replaced with better ones. Out of the shambles of the evening his own image emerged ever more clearly as that of a zealot who interrupts others, then speaks twice as loud as those he has interrupted and, to top it all, flails the air with his hands too often and too violently—he was the only one who had knocked over a glass that evening—and visibly sweats in the grip of hectic emotion. And then, if the hostess doesn't stop him with all the authority at her command, this uncouth choleric goes on talking until, in the most idiotic manner, he has insulted every person in the group, or at least a friend of every guest. And this was the man to whom Mrs. Reinhold had wanted to pass on a tip!

Of course he would rather have behaved differently. He hadn't behaved the way he would have liked to. Things had gone wrong. But he couldn't tell that to anybody. Just as he often ordered the very thing he didn't want to eat, so he often behaved in the way he didn't want to behave. If Mrs. Reinhold had meanwhile told Kaltammer how Mr. Zürn hated and reviled Jarl F. Kaltammer, she hadn't told the truth. He didn't hate either Kaltammer or Paul Schatz. If he yielded to the feeling that arose in him whenever he met Kaltammer or Schatz in person, he would have to say that he was invariably attracted by each of them. He invariably felt won over by each of them. Should he have admitted this? Now, at this very moment, he should be sitting on Mrs. Reinhold's terrace, and she should be quizzing Gottlieb about *him.* Now every one of his phrases would be just right. Now, quite uninhibited, he could become caught up in a speech—at first a bit mendacious but becoming more truthful with every sentence— glorifying his competitors. The conquered know a happiness of which the conqueror can have no inkling. That would be his theme. And he and his audience must become convinced that, since the moment when the principle that "one must love one's enemies" was expressed for the first time, no one had offered such living proof of this principle as Gottlieb Zürn. And the luster of this speech would reach Schatz and Kaltammer, dazzle them, so that they would come to him and instantly embrace him. But perhaps it wasn't too late. He made the speech now. In the dark hotel bedroom. The important thing was that he felt able to admire Paul Schatz. And Kaltammer too. That was enough to make him feel better. To give him a sense of infinite release. Why hadn't he rehearsed this panegyric long ago? Since it was in demand everywhere. At every step one encountered admirers of Schatz and Kaltammer. Without joining the Schatz/Kaltammer admiration society, there was no getting ahead. Besides, he really did admire them. So what was stopping him?

The fact that on the other hand he didn't admire them at all, or even envy them, but, on the contrary, from his innermost arrogance despised them both in all their perfection, was something he needn't tell anybody. Was it arrogance? That's what other people would call it, but he wouldn't. He despised the two men because they lacked shame. Take it or leave it, that's how he felt about them. He must keep that to himself. It would be regarded as jealousy and resentment. But whenever it had been necessary to react to one or other of them hadn't he always done so with envy and resentment? He had. His profound invulnerability to the strength of these two men was something he had always kept hidden. Now for the first time he saw to what enormous extent he had adapted to other people's expectations. He even did things that could only lower him in the opinion of others. Since he was convinced that other people believed he could only react to his superior competitors with envy, hatred, and a sense of inferiority, he expressed envy, hatred, and a sense of inferiority whenever the conversation turned to either of those two. Were he to show any other feelings, they were bound to believe he was lying. One can't present the world with something it doesn't expect. So no panegyric for Schatz and Kaltammer after all? No. So he did have the proper reaction on the terrace? He should have been more explicit in conveying the most despicable antipathy; that way he would have made the other two greater and himself lesser and thus confirmed prevailing opinion. Favorites are favorites, that's all there is to it. He was not—and he really was conscious of this through and through—a favorite. Not even his own. And people notice that. They only love someone who loves himself.

Gottlieb felt that his ruminations had landed him in a witches' cauldron. Did he love Schatz and Kaltammer, or didn't he? That was the only question which counted. He wanted to stretch out in bed, to curl up again, but he didn't want anything to do with this question. He was afraid of the answer. He suspected an answer. And it would be devastating. My God, he almost cried out, don't tell me I'm going to have to like them! But he would like to. And he could. And . . .

Sometimes, when in the grip of inner turmoil, Gottlieb Zürn would address his children. He felt like doing this now. Dear Rosa, Magda, Julia, and Regina, he said softly into the darkness. Perhaps he had lost sight of himself with all that camouflage. Always looked somewhere where he didn't mean to look. And there was nothing to be learned from him, he said, except how things should not be. That he could guarantee. He always gave way to the opposite of his own wishes. Maybe he had always had the wrong ones. Good-night.

He took another shower. At some point he finally fell asleep. When he awoke it was still dark. He hoped it was at least past three. He didn't dare look at the time for fear it might be only 12:30. Falling asleep had long been something he had to require himself to do in the same way that he fulfilled the demands of his job during the day. What in God's name was I spouting there last night, he said softly into the dark room. He was back at the Reinhold party. In a whimpering tone he said: What in God's name was I spouting there last night? Then he said: I'd like to clench my teeth till they crumble and my mouth looks like a forest after a tornado. Stuttgart lies in a trough, he thought. Even at night there's no air. His nose felt swollen shut. He forced himself to breathe regularly. He fell asleep.

He awoke from a disagreeable dream. Although it must be pointless now, he had been running with all his family through the Nuremberg railway station. The train was supposed to be on platform ten. They were all wet, dirty, covered with mud, construction was going on all the way into the station. There was no time to buy tickets. He pulled Regina, who could go no farther, through the air. Suddenly she struck her left foot against a steel spike that pierced her foot halfway between ankle and toes. A hole in her dirty, muddy shoe. A hole in her foot. Blood spurted out. He kept pulling the family on. Regina screamed. So did he. He stopped because bits of flesh were shooting out of the bloody hole in time with the beat of her pulse. He knelt down to tie his clean handkerchief around her foot, but without pulling off her shoe. A woman said: Don't forget to take off her stockings later. They all climbed up onto a buffer stop. The train—but he had known that—had gone. It now occurred to him that the hole in Regina's foot was at the very same spot at which the nail had been driven into Christ's foot. At the top of the cross he saw Paul Schatz's initials: PS. That made him think: Paul Schatz = Christ.

What he was feeling in his left side—of course it wasn't a nail—but when one felt the stab one thought of a nail, of a hot—no, needle, not nail, of a hot needle. It would feel good to move his left side so as to spread whatever was stabbing. He tries massaging it. That helps. When he stops, the stab returns to the spot with such hot sharpness that he dare not move. Suddenly he is scared of making any movement. A feeling that, as soon as he moves, the stab will become unbearably painful. He should be able to move around the stab. But how? The stab was watching over him. Not missing a thing. Activated by every car. Every thought. Everything facing him. Gottlieb promised not to attempt anything more. He felt he must offer sacrifices to the stab. Immediately. Why did he have to go and see Mrs. Leistle! Ridiculous. At nine or ten o'clock he'll take the train home. He'll go for a swim, sing with the kids, drink some mellow wines, and sit in the shade of his trees. The very thought that this was merely a vision which he needed at the moment but which in reality—by morning, in daylight—he would, as so often, have to reconsider, even the slightest attempt at such deception activated the stab, drove it deeper; it was not inconceivable that the stab would reach a target. Gottlieb let everything slide. He no longer had any plan. Immediately he noticed that the stabs from the noise of passing cars grew less violent. He sensed that at last he was on the right track. The easier you breathe the more certain you can be that you are now moving in the right direction.

Outside it was light. He could actually feel resolve and strength increasing within him from second to second. When, without looking at the time, he sensed it was about eight, he got up without effort, dressed, had breakfast—only tea and bread because he wanted the taste of pure tea and pure bread, nothing else, also knew for certain that he wanted nothing else—paid his bill, left the hotel, heading not in the direction of Killesberg and Parler-Strasse but toward the railway station. But as soon as he crossed the street he stopped in front of the windows of the rug store that he had studied the previous evening. He stopped in front of the same rug, a Kashan with pale stems and flowers sharply outlined on a dark blue ground, singly in the center and more intertwined closely around the border. He walked on as if unconcerned. Went back again. To the spot where the rug showed to best advantage. He knew he was hooked. He went in. He heard: "Eight thousand two hundred ninety" and knew that he should name some figure below that but not how much below, and he didn't want to lose face in front of the young man who seemed such a paragon, so, after fingering the rug and pretending to be an expert, he said he would take it. He paid with a check. He was told the rug would be delivered within a week.

Before taking the underpass to the station he entered a camera store and bought a Polaroid camera, ten packages of film, and the same quantity of flashlights. "Five hundred and twenty-one," he heard. Here, since he was taking the goods with him, he paid with his Eurocard. Then he ran to the ticket counter at the station. He was lucky. A train was leaving in six minutes. One second class, one way. Because he wanted to economize. But also because today he wanted to travel in his own class. Today he could afford to do that. Today he wouldn't have cared if one of his clients had walked past and either impudently looked in or shyly looked away. Gottlieb Zürn would have waved to him. Cheerfully. Lightheartedly. Today at last he felt once again that nothing could happen to him. He felt more independent than he had for a long time. It wasn't altogether new, this feeling of happiness. But today it was unusually strong. Probably because he had turned his back on something really important. He had felt something of this mood the day before yesterday, when he had tried to phone Baptist Rauh and couldn't reach him, that feeling of happiness when something remained undone. As soon as he was sitting in the train—on the platform he had just had time to phone home to tell them when to expect him—his exalted mood grew even more fulminating. As the train drew out of the station—Gottlieb was alone in the sun-filled compartment—he felt blissfully secure. Everyone wants to get out of the zone of pain and suffering. He was out. Only those who cease to do anything cease suffering. Those who act suffer.

Böblingen! Böblingen! he heard from outside, and couldn't remember that any word had ever made him happier. It was 10:21. In the countryside, cranes like idle gallows. On across the autobahn, on across the cars racing south. And into the forests. With all his thoughts pressing upon him, Gottlieb leaned into the curves taken by the fast train. In his mind he was helping the train along. He saw himself in search of a delusion. His mistake all through the years: wanting to create an illusion that looked like reality. He should have been looking for something wholly delusive, faith-inducing. Swinging homeward through the valleys he had a vague notion of something as improbable as the immaculate conception. Anything that failed to attain this degree of improbability was no good. So what has he achieved in this way? His only accomplishment so far: he didn't go to see Mrs. Leistle. He knows he will lose the security now filling him. But he must make this second of security lasting, memorable. He must be able to say at any time: like that Saturday on the train between Stuttgart and Singen.

Now the figure "8,811" hit him. Against his will his purchases had added themselves up. He had to face the consequences of his impulse. An attack of impulse-buying. Thinking of Anna. Himself with Anna. In the coils of that rug. He had had to buy the camera because he wanted to photograph Anna without having to leave the film in town to be developed. That's what these cameras were invented for. Or was he just the fifteen-year-old again, no, the twelve-year-old? Last evening, standing in front of the store window that displayed this camera, he had imagined that in every house in Stuttgart people had long been equipped with such cameras and were constantly using them to produce the most incredible pictures. Only he didn't have anything like that yet. And at home he couldn't buy that kind of a camera. The saleswoman would know at once what he had in mind. He was looking forward to the evening. Anna, you'll see. . . . But the money: instead of earning he had spent.

Until he had firm ground under his feet again he mustn't think either of his purchases or of Parler-Strasse. He recited resolutions to himself like a criminal shortly after the deed. If just this time, just this once, disaster can be averted, he promises never to do anything like it again. The worst part is the feeling that it has happened more than once. While he was traveling. This impulse-buying. And each time it gets worse, more devastating.

8,811 marks. Without his . . . That means not only is he incapable of learning anything but he must reckon with increasingly bad decisions. He mustn't think of his family. For him, whatever he had done or not done was bearable. Necessary. Satisfying. But how would he explain that at home? The compartment door rattled malevolently. Herrenberg Church, that monster hen, reminded him of his family. A sunny day. Even though along its edges the sky is resting on clouds, white ones. Corn is the only crop still standing. Eutingen, Württemberg. That must mean they're about to enter Baden. Still some fields of clover with purple blossoms. Because he always sits with his back to the engine, everything he sees drops behind. Along the shoulder of the valley. Down below in the green fields the Neckar twists and turns. Down to Horb, spreading across the valley. But then it suddenly narrows. A green gorge. Single track. Then right away freedom again. The rails swing on an embankment along the curving valley floor. Neckar, road, and railway accommodate each other between steeper slopes, fir-clad. Aha, bee colonies are at home here. Neckarhausen is at home here. The Neckar gets smaller. The train travels toward its tapering. Tall willow trees try out their silver in its green. The Steeb Works, dead on Saturdays. Sulz, 11:15. Although he is sitting so that he seems to be merely moving away from somewhere, he must admit that he is also moving toward somewhere. That's what the recumbent cows, those monuments to pensive, thorough chewing, are trying to tell him. And each curve reveals where you have just been. The Neckar is beginning to show more rocks than water. Oberndorf 11:30. The valley stands around and is silent. Today no one is at home in Oberndorf. Here comes the train going the other way. Gottlieb could go back to Stuttgart on it. Ridiculous. But he is ridiculous too if he arrives home and informs them: I haven't got the contract, but I've spent 8,811 marks. He would secretly take the camera into the bedroom. Ridiculous. To be ridiculous is not ridiculous. In any case no more ridiculous than not being ridiculous. The Neckar must submit to being slowed down by the rocks it has placed there itself.

A few more times, river and road and rails vie with each other for the upper hand. After high Rottweil the meadows increase, the slopes open out, the forest no longer covers everything, and Württemberg puts in a brief appearance again. A girl sits under a bridge letting the Saturday train roar past her. So that's all it does. Although it has to put on the brakes for a station, first a quick dash across the Danube. Tuttlingen. An announcement that this train will go on to Constance. But first there is an exchange of passengers with the train from Munich to Freiburg and the one from Freiburg to Ulm. When all three trains arrive, a Saturday silence will descend here too. There is an electrical humming. Train doors being slammed resound like church doors. Between stations the train stops again. Not on his account, mind you. He's glad to get there as fast as possible. As far as he's concerned, they can hurry like the end of a symphony. A coil of wire, waiting to be used, lies there over the weekend, a circle in the sunshine. After one has had to endure the racket of the Zürich-Stuttgart express, the train is allowed to rumble on. Only now does it become clear that it had been waiting in Hattingen rather than out in the open. Then for so long through a tunnel that a new landscape must be expected. And there it is, free, wide, with cautious rises. But immediately back into the forest, then high across a precipitous valley. The train becomes cautious again as if it might plunge over the side. Yellow-gray layers of rock reveal the strata being traversed. The track crosses over the valley at a great height and is crossed higher still by the autobahn. Gottlieb was surprised to find himself thinking "At last" as the train left the probing valleys behind and shot out into the Hegau and now—a full-fledged fast train raced between those veterans of volcanoes and made a beeline for Singen. There's my friend the Hohentwiel!

Singen means preparing for Radolfzell. The corn finds open spaces at last. NO POWER FOR NOBODY! has been scrawled on the wall in revolutionary red for the benefit of people changing trains. He was ready to like the slogan until it occurred to him that Kaltammer would be the one to like it most. So he withdrew his approval. Once again he was in the region that was Kaltammer-free on Saturdays and Sundays. In all his years in the area, Kaltammer had intoned on the terrace, he had never spent a weekend here. On Saturdays he was to be pictured beside Burgundian fireplaces. From Radolfzell a really tiny little train rocks its way home. Everyone is squeezed into one long coach. Kids try out their toys and at the top of their voices explain everything they are doing with their hands, to double the fun. The girl whose hair has fallen forward on both sides is doing her best to read the illustrated weekly that the joggling train keeps knocking aside. Some balloons are along for the ride too. On a girl's T-shirt, embroidered with her own hands: San Franzisko. Weary-eyed, an old man sits beside an old woman. The benches are so close together that knees must be placed between the knees of the person opposite. The bone-rattling little train hastens past the scaffolded spire of Sippling Church and for several kilometers preempts the shoreline that must now be worth ten times as much as this veteran railroad.

Gottlieb was enjoying the little train's sense of purpose. His gaze slid along the Bodanrück, the ridge of hills that had accompanied the train for the last few kilometers on the other side of the lake arm, green-furred slopes that seem always to rise out of the water as if on the first day of Creation. As the train traveled along below the steep sandstone wall supporting the plateau with the Reinhold villa and its fateful terrace, Gottlieb jumped up, looked out toward the station, sought Anna in the shadow of the building, that figure of gentleness that always stayed close to walls and in shadow, and saw, much farther from the station building than Anna would ever choose to stand, Rosa waiting for him in the sunshine. His disappointment turned to happiness.

Rosa showed her emotion in the mocking manner that had been established between them. Solemn greetings or partings were not customary in his family. Even with his mother such things had not been possible. Only once had he ever touched his mother's face: as she lay in her open coffin and, for one moment, he had been alone in the room with her. Without ever putting it into words, all the members of this clan were agreed that a minimal expression of emotion suited them best. Usually one member would touch the other briefly with two fingertips at some insignificant spot. Rosa was more than pale. And had even put on pale makeup. Probably to hide the fact that she was pale. "My, you look pale!" he said and could have kicked himself for his lack of self-control. She flinched at his words as if he had hit her. Whereupon he quickly added: "Or have you just used very pale makeup?" In a flat, artificial voice she said: "Just a bit." It also sounded much too formal.

She drove. He kept his eyes off her. She looks as if she's filled with tears; wherever she was squeezed, they would spurt out. She couldn't introduce Max Stöckl right away because he was just in the midst of his meditation. In the shade of the candelabra-branched sumac tree a naked man was seated in the lotus position—or was he wearing something, hidden by his posture? With his thick black hair, worn in the manner of King Ludwig II of Bavaria, his luxuriant beard trimmed exactly like that of another member of that clan, he looked like two Wittelsbachs rolled into one.

On the terrace flagstones, stretched across newspapers that Rosa and Max must have brought, Magda lay studying the employment ads. In her right hand, the scissors. She was demonstrating her concentration so pointedly that he knew he would have to put the first question to her. She had already found a few interesting offers and read aloud: " 'Jeune fille au pair qui s'occupe de l'enfant, consciencieuse et de bonne éducation.' That's what a *couple suisse* in Parly, fifteen kilometers from Paris, is looking for. And listen to this one!" Her voice was brighter than it had been for a long time. It was as noticeable as if the sun were shining again for the first time in many days. At ease and relaxed, she lay there in her bikini on the rough granite slabs. Not a trace of the rigidity of the last few days. In a voice almost shrill with enthusiasm she read out that the firm of Theis & Co. in Munich was looking for a filing clerk. No experience needed. Gottlieb, who was still holding his suitcase, said that must surely be a dull job. That was precisely what appealed to Magda. She always said "Thé-is," although he had told her at once that it was almost certainly pronounced to rhyme with "ice." But here was the best of all, she said, pulling out from under her thigh a book about employment in the public service and reading aloud the paragraph on administrative employees in the Justice Department. She was thrilled by the fact that one could get a job there as a clerk of the court. Grade-10 education was enough. Gottlieb said in that case surely the right thing for her would be a career

as registrar, which required grade-12 education, two years'
practicum, and a three-year university course in administration in Berlin. She returned to employment as a court clerk.
She wanted something where a person could watch others and
have no responsibility. After all, it wasn't the pay that interested her, she said quite matter-of-factly; perhaps a trifle
imploringly.

Rosa and Anna had set the table for lunch. Armin and Julia
came up from the lake. Rosa looked at her watch and called
out: "Max, that's enough for now!" Gottlieb went inside,
walked upstairs, hid the camera behind the curtain, changed,
and met Max Stöckl, who was rebuking Rosa for having called
him so rudely. Meditation couldn't be switched off like a TV
set! Because Anna had told him on the phone that Max always
spoke in a very loud Bavarian dialect, Gottlieb had pictured
him taller, brawnier. Brawny he was, but in a more light-
weight, athletic way. His hair was blue-black. He might have
been a younger brother of Anna's. Until he opened his mouth.
Gottlieb didn't mind this Max fellow's loud voice. Also at the
moment he found this unstoppable torrent of words if anything quite agreeable.

Anna had asked him only one quick question: "How did
you get on?" "Time will tell," he had answered. And why
wasn't he asking how she had got on? Her first question had
already been worded in such a way that he ought to have
completed the symmetry by asking: "How about you?" He
now did this. She had sold the mill, here you are. And held out
the signed interim contract. All this in a quick low voice. Max
Stöckl was still talking to Magda or Rosa or to the company at
large. He was talking about careers. Obviously he hadn't been
slow to grasp that this was a topic of interest in this family at

this time, and luckily he knew more about it than anybody else. After glancing through the interim contract that Anna had signed, Gottlieb could only shake his head in amazement and smile happily. Three percent plus value-added tax. Well, hadn't they asked about the autobahn? Anna had reassured them. That was justified, wasn't it? More than five hundred meters away and half hidden behind the hill. And so fast? Yes, she had told them about two hot potential purchasers. She was justified, two parties had phoned. Hot? Well, warm. Tomorrow at nine the father who was buying it for the young couple would be here. He was flying off to Majorca for a month. Hence the urgency. And because the young people couldn't wait. Someone had also phoned about the Immenstaad apartment. What a woman. That would be the first sale in a month. From the vendor a fee of 10,000 marks, from the purchaser 13,200 plus value-added tax. What a woman. He looked at Anna. With an almost imploring gesture she indicated that he was to concentrate on Max Stöckl. She and Rosa brought in the meal.

Gottlieb heard with amazement that Rosa must give up the study of law or had already given it up or—under Max Stöckl's influence and guidance—was about to give it up. Rosa must become an actress. And Magdalena, with whom he'd talked for four hours last night, right after his arrival— after first managing to pry her out of her room, he remarked to Gottlieb Zürn—Magda must study law since she had precisely the qualifications that Rosa lacked: the need and the ability, with the resources of a ready-made vocabulary, to rob every event of its uniqueness and turn it into a case, and, with no personal involvement, to choose the optimum solution for the case from among all the solutions that were available. That was the very thing Rosa would never achieve and Magda would always achieve: the passionately impersonal operation. On the huge platter, swimming in herbs and vegetables, lay what was at least a four-pound steelhead trout. Anna managed to interject, when Max Stöckl had paused for breath, that, since she had been busy selling the mill, Rosa had done the cooking. Gottlieb expressed his admiration of the creative cook in pantomime, since Max Stöckl, who could efficiently combine everything with everything, was talking again without missing a bite. Even while they were having their coffee, he went on talking. When Julia got up because she wanted to take Armin to the training center, Max Stöckl, who had obviously recognized and solved her problem too, told her in heavy Bavarian dialect: "Now just listen to me and don't transfer your fear of shooting to him, you'll see how much success you'll have then." And back to Magda: "Whatever you do, don't drop out before graduating, whatever you do." To Gottlieb Zürn: It was quite clear that Magdalena only wanted to escape from school because she was scared that in two years, after graduation, she wouldn't get a job. But that was precisely the ploy of the people who were fanning such fears. These scare tactics were designed to drive as many kids as possible away from high school in order to recruit cheap labor en masse from among the intimidated. That's why it must be Magdalena's tactic to hang right in there in school. To fight for every grade to the second decimal point. If she dropped out now, everyone who looked at her papers during the next, decisive ten years of her life would ask why she dropped out a year and a half early, and it would be impossible to explain on each occasion just how she had felt at the time. Gottlieb nodded.

He continued to nod when Max decreed that Magdalena would have to graduate if only because she would make an ideal attorney. The operative intelligence par excellence. Gottlieb thought: Imagine a cameraman being so articulate, unbelievable! Magdalena smiled mysteriously. She must have undergone a thaw since yesterday. Suddenly she seemed to enjoy being discussed. Gottlieb considered what he could do to show this Max fellow how grateful he was to him. He really wouldn't have known how to cope with Magda's rigidity without the all-thawing torrent of words issuing from those black ornamental whiskers.

As the day went on he realized that Rosa had played an even more important role than Max in the thawing of Magda. She had been present at their nighttime conversation. Although nothing had been solved yet—this fanatical search through the job offers was enough to show this—contact had been reestablished, one knew where Magda was. As soon as they left the table, Max Stöckl expounded on Rosa's future. It was almost a consolation that his involvement seemed to be a strain on him too. Beads of sweat shone on his forehead and upper lip. He frequently thrust his face at Rosa as she sat beside him, his mouth open as if he wanted to take a quick bite of her. And then he would do something of the sort. Should Gottlieb draw his attention to the aromatic plum torte, its slivered almonds deeply embedded in the plums? Max not only put his arm around Rosa, he kept drawing her toward him as if to drag her away from someone pulling at her from the other side. Rosa showed the family that she was parrying this display of emotion with the clowning developed hereabouts for such situations. But gradually her attempts to fend off his proprietary zeal with good-natured clowning began to seem forced.

Gottlieb Zürn was also often reminded of Kaltammer's diatribe against dialects. If the Zürns were to speak their Alemannic dialect with as little restraint as Max his Bavarian, conversation would be impossible. Apparently only one dialect at a time is possible, and it suffers no other dialect but itself. Probably dialects should simply stay at home. Away from home they acquire something domineering. Instinctively each member of the family made an effort to speak High German to Max Stöckl. Only Rosa, poor girl, seemed to feel obliged to demonstrate that there was a bridge between Max's Bavarian and the local or any other language. The result was a feeble version of the Max Stöckl language. It hurt Gottlieb's ears as well as his soul. So if this fellow were to become a son-in-law, they might have to have a talk about whether what he was producing in the way of language was really necessary. When he was in foreign parts. And for him this region, "if you don't mind my saying so," was a foreign country.

"From where you sit, you just can't see it, no, truly, take my word for it. Look, I've been nearly ten years in this business, during that time I've made more'n twenty films. I think I'm in a position to judge. How many broads d'you think I've had in my lens? I tell you, this Rosa, this girl, she's a real winner. You can't see that now, 'course you can't. You're her parents. But with me it's different, see? I have to have the eye of a pro, a trained eye, get me?"

He went on to explain convincingly why most other cameramen were duffers, bunglers—yes, if you considered how much they ruined, out-and-out criminals. Certainly almost all the directors. He was aiming to be a director. "D'you think I'll go on busting my ass for those dilettantes? No way! Apart from there being so many ninnies in those jobs that someone simply has to come along someday and take a hand. Film, d'you know what that is? Film—no, there's no point trying to tell you, you've never even seen a film, you can't possibly have seen a real film. Film, let me tell you, film is something you have to *make*. Not talk about. Those jerks all talk far too much. And I make films. You wait and see. Man, the films I'm going to make, they'll knock you for a loop, the lot of you!''

Despite the gentle clowning with which Rosa accepted Max Stöckl's vehemence, she was proud of him, that much was obvious. Gottlieb could understand that. He radiated something. Gottlieb was touched not so much by the enthusiasm that gripped Max as he spoke as by his earnestness. In the course of the day and evening it was possible to gain some inkling of the multiplicity of his interests and the total involvement with which he approached everything he did. He refused all alcohol. That sort of thing impressed Gottlieb. And has never smoked in his life. And the way he's preparing for his career as a movie director! His masters are the Japanese. But one can't simply be taught by them. That, he says, happens only via one's existence. And he provided the family with the latest in religious teaching. So Gottlieb drank his Hagnauer alone. It was as if, by so doing, he was taking leave for today of Anna, who was drinking mallow tea, and would not be meeting her again. It seemed that at least from now on they would have to worry less about Rosa. Max Stöckl was obviously itching to build a life with Rosa. What impressed Gottlieb most was that Max Stöckl claimed to have found in Rosa's nature something like a source of strength. Something that had never emerged before. Something entirely untouched, recognized by him alone. A kind of supervirginity. And that, according to Max Stöckl, was so unique nowadays that, if you could only capture that fabulously pure radiance on film, you'd have your hands on a world-class movie. For movies, ever since their existence, had done nothing but exploit women. Never yet had a woman "unfolded" on film. Did they understand—not exposed herself but unfolded? The demands that human development had placed on the woman were more diverse than those placed on men, hence woman was more differentiated than man. But that was something people didn't know. At least not in the film world. That's where he saw a challenge. For himself. For Rosa. For them both. Right, my girl?

Strangely enough, Gottlieb, while listening to Max Stöckl, kept thinking he had done the right thing after all in retreating from his begging trip to Parler-Strasse. It was not desertion, it was self-respect, self-realization. Max Stöckl built everything on a sense of self. He expressed it this way: a person must have the courage to be interested in himself. He was convinced that within the next ten years the entire profession would capitulate to him. To him and Rosa, of course. Without Rosa he couldn't even imagine the beginning, which would also have to be the breakthrough. As he opened the second bottle, Gottlieb was on the point of telling Max Stöckl and the family all about his behavior in Stuttgart, as confirmation of everything Max Stöckl had been expounding. But an unaccountable inhibition prevented him. This was Rosa's evening. The years of being unacknowledged are behind her. Instead of misgivings, prospects of triumph. The way he had behaved in Stuttgart was also a triumph. The longer he listened to Max Stöckl, the clearer this became. Those reckless purchases—it was almost a shock to be suddenly confronted again with the figure of 8,811—that unhesitating desertion from the field of battle, that ecstatic journey home, all was triumph. He saw himself in a lightning-fast movie that could never be made, flying through valleysforestsriversbridgescurves out into the plain, landing here between sandstone and lake with Rosa standing free in the sunshine; and in his all too instantaneous fear, which he probably transferred to her, he had not realized how happy she was. He loudly toasted everyone. They all smiled a little. He was, after all, the only one drinking wine. And no one begrudged him that. What a lovely evening. On the terrace. Another warm night. Only Regina was missing. Her day had passed quietly. No fever, no vomiting. What more could one ask?

Gottlieb Zürn was looking forward to the bedroom. The camera was lying behind the curtain. To hide his expectations from everyone, he picked up the newspaper saying he hadn't even looked at the real estate pages yet today, the first time in fifteen years that this had happened. Then he asked Rosa not to forget to turn out the lights. Max Stöckl immediately burst out laughing and cried: "Just like my old man!" He actually leaped up, made his way around Magda, danced around on the terrace to demonstrate how his father used to come up to him in a conspiratorial manner and say in a solemn, urgent whisper: "Max, don't forget to turn out the lights!" This performance proved that Max Stöckl could reenact something with perfect accuracy. How old was he on Gottlieb's scale? He coincided with himself. He was thirty-seven, had been for quite a while. Gottlieb wasn't absolutely sure.

As he entered the bedroom with Anna, Gottlieb didn't dare fling the newspaper into the corner, which would have been the right place for it now; instead he laid it carefully on his bedside table and undressed without looking at Anna. Since he had been drinking but she hadn't, it was up to him to adjust to her as best he could. Or should he simply bring the camera out from behind the curtain and take a series of pictures of Anna before she could disappear into her nightgown? He could simply parody Max Stöckl. There would never be a more favorable moment for introducing the camera into the art of interrelating in their bedroom life.

In a voice of forced calm Anna said, almost as if to herself: "Rosa is pregnant." Sometimes Gottlieb Zürn felt that, when she wanted to avoid him, Anna would make obstructive remarks. She never needed many words for this, neither gestures nor volume. They were usually sentences like this one: Rosa is pregnant. Such words must have an impact. They must convey that they could not have been spoken earlier and must not be suppressed any longer. So there was no choice but to utter them at this particular moment. Under no circumstances must they be open to the charge of being obstructive. The ones that worked best were those in which Fate called the shot. As, for example, in the sentence: Rosa is pregnant. All right, *Eroica*, it's your turn now.

Much as he could see himself as being close to fifty—he had been training for years for this event and in the years still available for that purpose would go on training—the word *grandfather*, as applied to himself, sounded ludicrous. He hadn't yet solved the problems of having become a father. He needed to ask for more time to practice. Twenty years are not enough. He demanded twenty-five. And Anna? Anna can cope with such things. In Gottlieb's age scale, Anna is the miracle. She is at home in several ages. For days on end she can be a reliable forty, and as soon as the pressure decreases— provided she is free of worries—the seventeen-year-old blossoms forth, and within a few hours she is completely enveloped in the age of seventeen. In Anna, this stroke of Fate would arouse dormant capabilities. Terminology had little power over her. She could be down-to-earth. But—and this explained why the information had been given tonelessly and without rejoicing—she lacked confidence in Max Stöckl. He needed Rosa, but he couldn't be anything to Rosa. Fifty students had applied as extras, but this uptight fanatic seizes upon Rosa. This again was Anna's choice of words. He needed Rosa because without her he couldn't endure his own ideas. To Anna he seemed to be wound up tight and then locked. Had Gottlieb been observing Rosa? She'd been on the verge of tears all the time, hadn't she? But because Rosa was pregnant Anna had said nothing. But he, Gottlieb, should have said something! He had behaved disgracefully. But, he said, how could he have known Rosa was pregnant? Besides, for him that wasn't a son-in-law but a . . . a discoverer. Rosa's discoverer. Anna made noises of contempt. Gottlieb had behaved disgracefully in not instantly protesting when that fellow said Rosa must quit studying. She hadn't been able to say a thing because she was thinking all the time of Rosa's pregnancy. But Gottlieb! *He* should have defended Rosa's education! For years they had discussed, and then established, that nowhere could her talents develop more naturally than in the field of law. A judge, juvenile-court judge perhaps! And now? With not so much as a word was he defending the result of years of thought and planning.

He didn't want to force Rosa, he said weakly. Anna: "But it's okay for *him* to force her, is it?" Rosa had brought him here because she didn't know where to turn. Rosa was watching closely to see how her parents would react to this poor fellow. And what did she see? Her father immediately succumbs to him, lets himself be hoodwinked, silenced. Rosa had been expecting help. He had totally deserted her. That was disgraceful. So it's disgraceful, he said morosely. And after a time: "Why don't you suggest she have an abortion, then she'd be free again?" How could she suggest such a thing to Rosa? But of course, if Rosa brought up the subject. "*I* can't bring up the subject," he said, and was glad to have finally said something that couldn't be criticized. Personally he hoped everything would turn out all right. Anna uttered a gasp of exasperation. She was lying on her back, her eyes wide open; she was working. He supposed the kids could be glad to have a mother like that.

He turned on his side and lay staring for a while at the curtain hiding the camera. Then he briefly stroked his sex organ as if it were something placed in his care to which he owed consolation. Anna was right. Poor Rosa. Apparently he had misjudged that bearded pedant. The truth was, he was no judge of human nature. . . . Anything more idiotic, more grotesque, than this imperative to propagate can't possibly be imagined. Although in this room nothing was now more impossible between Anna and himself than sexual intercourse, he could think of nothing else. He even had to allow a certain fury toward Anna to gather momentum because once again she had prevented it. Perhaps things with Rosa and Max were quite different from the way she had described them, and she had only described them that way because she wanted to keep

him at arm's length. The more clearly one realizes something,
the more impossible it is to prove it. But wasn't she right not to
let him come near her? She invariably senses everything before
it is put into words. How he had left Stuttgart—she was fully
aware of that. What she didn't know was that he considered it
a triumph. He would have to tell her that. But for her at the
moment there was only Rosa and Rosa's plight. Anna was
right, nothing was more important than Rosa. Forgive me,
Anna, he thought, forgive me for being furious with you
because once again you prevented it.

When Anna turned out her light, he remembered the newspaper. He switched on his light. He always looked first for his
own ad; it had not been well placed. And only then did he
read what Paul Schatz was doling out to the public today. A
sermon on notarized fixed-price guarantees. *For many a
would-be purchaser, the real estate sector is slippery ground.
He looks for a firm foothold. The notary offers his services as
the perfect solution.* Well well, thought Gottlieb Zürn. But
after reading the sermon he was impressed. He was impressed
by the frankness with which Paul Schatz dispelled the illusion
that the notarizing of a builder's commitment implies that the
notary has some influence on the performance of the commitment. Paul Schatz didn't care a damn whether this made
pleasant reading for notaries or not. In fact he might well be
the notaries' favorite realtor because he was always urging his
clients not to appear before the notary in their shirtsleeves to
sign a contract. Whether one was disposing of real estate or
acquiring it, it was always a life-changing act. He associated it
with a wedding. Gottlieb thought: One more Saturday that's
turned out in Schatz's favor. So much achieved yet still no

recognition by his rival? On the contrary. Unreservedly? He read the Schatz homily once more. And this time he discovered today's motto placed by Schatz inside the black border that separated his ad from those of all the other agents: *To be good one must be better.*

The motto was more than Gottlieb could stomach. Once again he had been prepared to recognize, to admire even. But not now. He simply can't resist it, showing off, being unique. To hell with him. He glanced through the other ads. And what he found there drove him out of bed. The long column of JFK offers was headed by a JFK fanfare: *The chance of a century. Villa, 19 rooms, 5 social rooms, in unique park (4½ acres), exotic trees, tennis court; terrific marina (40 docks) with cabana. A property for property owners. Price: to be negotiated.*

"That's impossible," cried Gottlieb, "absolutely impossible." He read it out to Anna. His house. His listing. Mrs. Reinhold! Of course. Instead of giving Gottlieb the tip she had given it to Kaltammer, who had . . . Just a moment, the ad had been placed on Wednesday. . . . Yes but, since he always has his long column at the side of the page he still has time to make changes on Friday. Or he had had it all by Wednesday. But surely Mrs. Reinhold would prefer Paul Schatz. Most likely she had informed Paul Schatz first and then Kaltammer. But since Schatz worked more thoroughly and conscientiously than Kaltammer, Kaltammer had beaten Schatz to the post. And after Mrs. Reinhold had informed them both she had felt embarrassed that she hadn't included the realtor through whom she had bought her own house! So then she had phoned him, invited him, only then to tell him nothing.

He must write to her. She must get this from him in writing.

Inside his head, letters to Mrs. Reinhold took shape at break-
neck speed. He rejected one after the other. But then he had
one he hoped he would still approve of tomorrow morning. He
filed it away in his head. Till tomorrow. Suddenly Anna said:
"Did you hear that?" She had heard doors. "Imagination,"
he said, put out his light, and pondered from which point he
would now most quickly find the way to sleep. Again Anna
insisted she had heard doors. One of them had been the front
door. "Oh, Anna!" he said. "Good-night." Then he heard
the metallic click. That was their bedroom door. He sat bolt
upright, put on his light. Rosa. She went straight to Anna's
side, where she sat down on the bed. She tried to laugh but
with no success. She was fighting back her tears. She had had
a fight with Max. Now she couldn't stay alone in her room.
She was scared. Where was Max? Gone. She had kicked him
out. Because she couldn't stand him any longer. He had
insisted she have an abortion. She had said she couldn't
visualize such a thing yet. She hadn't said it was out of the
question. Simply that she couldn't visualize such a thing yet.
Then he'd said she wanted to destroy him, it was only too
clear. There were two other women at the moment who were
pregnant by him. A waitress and a girl from the ballet. He
took full responsibility. For a man to beget as many children
as he liked must no longer be a privilege of the aristocracy. But
at the moment these children must not be brought into the
world. In three years, yes. But not before that. The two other
women were more primitive than Rosa, and for them to balk
at an abortion no longer surprised him when even Rosa, who
had the advantage of far greater knowledge and understanding, refused to see the necessity of an abortion.

"So," said Rosa, "I'm supposed to have an abortion

because the other two won't!'" And, what's more, he was married. Despite the now wholly ludicrous nature of this information, she burst into loud sobs. Anna drew her down into the bed. Rosa sobbed even louder. She even verged on screaming. It sounded as if this tone were long overdue, as if she would have died had she not now been able to cry out.

F O U R

When Gottlieb Zürn got up at seven he saw that Anna
and Rosa were lying side by side, awake and silent;
they appeared to have spent the whole night staring into the
dark, as they were now staring up at the ceiling. And he had
slept and slept. He crept out as quietly as possible. As soon as
he was outside, he ran. Ran down and across the path and
into the water. Because no one was looking yet, he did the
crawl. Ludwig, now there was a swimmer, by God! The way
everything worked together when he did the crawl. When
Ludwig did the crawl everything moved slowly, but as a result
Ludwig moved ahead fast. Gottlieb felt that all his own
movements were violent and fast but that he didn't get ahead.
That's why he never used the crawl if anyone could have been
watching him from the path. For someone to thrash the water
like that and not get anywhere must surely be a comical sight.
Ludwig had always swum ahead, back again, and in a circle

around him. Gottlieb had always admired Ludwig, never envied him.

The last time he met Ludwig had been at the boat show in Friedrichshafen. By coincidence both had stopped in front of a Folke boat. Then at the fairground restaurant they had drunk a glass of red wine, and each had wanted to pay for the other. Ludwig was working in Paris at the time. In a *banque israélite*, he said. Since his father had been a Nazi he had decided that, if he should succeed in getting a job in a bank in France, he would not consider a *banque protestante*. "But your father wasn't a Nazi!" Gottlieb had said. "*Your* father wasn't a Nazi," Ludwig had said, "but mine was." "Your father was a block warden," Gottlieb had said. "Exactly," Ludwig had replied, and at that moment his chin had grown to positively frightening dimensions. When Gottlieb swam, he usually thought of Ludwig. They had spent hours swimming together. By day and by night. Ludwig and he were no longer friends. But if he didn't watch out he would start waiting for Ludwig again. He had done that for years. Then he had taught himself to think of Ludwig only as he did of his dead mother, his dead father, his dead brother.

When he turned around, far out in the lake, he saw, in a high silver dome of mist that the sun was just trying to penetrate, the delicate figure of Birnau Church standing on its own little hill. Were Anna and Rosa still lying so stiffly side by side? If he had had Max Stöckl handy at this moment, he would have strangled him. Instead of strangling him he had to write that letter to Mrs. Reinhold in which now he only mildly complained that she had given the tip to someone else.

Then he woke Julia. She asked for a ride as far as Andelshofen because she wanted to lay one more trail in the dewy grass for Armin before his test. Gottlieb had to be at the property ahead of the prospective clients. This would have been his principle even if it hadn't already been Dr. Enderle's.

As he rounded the corner of the barn into the driveway of the Baiten mill, he almost rammed a Mercedes. A local license plate. But wasn't the father of the young couple supposed to be from Kempten? A man lay on the backseat. Asleep or dead? Asleep. Although most of the face was covered by one arm, Gottlieb could see that the figure was that of Dr. Terbohm. Where was Barbi? He advanced into the courtyard that was enclosed by the main house, barn and stable, sheds and coach houses. The last miller had died four years ago. Well over a year ago the seventeen heirs, who lived all over the world, had agreed to sell and how to sell. Apparently they had had to go to court to turn out an incumbent, a pensioner, a distant relative of the Baiten miller's wife who had died twenty years earlier. A retired hotel porter from Zürich, he had moved into the mill and, according to the heirs, taken advantage of the old Baiten miller. Above all, he had induced him to make him his heir. That had to be contested. The proceedings had been curtailed inasmuch as Josef, the tenant, had hanged himself in the top attic. He had fallen to his death from the same beam the old miller had used to fasten a swing. Gottlieb had heard in the village that the swing must have been Josef's idea. It was assumed that the old miller must have been pretty senile or he wouldn't have taken Josef up on his strange proposal—Josef was apparently somewhat childish. There was no question that the two old men made frequent use of the swing in the top attic a great deal because often when wood or fruit was delivered and the stable hand wasn't around, a lot of calling and searching was necessary before they were found up in the attic. All the same, people say they tried to keep it a secret. And the very fact that Josef had been able to induce the old miller to use the swing apparently made it possible to have the testator posthumously declared legally incompetent.

After Josef's death the house stood empty. By now not a windowpane remained intact. The back door leading through the kitchen into the house had been torn off its hinges and could only be propped into the doorframe; inside it looked as if pillaging soldiers had made frequent visits. Prayer books, arch supports, chess figures, pipe cleaners, photographs, order books, chair legs, pieces of soap, socks, sparkling splinters from trampled Christmas-tree baubles. . . . The storage lofts were knee-deep in grain, and mice scampered about like ghosts. Barbi wouldn't be likely to go inside the main house. If she went anywhere it would be only the barn or stable. That's where things still looked reasonably inviting. The hayloft still half filled with hay. The feed passage stacked with hay bales. The broom against the wall as if it had been used only yesterday to sweep behind the cows. Or had Barbi walked along by the stream, toward the pond and the woods?

Before he could make up his mind which direction to take, Dr. Reinhold and Barbi appeared on the path from the woods, coming around the main house hand in hand. Dr. Reinhold's slight boyish figure and his large head created unmistakable proportions. Since neither of them had seen Gottlieb yet, he turned away and bent down to a rusty old boiler lying among the stinging nettles. Let them discover him, not he them. He waited for them to approach and recognize him before turning around. They had come almost straight from Constance, said

Barbi, a bit too eagerly: Judith had been playing there—really, she had no idea Judith could play like that! But now it was time to wake the doctor, the windsurfing regatta started at ten. Too bad, said Gottlieb, he had been hoping they were interested in the mill. He said it as if they were a couple. They didn't laugh. Gottlieb backed up his car, three drove off, two waving to him. "Poor Dr. Reinhold," Anna would always say on hearing of another of Mrs. Reinhold's emancipatory gestures. One knows as much about other married couples as about continents one has never visited. Should he alter the letter? There is some knowledge that cannot be used. But it was a splendid coincidence that the two Mercedes—one carrying Mr. Kristlein and the Gramers and the other belonging to Dr. Reinhold—had to crawl past each other on the narrow road from the village. Why doesn't one stage such action each time a property is viewed? There is nothing, nothing in the world, that makes an object so desirable as the discovery that someone else wants to deprive one of it. It was about time he incorporated that into his technique.

Mr. Kristlein immediately complimented Gottlieb on being so early on the job even on a Sunday morning. His daughter Irmgard asked anxiously whether those people had also been interested in the property. Gottlieb said yes, they had. Mr. Kristlein was not impressed. He shook his head. All this was fit only for the bulldozer. Nothing but an old dump, that's what it was. The son-in-law, Dr. Gramer, shook his head over his father-in-law's head-shaking but said nothing. No one except Mr. Kristlein said anything, and he kept reiterating that the old dump was fit only for the bulldozer. But Mr. Kristlein also wanted to make sure that Gottlieb Zürn would become acquainted with his own point of view as they walked through the house. He had built up a stonemason's business. Fifty years ago, with nothing more than a carton of underpants and socks, he had walked from Primisweiler to Kempten to begin his apprenticeship. And had started out at three in the morning. And had reached Kempten before ten. Now he has sold his business, which by this time employs thirty-two people. To the competition. They'd really had to cough up. So: he has money. But not for throwing away. He hadn't come by it easily enough for that. He is sixty-seven and worn out. Gottlieb protests. Yes he was, cried Mr. Kristlein, almost pugnaciously, worn out, that's what he was! And he wished someone would explain to him what his son-in-law, a vocational teacher, had in mind here among the stinging nettles. "To live," said the son-in-law defiantly from out of his reddish beard.

The daughter intervened and drew her father a bit away from Gottlieb and her husband. She had her father's delicately arched nose, the deep-set eyes with the eyebrows arching attractively above them. The two halves of her face were strikingly alike. A commanding effect emanated from this symmetry. Gottlieb had to shake his head; he wanted to escape this effect. Beside his tall, beautiful daughter, Mr. Kristlein did indeed look exhausted, worn out. The true racial difference is between young and old. As she walked back with him, her dress outlined her figure at every step. All right, Mr. Kristlein said, he knew nothing about timber, fair enough. He admits that timber is the most important aspect of this building. He has a friend in Tettnang, an old carpenter, he'll bring him over this afternoon, he'll examine the beams. On the way up to the woods and the pond, Mr. Kristlein stopped after a hundred yards. He refused to go on. Irmgard looked at him anxiously. She tried to pull him on. Didn't he think it delightful to walk among the mint and the wild geraniums? The stonemason refused. He wanted to drive as quickly as possible to his friend the carpenter. Tomorrow he's leaving for Majorca, his first vacation since 1945. The son-in-law hadn't said another word. Gottlieb thought that was smart. He had also noticed that there was no need to put on an act with this man.

Since Gottlieb had indulged for weeks in the hope and illusion of buying the Baiten mill for himself, he knew that this property was worth more than the price being asked. If it hadn't been for the threat of the autobahn coming through this valley, a buyer would have been found long ago. With his citizens' initiative, Paul Schatz had forced the autobahn farther and farther back from the lake until it had finally landed five hundred yards in front of the Baiten mill. The people around here weren't as clever at fighting back. For the time being they had the dirty end of the stick. And probably for good. Gottlieb would have bought the mill in spite of the autobahn. He had left it up to Anna to prove to him that they couldn't afford this kind of property with its woods, meadow, and pond. There was no way of financing purchase and renovation by renting it out. Anyway he would only have bought it to have it. To Anna, that was almost unbearable, to own living space and then let it stand empty: that went totally against the grain.

The three drove off. They would meet again at five. The young couple had again asked Gottlieb in a whisper to promise not to do anything before five. He was happy to promise. Dr. Gramer was extremely tense, that much was obvious. At the moment he couldn't imagine his life without the Baiten mill.

His wife was doing her share. For his sake. He wanted to be here with her. Alone with her among seven buildings and seventy trees and reeds and grass. Several times he had held her close and inclined his head toward her. Always at places where he could imagine doing something with her. Gottlieb Zürn had long known that houses and properties are bought mainly because a couple has a mental picture. In his experience it was mostly the man who had the mental picture. The women were usually more interested in how much sun the balcony got, how far the children had to go to school, and how far away the stores were.

Gottlieb had carefully avoided mentioning the interim agreement signed by the couple. He didn't know whether the old man had authorized them to do so. Actually their signature was enough to ensure the commission from the buyer. Under Paragraph II of the printed agreement, already countersigned by the vendor, was printed in bold type: *It is hereby agreed that responsibility for payment of the agent's fee lies with the party failing to complete the agreement according to the above-stated conditions. . . .* Although Gottlieb had a feeling that nothing and nobody could prevent this stonemason from tearing up such a paper under one's very nose.

At home they were all sitting silently around the breakfast table. The place where Stöckl had been sitting yesterday was empty. Gottlieb sat down there. Rosa's pale complexion looked roughened. To bring about a change in mood, he said with all the malice he could muster that Anna's client had already partially withdrawn. But no one was interested. At least Anna could have said: "They signed, so they have to pay." Then he could have said once again that he was proud of never yet having sued for payment of a commission. Should he bring up the subject of Stöckl or not? How much did Magda know? She was sitting rather as she had sat before the thaw. Had it been only Stöckl who had moved her? The telephone rang. A Mr. Fichte. He and his wife happened to be vacationing in the area and were thinking of buying an apartment in Immenstaad. Gottlieb arranged to meet them at two that afternoon.

On returning to the terrace, Gottlieb suggested to Rosa that she should be glad. But she *was* glad, Rosa said. Actually he would have liked to show off now with the JFK phrase: *Il faut célébrer les faux baptêmes*, but he remembered just in time that it might hurt Rosa's feelings. He put his arm around Rosa as never before and said: "Oh, Rosa baby." Anna said: "The main thing is, he's gone." Magda stared straight ahead as if to imply that she didn't want her presence either to prevent or to encourage anything. Armin came dashing around the unruly juniper branches and lowered himself humbly to the ground. And on his heels followed Julia, perspiring and complaining bitterly about Armin's poor tracking performance. Suddenly Gottlieb saw the whole world before his eyes: a system in which everyone expects too much of the other because someone else is also expecting too much of him.

The phone saved him from Julia's flood of accusations. Baptist Rauh. It was enough for Gottlieb to hear him say his name to know that Rauh's wife wouldn't go for it. As far as she was concerned, Lake Constance is not a body of water worth raising a sail on. She doesn't even want to look at it. She finds it depressing to think of constantly bumping into the shore. He now has the following suggestion: if, after sizing up the situation professionally, Gottlieb Zürn is of the opinion that this property is worth more than the five sites with their varying views of Lindau, and if these five sites can then be sold for 900,000 marks, or preferably a million, Rauh will come, then he'll grab it, with or without Bruni. After all, he has had to make all his arrangements so far for his second, his true life without Bruni too. Sometime or other she'll come around to his ideas, or who knows what'll happen? Poor Baptist Rauh. And he invariably asked what the weather was like at Lake Constance. When the *Föhn* was blowing, he insisted on Gottlieb giving him a minute description of the tangible world of Lake Constance in all its dazzling closeness and clarity. Gottlieb Zürn looked through the open window at the dog roses and felt they were looking at him. Once again he studied the interim agreement he had filled out for the mill and which, thanks to Anna's persistence, was now signed. Anna had been right to press the young couple for a signature. In the real estate business people must be helped to make up their minds or they'll go on vacillating forever. Once renovated, the mill would be worth double in five years. The more land was associated with a building, the more it interested him. He would have liked to buy all the properties he dealt in. It was beyond him how people with money would ever buy anything but real estate. Not that he wanted to speculate. He wanted to own land. Anna, on the other hand: no more than one could manage oneself, whereas he would have liked to leave the land to itself. To leave as much land as possible to itself would have been his ideal. He often fantasized about a society in which the birth rate was falling. Nature recovering, a mild surplus, relaxation as a product of Nature, people holding their hands out to each other again yet hardly needing to travel since life is once again tolerable right where they are. There would be room and sustenance for grandfathers and grandmothers; the excuse that their pensions would always call for further expansion would no longer be valid.

It being Sunday morning he took his poetry books out of the drawer. Sunday morning, he found, was the best time for writing poetry. He also liked being devout. But now as he set about reading his poems, he felt a distaste for his words. Those weren't poems at all. What he read was merely laborious and vapid. He was certain he would never again find anything to his liking. And the more it had something to do with himself, the more repugnant it would be. Within the space of a few minutes, so it seemed to him, he had plunged to the lowest possible point and would never be able to pull himself up again. He admonished himself. Be content, he said, you're well off. What was wrong? His life was becoming more and more bearable, yet he was being assaulted more and more often by this weight of unhappiness. He wasn't in the least content. And contentment was the very thing he was gradually expecting of himself. Not that he was ever likely to be cheerful. But he was not prepared to put up with this feeling of unhappiness from which hardly a single day was now immune.

Was this the melancholy of affluence? He didn't dare discuss it with anybody; he was embarrassed at being so unhappy although he was well off. He demanded a calm attitude of himself. Again it felt as if he could never raise his head again, never move his eyes again, never lift the receiver again. And indeed, although several calls shrilled away right under his nose, he was incapable of moving his hand as far as the receiver. But it would never have entered his mind to blame life or the world or the human condition. Recriminations seemed ludicrous to him. Besides, he had a suspicion that it was his own fault. At least his own affair. Even at the worst moments he still knew how beautiful it was to be alive. It was just that this knowledge no longer had any power over him. He could not move, could not participate. Each movement would have merely made the burden more palpable. Not even banalities about death could stir him now. So it wasn't despair. The word *despair* had no more effect on him than *desk with pears*. He had no name for the presence weighing on him. It was something luxurious, imaginary, self-imposed. Something one must at all costs keep secret.

Suddenly he jumped up and went, almost ran, down the street to the mailbox. His letter was still in it. Tomorrow morning at 5:45 he'd be here when it was being emptied and ask for the letter back. He no longer understood how he could have believed it possible to write a letter to Mrs. Reinhold telling her what he was thinking. How ridiculous to point out to her that he saw a contradiction between her constant railing against people who crawled and kowtowed and her insistence that he find Kaltammer charming and Paul Schatz irresistible! Wasn't she the first to call a person neurotic who forced himself to like people he couldn't stand? So he believed himself to be following her instructions, as it were, if he clearly stated how repulsive he found Kaltammer and how disappointed he, Gottlieb Zürn, was at her having recommended Kaltammer to Mrs. Leistle. After reading that advertisement he hadn't even bothered to go and see Mrs. Leistle. Perhaps she would be good enough to explain to Mrs. Leistle why, with no apology, he had failed to keep his appointment.

Apart from the fact that it was idiotic, now that all was lost, to expose his weaknesses still further, nothing in that letter was quite true anymore. The very fact of writing it had enabled him to escape from the situation set out in the letter.

After lunch he drove to Immenstaad with Mr. and Mrs. Fichte. The others went to see Regina in the hospital. Mr. Fichte called his wife, who drove, Mudder. He was from Saxony and said he had only one interest left in life, and that was to spend a few nice quiet years with Mudder. He had worked all his life as a mechanic abroad, in South Africa, Singapore, Mexico, had saved up a nice little pile out of his expense accounts, which he had invested, and had only seen Mudder once in a blue moon, and never under a roof of their own. But as a result they had both remained in remarkably good shape, as everyone told them, and now at last they wanted to enjoy a li'l slice of the good life, eh Mudder? Just as long as it wasn't too expensive, that li'l slice, said Mrs. Fichte in a slight imitation of his Saxonian accent. This was where Gottlieb could chime in. It was his favorite theme: one's own roof, one's own land under one's own feet. Gone was the awkwardness at making conversation from which he so often suffered on such occasions. That so many should still be born and learn to walk on someone else's land where they have no say at all, this was the last great evil of the system surviving from medieval times, a feudal relic reminiscent of serfdom. All laws for the protection of tenants were so much hogwash as long as *de jure* there were still landlords. Yet even as he spoke he could not forget that he was a bit of a landlord himself. But he needed the security. Schatz, of course, snob that he was, lived in a rented home: no one, he would say, was as privileged as the tenant, so he meant to take advantage of this too.

Schatz had all the figures to prove it. Gottlieb simply couldn't understand it. No matter what the calculation, he found it unbearable to live on someone else's land. The Fichtes agreed. As they entered the first apartment the mood was cheerful and everyone agreed that the basis of democracy, the demand for equality, would have no meaning as long as there was one person still left living on someone else's land. Mr. Fichte pressed the button that shot his tape measure out of its case. Mrs. Fichte unfolded lists of the measurements of their furniture. The two of them kneeled and crawled around, calling out figures to each other in happy excitement. Yes, the big rattan table he had brought back from Singapore would fit! God Almighty, that was a weight off his mind! It would fit with all ten chairs. And the skins from Africa too. At last he would be able to dig them out of their packing cases. But Mudder is dead against having them in the living room. He can already see himself stretching out his legs here, his feet on the skins. But Mudder's idea is to have the skins only in the bedroom. Once again Erich Fichte crosses the room intended as a bedroom. Will the skins show to any advantage at all in here? Or would they be demoted, so to speak, to the status of bedside mats? Mudder didn't want that either, of course. In the den, maybe? Yes, he'd be more inclined to agree to that, let's take a look. The den is on the small side. Frankly, he felt that the TV corner with the semicircular couch could only be made comfortable if floor and couch were covered with skins. For God's sake, Mudder, for thirty years he's been traipsing around the world, now he wants his comfort. By the way, today was Sunday, the traffic wasn't too bad but—this sharply to Gottlieb Zürn—during the week, the truck traffic, what about that? Ask me another, Gottlieb thinks, and says:

"Oh, it's not excessive, you know." "But yesterday on the phone you told me there was no traffic noise at all." "*I* did? It was my wife, Mr. Fichte, not me, who spoke to you yesterday on the phone." The Fichtes are going to look into that on a weekday.

After the best part of two hours they have fitted their furniture and their mental pictures into each of the two apartments, and Mr. Fichte, who seems to be an expert all round, has checked the prices of the apartments with a slide rule and knows that the price of each of these apartments is 35,000 marks too high. Of course they had only just begun their campaign, they said: if they wanted to pursue the matter they would be in touch again. Both let out a deep breath. Apparently they had now completely cast off the spell of the two apartments.

Gottlieb was glad he had arranged for Anna to drive him home. He wouldn't have liked to share the Fichtes' tiny car again. For half an hour he sat in the grass beside the bus stop. Watching the cars chasing each other along the highway, it seemed hardly conceivable that Anna and the children would arrive in one piece. Should he condition himself to the thought that he and Regina would be the only survivors? But suddenly there they were, drawing alongside. With Rosa at the wheel. Rosa had damaged a car in the hospital parking lot; the Zürn car had suffered a crushed rear light and a bent rear bumper. Gottlieb said: "How could you! In a parking lot!" Since he had himself caused 13,000 marks' worth of damage two years ago, he was hardly in a position to yell at her. Wherever he looked, he saw expenses shooting up. Yesterday he had squandered 8,811 marks.

"Rosa shouldn't have been allowed to drive today," he said

through lips that barely opened. Moreover, he discovered that Anna had paid the Mercedes driver 350 marks cash on the spot for the damage estimated by the man himself. Because of the premium rebate. "You can claim that as an expense," she said. "No," said Gottlieb. "What we could have claimed is the increase in the premium on account of this accident." Anna said: "Damn." Rosa said they shouldn't have paid anything at all, they should have called the police. While backing out of her parking space she had seen the other man coming, so she had stopped and, when the other man hit her, she had been stationary. But everyone had immediately rushed out of the car and apologized to that joker, so there was nothing more she could do. "She was not stationary," Julia said somewhat stonily. Rosa yelled at Julia. She was *so*, she yelled at the top of her voice. Julia yelled: No one was going to shut *her* up, that really bugged her. Anna shouted that if Julia went on yelling at Rosa there'd be another accident. Magda—one could tell from her gaze fixed on some distant point—was oblivious to what was going on around her. Julia and Rosa went on quarreling. Gottlieb was glad when he could drop them all off and drive on alone to the mill.

Dr. Gramer was already standing there, the crimson bullet-head and purple nose of the old carpenter shining beside him. A shock went through Gottlieb when he saw only those two. And was told that, while having lunch at the Wheel in Tettnang, the father-in-law had slipped from his chair and been dead by the time he reached the floor. Only then did Gottlieb notice Irmgard sitting in the car, staring straight ahead, not moving. He couldn't bring himself to go over to her and express his sympathy. Dr. Gramer whispered to Gottlieb that he hadn't wanted to cancel the carpenter's inspection his father-in-law had wished for. They climbed up to the lower attic, then to the top one. The carpenter opened his pocketknife and stuck it into one beam after another; they were sound. A hundred and fifty years old. He admired the joints. An old wall of the north gable, which had long since been refaced on the outside, particularly appealed to him because the wall was made of latticed wood and mortared with clay. That was called "knitted," he said. As they walked back through the mill section he said approvingly: "And mill chutes for five granulations!" The only brittle timbers he found were in the kitchen and the still, but even the most brittle was good for at least another fifty years. He would have said so himself to Karli, his old friend, but that was life, wasn't it, you wanted to tell a person something, and there he was, dead. Dr. Gramer said it might now take a couple of weeks longer to complete the deal but, since there were no problems over the estate, a maximum of three weeks.

Julia was blow-drying Rosa's freshly washed hair. It was a lovely sight. But Magda was again lying on the sofa, staring up at the ceiling. He was told that Rosa had tried to persuade her to wash her hair, whereupon she had said she would do so as soon as she could manage to be a grown-up. And to Rosa she had said: "You make yourself look pretty because you're grown up. I can understand that." If Stöckl had stayed, Gottlieb thought, she would have too. Nobody mentioned Stöckl. Nobody mentioned Rosa's condition. He hoped Anna had had a talk with Rosa. It might still turn into a proper Sunday evening. Almost the whole family under one roof. No dramatic news about Regina. She had to assert herself against her two roommates. The Greek girl was so domineering. Apparently in order to compete with the Greek child's exotic quality, Regina had told them only her middle name, and in its English version. Acting out a scene of welcome she had at once drawn Anna down to her and whispered that her name was Mary. "That sounds very nice," said Gottlieb.

While they were at supper, Mr. Rauh phoned. Great news! Bruni had suddenly come around. She must have had some dreadful experience that she hadn't yet been able to discuss with him. And it must have had something to do with Hamburg because suddenly it seemed to have dawned on her that Hamburg might be overrated. He didn't want to say too much yet, but one thing was sure: his properties in Hochbuch, Motzach, Taubenberg, Rehlings, and on the Hoyerberg—he always recited the properties in the order in which he had acquired them—were not going to be sold. He wasn't about to get rid of five properties that all had a view of Lindau lying in the lake backed by a wreath of mountains. Evidently Baptist Rauh was capable in his mind's eye of looking at the island of Lindau simultaneously from all five properties. Gottlieb didn't dare bring up the fact that actually only one of those five properties was needed to see Lindau lying in the lake backed by the wreath of mountains. "If Bruni will do her part," whispered Baptist Rauh, "we'll buy the Swan Villa. Bruni has inherited some jewelry that's always kept locked away in the safe. What's jewelry in the safe compared to a house on the lake with a turret, four gables, and stained glass?" "And a flagpole terrace on the roof," Gottlieb quickly interjected. "Crazy," said Baptist Rauh, softly and slowly. As soon as Bruni admits the full extent of her disillusionment with Hamburg, Rauh will call him, and they'll fly down. If a serious buyer should turn up, Rauh wants to be phoned immediately, is that clear? Perfectly clear.

On his return Anna was just saying that, when she had Rosa, she thought the child would belong to her for the next twenty years, and that had seemed like a lifetime. And how quickly it had all passed! Nonsense, Gottlieb wanted to exclaim. He pressed the button for the news. Rosa immediately got up and said she must pack her things if she was to catch the last train to Munich. The more Anna urged her to stay, the more relentlessly Rosa insisted on leaving. Anna and Rosa left the room still arguing.

One news report hit him hard: five major economic institutions were saying that the trend indicators had been wrong. Things were already on the decline again. Increased unemployment. Tax revenue from wages below earlier estimates. That touched him at the very spot where he had wounded himself yesterday by buying the rug and the camera. He could have screamed. The mistake he had made with that buying spree was escalating by the hour. What if the real estate market went dead as it had in '75! A two-room apartment shown ten, twenty, fifty times, and no deal! All it would need was for the gentlemen of the Federal Bank, imagining a nonexistent boom, to tighten the interest screws. At least he can be sure of the 13,000 from the mill purchasers. But only because the sole opponent of the purchase fell dead off his chair. Plus the fee from the vendor: 10,000, if Gottlieb manages to sell for 440,000. So he can count on 23,000. And of that he has already frittered away 9,000. And 23,000, when looked at more closely, is nowhere near as much as it used to seem when there was virtually no prospect of getting 23,000.

With the 60 to 90,000 for the Swan Villa, the months from

now till next season would have been snug ones. Every month they need more money. A thrifty wife, an excellent manager who always gets the most for her money, four thrifty-to-stingy children, and each month costing more than the previous one. Sometimes he was gripped by the fear that they were simply losing the money. Maybe he and Anna lacked the watchful eye, the tight hand, that were so essential. Maybe from time to time he or Anna absentmindedly puts down a hundred-mark bill on the windowsill and the wind blows it away. Or to the delight of underpaid junior clerks they leave fifty-mark bills behind on the counter. Sometimes he has a vision of the house with a conveyor belt, no wider than a letter, that continuously carried bank notes out of the house. What couldn't be taken from him in cash was wrested from him in monthly payments. That rug! That camera! Instead of spending 88.11 marks on knickknacks that would have delighted all the kids and Anna and filled the house with cries of joy, he had used 8,811 marks only for himself. Could he do more against himself than buy so much? Yet he has done it *for* himself. But the only thing one can do simultaneously for and against oneself is buy something. The more expensive, the more beautiful, the more unjustifiable, the more it is experienced as something done for and against oneself.

He and Anna drove Rosa to the station in Friedrichshafen. Rosa wouldn't allow them to discuss anything to do with herself. She looked terribly pale and determined. As the train moved out, they waved to her. From behind the closed window she tried to wave back. But because her wrist apparently refused to bend, the wave became a movement of rejection. "We shouldn't have let her go," Anna said later. But there had been no holding Rosa back. Tomorrow she planned to go first thing to the doctor and then to Pro Familia to get a social-counseling referral and a certificate of pregnancy, then an appointment at the clinic.

Gottlieb tried to turn the experience Rosa was facing into a sort of visit to the dentist. He wanted to create a protective layer to ensure that he and Anna could have the rest of the evening to themselves. Anna seemed cooperative. Magda and Julia had already gone to their rooms. Gottlieb poured some more wine. He was aware of a growing ability to imagine himself and Anna alone in the world. That was the basic requirement. Without that, nothing worked. In an optimistic distortion he told her about the viewings, about the stone-mason's sad fate which had had such a favorable outcome for them; about his unavailing patience with the dallying of the Fichte couple; with evident relish he told her how early that morning he had seen Dr. Reinhold, so often pitied by Anna, returning from the woods and meadow and pond hand in hand with Bärbel the suntanned windsurfer. Anna told him about Regina and Rosa; he made light of many of her worries, and indeed she seemed glad of some relief; the art of inter-relating was blooming; his thoughts were already on the camera behind the curtain. But when they entered their bed-room and he watched her undressing, Anna said: "If only it were all over, then we could breathe easily again." She couldn't rid her mind of the ordeal Rosa was facing. He tried at once to make light of it and so render her immune to the assault of suffering from Rosa's direction, but she shouted at him despairingly, imploring him to stop, she couldn't stand it; her instinct was to drive off that very moment to Munich so she could intercept Rosa at the station. She shouldn't have let Rosa go. And if Rosa did have to go to Munich, she shouldn't have let her go alone. Rosa couldn't endure the ordeal facing her in the next few weeks alone. But then Gottlieb had found that Max Stöckl such a terrific fellow. Oh my God, my God. . . .

He switched off the light. Again he wanted to be furious with her. She had ripped away the protective layer he had tried to create so they could have their requisite sexual intercourse in a capsule of illusions, as it were. Ripped it irremediably. On noticing that he was watching her undress, she had dealt the first blow against his structure of illusions. He was tempted to believe that she was merely using Rosa's suffering to keep him at arm's length. The previous evening he had succeeded in amassing a fury. Now he did not succeed, in spite of what he felt to be twenty-four hours' additional reason to be furious.

At five o'clock he got up, at 5:45 he was at the mailbox and persuaded Mr. Nothhelfer to give him back his letter to Mrs. Reinhold. Fortunately he had already been on his way home from the Baiten mill when he remembered to mail it, otherwise the letter would have gone and Mrs. Reinhold would have had a chance to laugh at the feebleness betrayed by his complaints. Gottlieb was obliged to put up with Mr. Nothhelfer's ransacking the contents of the mailbox for the Zürn-Reinhold letter with a zeal that implied he was doing Mr. Zürn a favor so immense as to be beyond Zürn's power ever to repay it. Gottlieb thanked him with all the enthusiasm that was expected of him. Back in his office he placed the letter in the drawer where he kept retrieved letters. He never opened them. Once again he experienced that same sense of triumph he had felt two days ago in Stuttgart after he had succeeded in passing up Mrs. Leistle. To initiate something, and then reverse the process in good time, gave him deep satisfaction.

There was nothing like a swim to supply the lift required for one's daily start in life. After ten strokes he could barely remember the difficulties of starting life anew each day. He always became cocky, timeless, in the water. Today the mist was already denser. Birnau Church a slender shadow in a September silk of sun and mist. The distance, too, a silk. Poor Rosa. Anna must always first demonstrate what it means for a person to undergo a certain experience. Without her prompting, he would often have no empathy whatever.

At breakfast Anna made it plain that she didn't want to be reminded of last night. She read the paper as if searching for something. Three times she interrupted her grim concentration on the paper and, by reading a few lines aloud, indicated that, though she might wish for contact, it could not be more than the kind created by reading aloud news items. True, these were of a sensational nature. Dr. Terbohm's first wife had been found dead in her apartment; she had apparently stopped eating, starved herself to death. Dr. Terbohm's second wife has won the windsurfing championship. Judith Reinhold's first public recital ended in enthusiastic applause. While reading the review of the concert, Anna was caught up in the raptures with which the audience had infected the critic. Gottlieb would have gladly suffered this paean of bespangled words had it been Julia or Magda who was being glorified. In order to discount the paean he pointed out the style. Would Anna really want to accept the opinion of someone who described Miss Reinhold's "Schumann touch" as being of a "sensuous, delectable slimness"? And what did he mean by "unstilted, bravuresque modesty"? Or: "technical problems are beggared under her jubilant fingers"? No doubt Anna, herself once the pupil of a master-teacher, could explain that to him. Anna refused to let her unalloyed delight in Judith's success be clouded. She would send Judith some flowers. After all, Magda was in Judith's class, Anna said, and there were times when they had been friends. Had been, said Gottlieb. She was going to send the flowers anyway, she said. Gottlieb pretended to relent. Perhaps it was even a good idea to shame the Reinhold house with a bouquet.

The telephone rang. He was afraid it would be Baptist Rauh announcing that he and his wife had already booked their flight. It was Rudi W. Eitel. He spoke in a slow, soft, hesitating voice, deeper than ever before. He's in a bit of a jam. Has somehow got involved with a bunch of fellows from Berlin. Some kind of tax-shelter proposition, you know. If he's going to be spending a few short weeks on this lousy continent, he might as well take a hand in the fun and games around here, right? So he'd let himself be roped in by a cousin of a former Bavarian minister of finance—you know how it is, they had been classmates at Stella Maris. A proposition of substance, that's for sure, though for Rudi W. Eitel's taste a bit too conservative. Fifty thousand prospectuses offset-printed, okay, but everything only over the counter. Now they're in trouble. There was a bad apple among them. Now it's a matter of jacking up the kitty, otherwise you're out and you can kiss good-bye to what you've put in. At the moment that would embarrass him, to say the least! He's got it all together for a new shot in the arm except for a ridiculous 5,000. But that's the joke, isn't it; it always hinges on a ridiculous 5,000. Because of a ridiculous 5,000 which you don't happen to have at the moment, but next week, when it's too late, will have ten times over, you stand to lose a whole leg and maybe even your backside too. He's already been talking far too long. Here he's been talking for half an hour all on account of 5,000. Must be this lousy continent. Okay: so Gottlieb'll get forty percent interest and in one month he'll have that sweet little bundle back plus interest. So for now his old pal Rudi W. Eitel would find that 5,000 trifle damn useful.

Although, while Rudi was speaking, Gottlieb would have had time to think up an answer, when Rudi finished he had none ready. Once again he had merely listened. Jesus, that's really tough. If he had been given that listing—Rudi would remember, he had told him about it on Wednesday at the Lazy Bones—if Kaltammer hadn't snatched it from under his nose just as Helmut had prophesied, he, Gottlieb, now that he had two keenly interested parties for the property, would have interrupted Rudi after his first few words and said: Rudi, come right over, the check will be waiting for you. But the way things were, Rudi, what could he do, his last deal had been on August 2, an August with no deals behind him and a September with no deals ahead of him, Rudi, and four wholly dependent kids. "Okay," Rudi said, softly and curtly. And once again, his voice slowly and softly dying away: "Okay." And hung up. To Gottlieb it was like a slap in the face.

That morning's next phone call: his cousin Franz Horn to inform him that Thiele had sighed once and swallowed once and then put it behind him. The Markdorf project is getting on his nerves. Thiele is running around with an expression of desperate resolve. They agreed to get together again soon. How about next Sunday? Franz's mother is celebrating her seventy-fifth birthday on Sunday, how about the Zürns coming over to Bodnegg that day? The Wigratsweiler and Torkelweiler families are coming too. A little get-together would do us all a bit of good. They hardly ever see each other. Suddenly the kids will find themselves without any relatives. Gottlieb was glad the subject of the Swan Villa hadn't come up again.

In the afternoon he and Anna went to see Regina. The Greek girl was no longer there. Jutta, the girl with the two fractures, was cheerful. Regina drew both her parents down to her. In whispers she tried to rid herself of her disgust over the violence to which she had been subjected. She contorted her face into grimaces, pummeling Anna and Gottlieb tensely and fervently with her fists. First the filling of her bladder with the contrast medium. She showed them how she had lain there with her legs drawn up and together. How they had spread her legs apart. She wanted to leave right now! Anna and Gottlieb must take her away this minute, to the North Sea and to the island of Mainau and to the municipal park. It took them more than two hours to persuade Regina to stay where she was and let her parents leave.

At home he signed the forty-one letters that Mrs. Ortwein had typed. Outside, as she walked by, Mrs. Constabler said to Isolde in her slow lilting voice: "You can go down to the water, if you like." And Isolde asked back: "Aren't you going down to the water, then?" And her mother: "You can go down to the water, if you like, I'm not going shopping yet." For an instant it was vouchsafed to Gottlieb to look over the fence into Paradise. At supper Magda again answered every question with "What for?" Julia was obviously annoyed to have to spend the evening, or her life, in such a family. But when Gottlieb tried to ally himself with her against the prevailing mood, she refused to cooperate. She sat there eating grapes, blowing the pips into the hollow of her hand, and said: "Bull."

When Gottlieb and Anna were lying side by side in the

dark, it occurred to him that he hadn't even obtained the Mannheim couple's address. For his index cards. Madness! Those people are looking for an apartment here, they contact him, and he doesn't even ask for their address. Incredible. What next! Now he can't even remember their name. Now he can't even get their address through directory assistance. What *was* their name? It's impossible. With his memory! He had to say it out loud. Anna was still awake anyway. He told her the reason he was worried. "It might mean fifteen thousand marks, Anna." Anna asked why he didn't simply say the first letter. Inexplicably his lips, under the quiet power of Anna's suggestion and after a brief groping, formed the letter *F*. Tentatively he attached all five vowels to the F. After the fifth vowel Anna said just as quietly: "Fichte." "Yes," he cried, "Anna, that's it! Believe it or not, you're right, that's the name, Erich Fichte. By God, Anna, you did it again!" "You needn't go overboard," said Anna. And after a while: "It's your own fault if you don't use me more often as a medium."

Now he was going to see how often she could do that, he said. "The last time was in June, in Munich when we had a quarrel on the street on the way to the beer garden because you kept insisting on going into one more store although Regina and I were absolutely ravenous and dead tired and left you behind and sat down in the beer garden and had something to eat and drink, and you didn't come and didn't come so we finally paid and went back the way we'd come, couldn't find you anywhere, but then when after another hour we returned to that huge beer garden, there you were among a hundred tables sitting at the very table we had been sitting at before, and not on the chair Regina had been sitting on, and not on the chair I'd been sitting on, but on the one to the right of my chair where you would've been sitting if we'd gone there together." She said nothing. He sought her temple and kissed it. When he moved over into his own bed she made no attempt to keep him back.

Whenever he drove anywhere with Anna, he usually arrived too late. So, too, at the auction. They could barely manage to squeeze through the door of the Blue Drawing Room, where the auction was being held. Sofas and armchairs stood against the walls. Whenever the auctioneer offered something of special interest, Gottlieb helped Anna to climb up onto a delicate little chair so she could see the object for sale. For seventy-five marks he acquired one lot consisting of an art nouveau bowl plus various items such as sugar tongs, a napkin ring, et cetera, without having a proper look at it. He very quickly became greedy. The first time the hammer came down for him and he had to call out his name over the heads of the crowd, a woman standing right in front of them turned around and said hello: it was Mrs. Schneider. She was there with two of her friends who were on vacation with their families in Nonnenhorn. Although she had spoken hurriedly as if from a departing train, she was interrupted by one of her friends, who had apparently hurried off to get some more money from the husbands who were sitting in the café. "There, Susie," said her friend, "five hundred, that's all I got." The third woman, who was fixedly following the auction, hissed across without taking her eyes off the wall lamps being held aloft by the auctioneer: "That's the ones, I've got them in my bedroom, you can go for those, they're lovely, the others with the flowers are kitschy, but not those, they're the very same as I've got in my bedroom." Mrs. Schneider joined in the bidding but didn't get the lamps. Her friend hissed: "You must fight back, Susie, don't be so bashful!"

In the midst of the crowd a baby was squalling. Mr. Kant, the auctioneer, called out: "Can't you nurse it and keep it quiet?" And without pausing for breath he went on: "One four-stranded coral necklace, thirty-three, thirty-six, thirty-seven, thirty-eight, forty, now s'pose I go up one mark at a time; remember, I don't expect too much, do I hear fifty-one, fifty-one, fifty-one, sold, one cross, I understand the missing emeralds can be obtained in Pforzheim, one terra-cotta stoup plus crucifix plaque, lower part of bowl shaped like girl's head, Italian I'd say. . . ."

An unmistakably firm voice, apparently from the front row, corrected him authoritatively: "South Tyrol!" Paul Schatz! Gottlieb felt the sweat break out under his arms. There were also a few antique dealers standing in the front row and doing most of the buying: one of them took the South Tyrol piece. For 110. As well as the reddish-gold enamel bowl filled with minerals. For 75. And the album of postcards spanning the years 1909 to 1925. Mr. Kant reads out greetings from Manila, San Francisco, Paramaribo. For 95. Another dealer, a young giant with a Bavarian-accented girl's voice and classic Beatle haircut, acquires stacks of old paintings—Mr. Kant praises the frames—for 110. A silhouette of Weissferdl the comedian goes to the dealers only after some resistance by a woman. When she has to give up she says: "What a shame, he's my uncle." Mrs. Kant, whom he addresses as Jakobine, and an assistant, Olga, lug in one item after another from an adjoining room.

Now come the rugs. Because people at the rear are complaining they can't see, a man up front gets onto a small table and has the women hand him the rugs, which he proceeds to hold aloft. Gottlieb nearly cried out: Eberhard! For that's who it was. Grinning as he used to beside the blackboard after scrawling his brilliant concatenated formulas. The greasy black curl hung over his round shiny forehead just as it used to. Even a few pimples had survived. He scored a great burst of laughter when, after the first rug had been knocked down, he turned it around to reveal that on the other side it was nothing but a rag. Had he already noticed that the Mr. Zürn who had acquired the sugar tongs et cetera was his schoolmate Gottlieb? Gottlieb felt embarrassed. But Anna meant more to him. And Anna wanted to take something home from here. So did he. If only dear Eberhard had seen to it that Gottlieb had been given the listing! If only he hadn't let himself be declared legally incompetent! Anyway, life must go on! Now it's the Zürns' turn, dear Eberhard! In the days when your people were giving chamber-music concerts in this house, the Zürns and the Ehrles and the Völkles and the Krezdorns and other relations were dying miserable deaths in Russia and elsewhere. And even earlier, when the regimental band of the Lindau garrison marched here to enhance the festive occasions of this house, Gottlieb's and Anna's ancestors were working their heads off under inhuman conditions or were at the front at Verdun and never came back or, like his father, came back as wrecks. So don't take it amiss, dear Eberhard, that we're cleaning you out like this. I'm sure it reminds you of scenes from animal movies where in the end you see many small creatures in the wilderness devouring a bigger creature while quarreling obscenely over the carcass.

And that quarrel followed, so to speak, on the spot. An

Empire chair had gone for 400 marks to a Mrs. Feuerstein who, instead of bidding herself, had Claims-Maier bid for her. He was apparently her adviser on authenticity. Gottlieb had recognized the martial voice immediately. He seemed to be an old hand; he got everything he wanted. And after the auctioneer's "Sold!" he invariably named the person to be billed: "Mrs. Feuerstein!" This name, which he always shouted quite triumphantly, sounded in Claims-Maier's Swabian dialect like "Foiershdine." He also frequently outbid Paul Schatz, who would thank him two or three times for having been outbid. "Ah yes, those sour grapes!" Claims-Maier would then call out in his Swabian tenor. But when the important Empire chair was knocked down to Claims-Maier, Schatz protested. He had still had his hand raised, he said. Perhaps Mr. Kant had been annoyed by Schatz's comments and deliberately overlooked Schatz's bid. But as an auctioneer he must obviously have acquired the habit of regarding his own decisions on auction matters as infallible. That was why he ignored Schatz's protest and entered the triumphantly shouted "Mrs. Feuerstein!" on his list. All Paul Schatz could do was call out: "At least it's not genuine!" Now Kant had to pick up the gauntlet. He called out: "Certainly nineteenth-century, don't pin me down to 1820." Paul Schatz, who apparently would have liked to see himself seated on that thronelike chair, to Claims-Maier: "I'd take it anyway!" Thereupon Claims-Maier: "Four-fifty!" "Done!" said Schatz.

Now Mrs. Feuerstein took a hand and cried indignantly: "I have three apartments, remember?" Loud laughter. That was too much for Mrs. Feuerstein. Mr. Maier only had her authority to buy, not to sell, she said. She couldn't appreciate the victory Maier had just won over Paul Schatz, who had been forced to acquire something from Claims-Maier's hand that he had been unable to get when he was trying to acquire it against him. Now Paul Schatz could do his stuff: Certainly, if Mr. Maier has overstepped his authority he would be only too glad to return the chair to the lady. Claims-Maier shouted: "Over my dead body!," then turned to Mrs. Feuerstein, who could not be seen because she was sitting in the front row. This chair, he insisted, was just as surely a mere Empire imitation in the old-fashioned German manner as he was a great-grandson of the poet Uhland. He strongly advised her to allow Mr. Schatz to keep this fake and to pocket the fifty marks clear profit.

Mr. Kant ended the squabble by putting up a Louis XVI chest, damaged, for 2,400. Schatz now had his revenge. He didn't give Claims-Maier a chance. The antique wardrobe, hardwood, inlaid, went for 15,000, also to him. The rustic closet with its original painting, for 3,000, went to the handsome mushroom-head. A Louis XVI chair, for 750, to Paul Schatz. Although Claims-Maier continued to bid too, each item was knocked down to Paul Schatz. Then Claims-Maier would utter shrill sounds of mockery. "We've really got him going now, haven't we!" he shouted, and everyone laughed. From the front a stern voice to Paul Schatz: "Must you take everything?" "Sure, I've got three divorced wives!" Paul Schatz called out gaily, prompting an even greater burst of laughter. Since they didn't know that Paul Schatz really was married for the fourth time, people probably thought he meant to mimic Mrs. Feuerstein with her three apartments.

Now for the lamps. Gottlieb immediately helped Anna up onto the little chair again. A baroque candlestick, for 390, went to him. Two little lamps on Biedermeier stands, for 200, also went to him. But two alabaster lamps were taken by the dealer with the girlish voice. Next came an art nouveau lamp, consisting mainly of a naked female figure, ecstatically curved and bearing the shallow lampshade on her palms. She arches her head far back; this is supposed to make the ardor with which she offers the lamp seem overwhelming. Gottlieb at once rejoined the fray. Since Gottlieb had already acquired a number of candlesticks, wall sconces, and lamps, Mr. Kant looked in his direction. After all, he could, if he wanted to, overlook a person. Gottlieb saw that Anna wanted this lamp. Such women appeal to her, Gottlieb thought, art nouveau women. But perhaps they weren't like that at all. Of course they weren't like that. But in those days people longed for such women. Or, only in those days did they dare admit to the kind of woman they longed for. No, not really. People admit that today too. In those days infinite tenderness was openly expressed. Since it must be assumed that images of women have almost nothing to do with women but a great deal to do with the men who design them, he preferred the art nouveau man to the man of today. He hoped he would have done better in those days.

After 1,000 marks, Paul Schatz and Gottlieb Zürn were the only ones still bidding. They raced up the ladder of figures being built for them by Mr. Kant with his rapid-fire calls. At 1,500 Gottlieb felt Anna's hand on his shoulder. But he couldn't stop. He had a feeling that the lamp figure was counting on him not to let her fall into the hands of Paul Schatz. At 2,000 Anna punched his shoulder. At 2,500 she pinched him, and pinched him harder and harder until, suddenly realizing that Paul Schatz could drive up the bidding till Gottlieb was wiped out, he dropped his hand at 2,950; the spectators let out their breath. Paul Schatz ritually gave Mr. Kant his name. Jakobine carried the art nouveau woman across to the other items already acquired by Schatz. Claims-Maier called back over the heads of the crowd: "Good for you, Gottlieb! Congratulations!" And because with his tenor plus Swabian plus temperament he imbued even the shortest sentence with something playfully martial, people laughed again. Paul Schatz was the winner, but he was now also made to look a fool. Since Claims-Maier had already established himself at this auction as an expert, his remark could only mean that Gottlieb had mischievously driven up Paul Schatz and then, as in a poker game, got out in the nick of time, with the result that Paul Schatz had to pay far too much for the lamp. Gottlieb was not pleased. Now he not only didn't have the lamp, he had also aroused Paul Schatz's ire. If he believed that Gottlieb had deliberately taken him for a ride, he was bound to be furious. Gottlieb should have immediately countered Claims-Maier's remark by saying that he genuinely wanted the lamp. But his rejoinder should have also contained some kind of joke. And with so many people around he couldn't think up anything of the kind right away, so he preferred to say nothing. That Claims-Maier! What a clown! Again he'd pushed him into a position against Schatz. And he, clown of all clowns, had let himself be pushed.

Up front, Kant's voice announced a painting by David Teniers. "Here we have a painting," said Kant, "early seventeenth century, rocky landscape with clouds, in the background sheep with shepherd, in the middle ground a gypsy woman reading a peasant's hand, let's hope it's something nice, fifteen thousand." That went to a dealer so fast that it looked like a put-up job. Jakobine and Olga were already hauling in the next painting. In an ornate gilded frame, almost life-size, Mrs. Bansin. Bare shoulders, pink dress, probably batiste. Dear Eberhard had inherited his round forehead from her. One leg—the painting didn't quite reach to the knees—was placed slightly in front of the other. This and the challenging gaze, and the lips already pursed slightly askew, like a crossbill, in a way that would later look as if upper and lower lip were trying to pass each other, gave Mrs. Bansin a brilliant, adventurous appearance. Mr. Kant mumbled briefly that this was the lady of the house, painter Fiete von Losswitz, I'm offered 110—and quick as a flash, unstoppable—going, going, gone. And even gave the name himself: Berta Fiegle.

Jakobine and Olga had already put away the painting and brought in two fur coats. A mink and a Persian lamb. But before Mr. Kant could get started on his figures, Mrs. Feuerstein said from the front row: "No, we can't have that. Leave the poor woman with something." Whereupon that stern, official-sounding voice: "You're a silly chatterbox." Mr. Kant had already drawn breath again when Paul Schatz intervened. The very first sentence contained the word *indubitably*. He fully concurred with Mrs. Feuerstein's objection. Not in order to flatter Mrs. Feuerstein—even though she had as many apartments as he had divorced wives—no, he was thinking of Mrs. Bansin, whom he knew only from hearsay but whose fate went to his heart. He had heard that Mrs. Bansin was going to spend her last years in the Allgäu Mountains; what, apart from going for walks, could she do there? And for eight months of the year it was cold. So anyone who deprived her of her coats would be depriving her of the only thing that made life bearable there. Applause. Paul Schatz was a hero. Mr. Kant said: "I ain't aiming to harm the lady." Dear Eberhard carried his mother's coats back into the adjoining room, calling out: "Knowing my mother, she'd rather have had the money, but whatever you say." A few people laughed.

At one o'clock Kant broke off. They would resume in an hour. Gottlieb pushed his way through the crowd as it streamed out, avoiding Claims-Maier and Paul Schatz, and invited dear Eberhard for lunch. Eberhard beamed with pleasure at the sight of Gottlieb. He spoke his mother's upper-class Swabian. His Pomeranian father had had no effect on his speech. He went to fetch his basset hound, who was lying on a silk cushion in the next room.

On the way to the restaurant Gottlieb asked whether dear Eberhard was satisfied with the auction. Dear Eberhard stopped, turned to face Gottlieb, and said he was happy because everything was such an obvious swindle. Fortunately the auctioneer was not trying to behave as if this were an auction. Anyway, it was only the things that the banks and the attorneys had left for the mob. And he would have found it distasteful to pretend at this point that it was a serious auction, whereas he fully approved of this amusing bargain sale. The best part had been the way that Kant fellow had played Mother's portrait into Berta's hands. That Kant certainly had a sense of humor. Gottlieb remembered Berta, didn't he, Berta Fiegle, who had been their cook for over thirty years and who had been saying for thirty years that she couldn't stand it another week at Mrs. Bansin's. And now she's spending 110 marks on the portrait of her tormentor. His mother had been a horror for the kitchen staff because she didn't know the first thing about cooking but, in order to conceal that, had interfered all the more brazenly. But Anna, how come she still looked exactly the same? It was beyond him. On the one hand she looked exactly the same as when Eberhard and she had gone to the same piano teacher and Eberhard had always arrived half an hour early so as to hear Master Eisele playing duets with his favorite pupil, and on the other hand nobody could deny that time had passed since then. Anna said she could just as well ask him the same question since he still looked as if he would soon have to have his first shave. Gottlieb said he too had only met Anna when they'd passed each other mutely in the dark green corridor en route to the music room. Then, later on, it had apparently been a dreadful shock to Eberhard to see Anna with Gottlieb at the theater in Lindau. He had given up then and there. From that day on he had had the feeling that he must be terribly nice to Gottlieb, for then Gottlieb would be sure to speak well of him to Anna, and Anna would like him a little better.

Since the hour was almost up, Gottlieb had to ask outright whether Eberhard thought Gottlieb had a chance. Eberhard realized why Gottlieb had invited him for lunch, so Gottlieb was obliged to say: "Don't imagine that's why I asked you for lunch, it just occurred to me to ask how you stand with Aunt Hortense. I understand she's looking after everything now."

Eberhard said it was the attorneys who were looking after everything, and they gave everything to the person who greased their palms the most. "Obviously," he added, as if that were the most reasonable thing in the world. Because Gottlieb looked surprised, he said it made no difference who got all that money now: the tax department, the banks, the Leistles, or the attorneys; all that mattered was that a large sum of money be paid because that was the only way the whole property could regain its dignity. Those who would eventually receive the money were the victims rather than the beneficiaries of this process. In order to demonstrate the great value of the property, they had to behave greedily. Perhaps that's what they had become, too. The attorneys for sure. They were to be pitied the most, the attorneys. They were stuffing themselves sick from this deal, none of them would ever be able to recover morally. It looks like luck, acts like a disease, but is in fact a distinction. They have been chosen to restore our honor. The fact is that, since everything in this society is a matter of price, there must always be victims.

Gottlieb asked again how he stood with Aunt Hortense. She'd been here since the day before yesterday, so he'd been told by Mr. Dummler. Where was she staying? Eberhard hadn't asked. But, according to Dummler, she came here every day, by motorboat. Eberhard didn't want to see her, nor she him. She, too, was a victim. One might say he had all the advantages at her moral expense. It was easy for him to say: Look, my hands are clean. But she and the attorneys would have to soil theirs. It must needs be that offences come; but woe to that man by whom the offence cometh!

If George, the basset hound, hadn't grown restless, they probably wouldn't have managed to get away at all. They were late as it was. Eberhard pushed his way ruthlessly through the crowd, flailing his arms and shouting: "Make way, make way, for the son of the house, his favorite pet, and his last friends!" Gottlieb and Anna felt embarrassed. They halted. But Eberhard pushed his way toward the rear again, calling: "Make way, make way, the son of the house is coming to get his friends!" Then once more in the opposite direction: "Make way, make way, for the son of the house, his favorite pet, and his last friends." Embarrassing though it was, Gottlieb and Anna had no choice but to follow, otherwise Eberhard would have become even more worked up. He was certainly worked up, everybody could feel it; worked up in a terrible and incomprehensible way. Perhaps like a child brandishing a wooden sword, playing the part of Herod and forgetting entirely that he is a child. Anna and Gottlieb moved all the way to the front row. Gottlieb risked no more than a little nod at Paul Schatz, but Schatz at once held out his hand, shook Anna's hand, Gottlieb's hand, and laughed as if they had met here for some jolly conspiracy. Gottlieb instantly fell under the spell of this man again. What a fellow. That strong face. The way nose and chin strove to meet in a curve so compelling that one wanted to stare all the time at the spot where they might be expected to meet. This man is generous. He's not going to let himself be provoked by any pale, sweating, booming Claims-Maier. Deeply tanned and in the best of moods, Paul Schatz stood there in his suit with its old-fashioned blue-and-white stripes, enhanced by a pale blue waistcoat. The suit seemed designed to recall the sailor suits of childhood. It was all Gottlieb could do not to stare fixedly at Paul Schatz. He really did look like a work of art in his own right. If a work of art is something where one part enhances the other. He couldn't possibly be ill. Never. He could have saved himself the trip to Vienna. Probably just another one of those rumors. That was another thing about him. Wherever he went— wherever he trod, so to speak—rumors sprang up. All due to his fertility.

Now Gottlieb was glad after all that the son-of-the-house fanfare had invested him with a kind of prestige among this auction crowd. Gottlieb and Anna did not bid that afternoon. The three dealers, Claims-Maier for Mrs. Feuerstein, and Paul Schatz for his three wives, did most of the bidding. When Paul

Schatz had successfully bid against the girlish dealer for a small ivory object described by Mr. Kant as an erotic netsuke in the form of a fruit—"an oval opening offers a view of a copulating couple inside"—the stern, official-sounding voice in the front row said: "That must be for the fourth wife."

After everyone had paid and hauled their loot out to the cars, there were a few mopping-up operations. Mrs. Feuerstein berated Claims-Maier for having acquired only one of the two white armchairs with red upholstery. Claims-Maier said the back of the other chair had a crack. Never mind, she wants it. Claims-Maier ran after the young woman who was just loading the chair into her car. He pointed out the crack, talked, paid, brought back the chair. The young woman now had nothing. Mrs. Feuerstein was blissful. She embraced Claims-Maier. That looked hazardous because she was at least seventy-five and down to skin and bones and had to walk with a cane, apparently on account of a wooden leg. She was wearing white slacks and a long snakelike gold chain around the empty skin of her freckled neck. Because of her protruding jaws, her false teeth stuck out in front of her face. Homeric, Gottlieb thought. Claims-Maier introduced the Zürns to her. When she heard that Gottlieb was a real estate agent, she said: "No, no, nothing doing, I've got enough apartments. Come along Maier, we have to leave." Claims-Maier threw Gottlieb a look that pleaded for understanding and just had time to call out that the particular baroque candlestick Gottlieb had bought was genuine, all the others were fakes. Gottlieb pretended that this was quite obvious.

One of Mrs. Schneider's friends loudly berated Mr. Kant for not having any Scotch tape that she could use to stick the loose delft tiles to the coffee table for the ride home. Mr. Kant was surprised that anyone would expect an auctioneer to carry around Scotch tape. Waving a fat bundle of papers, he said he was now going off with these papers to the Baltic for a couple of weeks, to straighten things out. "Come on, Olga, get a move on, Jakobine!" "Will you look at that slave driver!" said Jakobine, clutching the cashbox to her bosom. He took the bundle of papers, Olga the little gilt traveling alarm clock from 1926 which he had knocked down to her for 70 marks in a single sentence that gave no opportunity for a counteroffer. At the sight of people hurrying by with their pictures, chairs, ministrant's bells, altar cloths, temple dogs, rugs, sofas, chests, and so on, one could only assume that some disaster must have occurred close by. The Zürns had bagged 3 lamps, 3 candlesticks, 4 wall sconces, 2 small chairs, 2 occasional tables, 1 chair, 1 ladle, 1 bowl containing silver oddments, 1 pigskin suitcase, 1 small porcelain fruit basket (slightly damaged). A total of 2,110 marks. After they had actually managed to stow everything away in the car, the chair- and table-legs sticking right and left out of the windows, there was scarcely room for themselves. They had taken part in a looting, that's how he felt. But when the Vikings, say, or the English had gone looting, they had felt justified. He was justified too. Absolutely. The only thing he regretted was that he hadn't acquired a lot more things. He wondered whether he would ever forget the naked woman arching her head back and holding out the lamp. When they had loaded almost everything into the car, Dionys Dummler arrived with Bubi, now in his sole care. He pulled him along on a string. "Pretty nice, all right, those things," said Dionys, "if a person only knew where to put 'em." Gottlieb, as always, had handed him the plastic bag with the two bottles. "Now Gottlieb, you didn't have to do that." Gottlieb asked: "How's the swan?" Dionys told him he now had two, the second one was better behaved, it'd had a rough time, got caught in a propeller; but, believe it or not, since it had lain there in such misery beside the fierce one, the fierce one was now only half as fierce. Gottlieb reminded Dionys again that he'd be looking in tomorrow morning. He went up to Dionys and said in a low voice: "I have to find out what they're cooking up, Dionys, d'you get me?" Dionys said: "Don't worry, Gottlieb, you can count on me."

As he drove off he overtook Berta Fiegle, who was carting off the oil painting with an even older woman.

Driving along the village street they were behind Schatz's dark blue Mercedes 300; at the wheel, Oswin, the Schatz chauffeur, who also came originally from the Balkans. Had they taken the art nouveau lady with them in the car? There was nothing about the Mercedes to show where it had come from. When they reached the permanently overcrowded highway, Gottlieb noticed that, by the time he and the Mercedes reached the intersection, there would be a gap in the stream of cars racing past that he should take advantage of. A hundred yards farther away, the next batch that would force him to wait again was already approaching. So he kept his eye on the line of cars bearing down and rammed his foot on the gas pedal so that, in the wake of the Schatz car, he could profit by the same gap. But Oswin, known for his stolid nature, had decided otherwise. Gottlieb plowed full tilt into the rear of the Mercedes. The heavy Schatz car was thrust six feet out onto the highway. But the gap had been sufficiently large to allow the next batch of cars time to cope with this obstacle. So there was no further accident up front. Gottlieb dropped his head on his chest. He never wanted to move again, ever. He could feel the edge of a table on the back of his neck. Anna was trapped under a chair. Since Anna and Gottlieb had their seat belts on, the furniture had bashed into them. He had heard nothing. Had he been unconscious? Surely an impact like that couldn't have happened without a sound. He saw Oswin and Paul Schatz approaching. Both seemed to be in good spirits. The trunk lid of the Mercedes had sprung open. Paul Schatz looked in and picked up parts of the art nouveau woman. He brought out the torso with its neck arched and one out-stretched arm lacking the hand. The torso had been broken at the waist. "Now we can share the lovely lady," he said, holding out the half to Gottlieb. Gottlieb thought of Schatz's remark that there was enough of Mrs. Reinhold to make two Wagner singers. It was as if Schatz wanted to shame him. Gottlieb couldn't respond at all. He was merely aware of everything that was happening. Schatz saw that the Zürns didn't seem to have come out of it as well as he and Oswin had. He beckoned Oswin. They opened the doors of Zürn's car and helped Gottlieb and Anna to extricate themselves from the furniture. Oswin brought over his emergency triangle and placed it on the highway behind Zürn's car.

Gottlieb could only keep looking at Paul Schatz and Oswin. He pointed a few times toward the highway, toward the intersection, toward the two bashed cars. He wanted to say: Oswin, Mr. Schatz, you had plenty of time to make your turn, why didn't you. . . . He noticed that the water from the radiator had leaked out of his car. He wanted to see how much damage there was inside. On reaching in under the dented hood to release the lever, he thrust his hand right onto a blade. His hand bled copiously. As soon as Anna saw Gottlieb's blood she seemed to wake up again. Oswin brought over a first-aid kit from his trunk. Anna bandaged Gottlieb's two cut fingers.

Gottlieb went into one of the new houses nearby. It was —he was counting on that—occupied by some people who hadn't been living in Mitten in his day and therefore didn't know him. He asked if he might phone for a tow truck. The man, wearing leather breeches, stood at the side of a house training a young German shepherd, which, being still disobedient, went for Gottlieb. Gottlieb did nothing to defend himself. The man watched to see how far his dog would go, then roared at it so that the dog immediately crouched to the ground. By the time Gottlieb returned, Paul Schatz had agreed with Anna that she and Gottlieb would ride with him. Although the Mercedes had a dented rear end, it could still be driven. "We'll leave the damage settlement to our offices," said Schatz. "The main thing is, no one's been hurt." Gottlieb refused to abandon his car. He could only make a dismissive gesture, shake his head. In the end Paul Schatz had to content himself with Anna. He would take her to see Regina, make a call in Friedrichshafen, and then take her home to Überlingen. Gottlieb was glad to see them go. Paul Schatz's friendly, helpful behavior was torture to him. He could have wept with happiness at his unhappiness.

At last Rupert Schobloch, who had towed Gottlieb away two years ago, arrived on the scene. "Well, Mr. Zürn, I hope this time at least you have collision insurance?" Gottlieb shook his head. Schobloch said: "What a man. It'll be seven thousand this time too." Gottlieb said: "Never! That bit of body work?" Schobloch raised both hands in supplication,

crying out as if in great pain: "Man, oh man!" He had lost
fingers on both hands and had a hard time walking because in
his own accident his hip joint had been smashed. He consoled
everyone he towed away with *his* accident. He hung Gottlieb's
car onto the hook, pressed the button of a switch attached to a
long cable that enabled him to carry the switch with him in a
wide circle; then his winch slowly pulled Gottlieb's car onto
the truck. Schobloch watched, checked, adjusted. Gottlieb got
in beside him. They were ready to go. Gottlieb felt an impulse
to giggle because here he was again sitting beside the
helmsman in the cadaver-removal robot. *Eroica*, he felt like
giggling. In any case, the evening at the Reinholds had now
played itself out. From this moment on, it was the accident
disc that would spin until . . . further notice. Looking back,
reconciling himself to 8,811 marks had been easy.

Just after they left Friedrichshafen, the two-way radio
screeched. Schobloch's wife reporting the location of a
wrecked car in Hagnau. Schobloch said he'd be there in a few
minutes. He hung this second car onto a hook in such a way
that it moved along on two wheels. The driver was already in
the hospital. "There, you see how lucky you are!" cried
Schobloch. Schobloch drove to the Zürns' house so that Gottlieb could unload his belongings, then on to the two garages to
get rid of the wrecked cars, and finally to Schobloch's place.
Rupert Schobloch talked incessantly, just as he had two years
ago, about the deal he could offer because he was the only one
for miles around who could handle two cars at once, which
meant he could charge the expense to the customer for whom
the insurance was prepared to pay, as long as he, Schobloch,
supplied the rental car.

After reaching home with the rental car, Gottlieb was able

to inspect the Swan Villa loot. Nothing had suffered as much damage as the naked lamp woman. Imagine Schatz immediately thinking of giving him half! He placed the piece of naked woman on the stone windowsill in front of his desk. Thus he would always have the fragment of ardor before his eyes. Each time he would have to think of Paul Schatz. The moment of collision had burned itself into his mind. Forever, as it were, Gottlieb would now look out onto the highway, see the next batch of cars bearing down on him from a distance of seventy to a hundred yards, step on the gas, and hang in his seat belt while thin smoke rose from the hood. Seven thousand, Schobloch the expert had said. Seven thousand plus 8,811 equals 15,811, between Saturday and Tuesday. And he had wanted to bawl Rosa out because of that parking-lot scratch! Why didn't someone hit him?

It was two hours before Anna arrived. Schatz sends his regards again. The accident had shown him that they had not nearly enough contact with each other. He saw Gottlieb's collision as a sign of Destiny and, obedient to Destiny as he was, he didn't intend to ignore that sign without a positive answer.

"I see," said Gottlieb.

"Regina," said Anna, "the state she's in! Covered with spots. She's been vomiting again. The doctor told her not to be so lazy and lie in bed all the time, she ought to get up. She was in tears." On her drawing pad she had drawn a freshly dug grave. With a wooden cross. And a wreath. Against the setting sun. And on the ribbon of the wreath her name. "Maria or Mary?" "Mary," said Anna. "Then it can't be that bad," said Gottlieb. Anna had been crying too, he noticed. They had been egging each other on again. But this time Regina hadn't ended anything by laughing. Anna said she wasn't going to leave Regina in there beyond Friday.

That evening Rosa called. She has an appointment at the clinic. For next Monday. Gottlieb's head shot up in the air, so light did it suddenly feel. Anna said the back of her neck felt as if it were filled with hot lead. She could no longer move her head. To Gottlieb, life seemed to rage.

F I V E

When something is nothing, everything is nothing. He had known with absolute certainty why these words, with which he had awoken, were true. Now he saw that he would never again be able to return to the point where these words seemed irrefutable.

Anna was lying on her back again, staring at the ceiling. Almost like Magda. Anna had hardly slept at all. She had made herself some cold compresses; these had reduced the pain at the back of her neck and head. Gottlieb left the room as if he had just committed a crime there. Very slowly he let himself down into the autumnal water.

This Wednesday the mill was absent from his ad for the first time in months. Mrs. Sonntag noticed this. Her lips twitched back from her teeth. Today she was wearing a sedate dark green blouse, closed tightly at the neck, and thus was of no interest whatever to Gottlieb. On the other hand, it pleased him that, through her clothing, she should so precisely express the breath of approaching autumn of which he too was aware. Last week's blouse would have been grotesque today. The fact that she congratulated him on selling the mill topped off his sense of acceptance and rapport. Unfortunately he didn't dare ask whether the Swan Villa was again included in JFK's ad or whether it might even be shining forth in Schatz's ad. His own latest offer was a former hop shed in Meckenbeuren. Not exactly in the best condition, the building, but 3,975 square feet of storage space on three levels. He pushed his bicycle slowly in the general direction of the barber shop. There was nothing in the immediate future where a newly shorn state could bother him. At the age of ten or twelve he had always wanted to spend the days after a haircut under a blanket. He was now on his way to the barber to prove to himself that he had abandoned all hope of an interview with Mrs. Leistle. Since hearing that she chased around in a motorboat, he was almost sure that his picture of her was quite wrong.

Suddenly the black-and-white Monteverdi Safari drew up beside him, and Mrs. Reinhold sang out her "good morning," the "morning" one octave higher than the "good." Then she laughed at an even higher pitch. How, where, when, who, or what must one be born to be able to laugh like that? He felt like throwing down his bike and driving off with her. But she already had her emancipation helper, Curly-Beard Giselher, as her chauffeur. But why shouldn't this woman have two chauffeurs? If her bulbous-headed husband could lead a Barbi by the hand through the dewy grass, then this woman *must*, to achieve a balance, have two men in addition to her husband. He would have loved to share her with Giselher

Curly-Beard. She was a woman for two. Which immediately made him think of the two Wagner singers with whom he had ruined everything. But had he really? Wasn't she laughing as if delighted to see him? Or is she practicing her voice? No, she thanks him at the highest pitch for the flowers. Anna has done it again. Now she has only waylaid him because she didn't tell him the other day that her cousin, Mrs. Leistle, was staying at the Hotel Bad Schachen this week.

In case he was still interested in the deal, she had made an appointment for him for the next day. Two o'clock, at the hotel. But the tip she had really wanted to give him: Hortense was so greedy for money that one could almost call it a money mania. She would follow whoever promised her the craziest possible amount. What she ended up with was not so important, since she had more than enough. "But give her the prospect of an unlikely amount, and our little Hortense is putty in your hands."

By this time cars were sounding their horns. Lissi Reinhold waved and called out a "Goodbye" across the Hofstatt that for a second turned the square into an opera stage. Giselher was ordered to drive on. The Monteverdi Safari moved off. Fatso, thought Gottlieb, and was aware that he loved Lissi Reinhold. He turned his bike around. No way that he'd go to the barber. A woman who chases around in a motorboat is not to be approached without hair. He pushed his bike home along the promenade. Outside the Lazy Bones, no Claims-Maier, no Rudi W. Eitel. The empty chairs were occupied by autumn. At this moment Gottlieb felt capable of saying to Rudi: Hold everything till tomorrow, maybe I'll be able to help you.

Anna told him that Dionys had phoned to remind Gottlieb of the appointment. He put his arms around Anna and drew her carefully to him and held her tight. He thought of the moment after the accident. Anna said: "I believe I've always misjudged that Schatz." Gottlieb thought of the sum Schobloch had mentioned. He went into his office, phoned the garage, and asked for the estimate. Seventy-two hundred if the frame wasn't bent. To check whether it was bent would cost 900; in view of this type of accident, they were obliged to check it. If, as was to be expected, it was bent, there would be an additional 1,500, so altogether 9,600 net. The current resale value of the car was 10,200, so the repairs were not recommended; instead, they would bend over backward and offer Mr. Zürn 3,000 for the wreck so that for 21,000 he could have a new car. Within a week. The repairs would take three weeks. For a while he sat there feeling that he was losing blood. He saw the conveyor belt that carried out the money revving up to top speed. He saw the hole in the bottom of his analogy boat getting bigger. So if he didn't want to sink, he had to increase his speed. But how?

Off now, to Mitten, to the Swan Villa, to spy on Mrs. Leistle and Paul Schatz. But could he still do that? After what had happened yesterday? Impossible. But if he wanted to get the Swan Villa. . . . In the hall he found Bubi tied by his string to the newel-post. Dionys was with the swans; the brindled one stood watching Dionys smoothing green ointment onto an ugly gaping wound at the base of the wounded swan's neck, then covering it with a piece of cloth and securing it; the swan was lying on its bed of straw like a stranded ship. As soon as the one with the infantile mottling saw Gottlieb, it reared up and flapped its wings. Gottlieb called out to Dionys that he was going to look for a spot where he could keep an eye on Mrs.

Leistle and Mr. Schatz. "Don't let them catch you!" Dionys called back.

Gottlieb hung the bag containing the bottles over the artichoke-shaped knob of the newel-post where Bubi was lying, and walked up the stairs beside the swan that raced upward under the naked woman's guidance. His hand slid along the gentle wooden grooves of the banister. Today, beneath an overcast sky, the yearning couple on the south window, separated as they were by stream, reeds, and swans, looked even more agonized than when their naked bodies had been brought to life by the sun. Gottlieb entered the Leda room, walked up the stairs behind the closet, opened the door at the top as well as the one leading from the third floor into the turret. Just in case. Or would it be better to clear out right now? If Schatz and Mrs. Leistle were to see him it would be embarrassing in the extreme, and the last vestige of any prospect of the contract would be gone. He had his appointment with the lady. And to clear out this time is neither victory nor defeat but simply good sense. That's all. Right. Okay. What are you waiting for? But he couldn't leave.

He walked down to the room with the naked Leda, who took pleasure in accepting the swan's arch of homage with both hands while her gaze was fixed exclusively on the children tumbling out of the eggs who had so appealed to Anna. Anna had been right. Anyone looking at this woman found his gaze directed by her to the tumbling infants at her feet. But Gottlieb had no difficulty directing his gaze back to her. After all, she was the largest, most naked, most beautiful part of the picture. The swan nestling up to her was almost entirely in her shadow, only a quarter of one wing catching the light. Gottlieb felt an urge to sit down on the floor in front of Leda's exquisite toes so he could feel as if he were sitting on the painted meadow and also stretching up toward her. The emptiness of the room, the roaring of the silence, this explicit, frontal nakedness: that a painted woman could have such an effect! He heard voices. A woman laughed. Mrs. Leistle. A man spoke. Paul Schatz. Jesus! He crept to the door.

As the two of them walked around the hall, out onto the south terrace, and back again, they kept crossing and recrossing his field of vision. Mrs. Leistle, taller than Schatz, wearing what looked like a tropical uniform. He couldn't have been more mistaken in his mental image of her. Every word they spoke was as clearly audible as if in a church. Schatz's opinion: "For a person who likes this, it's worth a lot of money." "How much?" she wanted to know. He laughed heartily. He wasn't the one to whom it was worth a lot. But he had no doubt he could find that person. His computer would do that almost automatically. If he fed it the particulars of this temple of romance, in less than five minutes it would spew out all the clients who were eligible or who might even be passionately looking for something of the kind. Then one would know what kind of client, hence what kind of price. But she wanted to hear some sort of figure from him. He laughed again. Why talk about figures? He could guarantee his ability to obtain the highest possible price for this noble pile. No one had the roster of clients he did. Without even trying, he could think of the former Greek naval attaché in London who had served under the colonels, didn't care for their successors, was just getting a divorce, the kids are in Switzerland, he's now designing sailboats, has radical ideas about yacht design, would like to locate his construction office plus testing dock on Lake Constance: this was the kind of buyer he envisaged. Or: a Düsseldorf client, beauty farms in Marbella and on Lake Tegern, wants to establish one on Lake Constance. But he, Schatz, couldn't compete with computer selection. Needless to say, for matching purposes he will feed the computer price limits, say 1.8 to 2.3 million. In his mind, realistic prices have to crystallize out of the interplay of object appraisal and client potential. There now: at the moment he is a little less interested in this house than in Hortense's motorboat. How about taking a run together to Romanshorn? A dip in the middle of the lake, then lunch at the Inseli in Romanshorn? If she wished to discuss nothing but prices on board, by all means.

Mrs. Leistle said she had a whole series of appointments. Lawyers, banks, real estate agents. What other agents, he wanted to know. She gave four names, among them J. F. Kaltammer and Mr. Gottlieb Zürn. She wanted to get it all over with in a hurry because she was spending the fall in Spain. He was fascinated by her having come here by motorboat. He adored women who could handle machines, since he was hopeless at it. Some people believed he kept a chauffeur as a status symbol. Not a bit of it. It was simply that he couldn't drive a car. At one time he had had a complex about it. Now he derived nothing but pleasure from being driven around. More and more pleasure. To sit up front in a car, horrible! But in the back, pure bliss. And what must it be like in a boat! To sit behind her, watch her lightly steering the powerful boat like that lady there with her swan. Had she ever had lunch at the Inseli in Romanshorn? "You might be missing the most wonderful afternoon of your life if you insist on your routine no." Gottlieb heard her laughter as they moved away. Imagine someone making the same proposal over and over again, when it had already been so explicitly rejected! He was now almost certain that Mrs. Reinhold had not given Schatz a tip. So she did regard Gottlieb as *her* agent. For her, Paul Schatz was an artist, a genius, somehow larger than life-size; her agent was Gottlieb.

When he drove next day to his appointment with Mrs. Leistle, he gave Anna a ride as far as the hospital. She was suffering less from the whiplash than from the infamous business facing Rosa. Gottlieb felt embarrassed in Anna's presence because he had dressed so carefully for his visit to the lady. Fortunately Anna made no comment. The demands of his job, he sighed hypocritically, deep within himself. He was afraid that under almost any circumstances he would enjoy dressing well. This time again it was the lemon-yellow trousers, the shirt of the very palest pink, the brandy-colored tropical jacket with the fine black check, the tomato-red shoes. He had looked at himself at great length in the mirror, rehearsed his mouth, his hands. After all, it is the crucial visit, Anna. Everything hinges on this hour and the next. He won't be granted more than two hours. We must reckon with losing. "Here we are, Anna, give Regina my love." Anna said nothing. Since Saturday night she had practically stopped speaking. He pretended not to notice. He didn't want to increase the misery by an echo. Let them all cling to him. The heavier they became, the sooner he would be able to fly.

On the way to Mitten he realized that he had dressed without paying attention to the weather or to the day's place in the year. He was dressed for a scorching summer. But today autumn was smoldering all around. His strength diminished in proportion to the distance from the lady. He had lost all power over what was going on inside him. Others were governing him. Collapse, why don't you? That'll show them you're not going to put up with it. Nervous breakdown, how does one go about that? You don't even know how to do *that*. This was the same road he had driven along, also in early September, to bring his mother the check for 10,000 marks. The first bonus granted him by Dr. Enderle. Looking back, he realized that with those 10,000 marks Dr. Enderle had bound Gottlieb to himself forever. That's what had made him a real estate agent. "Your agent's fee," Dr. Enderle had said. Dr. Enderle had never said "commission." After handing him the check he had leaned back in his enormous but immobile armchair (more of a throne than a chair), pulled out his huge crimson handkerchief, and at a distance of eighteen inches spat into the unfolded square. That was his way of ending a conversation.

In those days the Zürns could live on 10,000 marks for almost a year. But he took the check to his mother. How had Anna felt about that? Two kids already, a hard time making ends meet, and he goes and carries off 10,000 marks, just like that. By that time his mother had already built a house, contracted debts, though controlled ones, smart ones, debts precisely adjusted to the speed of inflation; a far cry from the madly proliferating, overflowing, devastating debts that resulted from each of his father's business ventures. "Debts must never be allowed to come to an end," his mother had said once she had grasped the philosophy of the economy that followed upon the Second World War. "If you make the right debts, they'll be paid for you by the government printing more money," said the farm girl from Wigratsweiler whose education had never gone beyond the school of hard knocks. By that time she could have managed without him, though she always kept herself in debt to the utmost bearable limits, living, as it were, with bated breath. Gottlieb had handed his mother the 10,000-mark check as if it were a twenty-mark bill. "Here you are," he had said, since those words seemed most appropriate for the pressing yet casual nature of the gesture.

He had done so without looking at her. He had a fever probably. She hadn't accepted the check. His demeanor told her that it was for a large amount. Indignantly, crossly, as if offended, she had shaken her head and scratched the back of her right hand with her left. "Don't be silly!" she had said. She must take it, he said. This commanding tone, which he had never before or since succeeded in using with her, was effective. Humbly she took the check. For an instant their eyes met. She looked tearful. Or close to tears. Pitiful. Beaten. By him. But he knew she felt good now. She positively floated in her state of defeat and subjection. That was her happiness. At that moment they were as united as never before and never again. That nothing of this must be said or shown was taken for granted. The subject had to be switched immediately to something trivial, something tiresome. The 10,000-mark moment must be only a moment. After all, nothing but money was involved. And money, by God, isn't everything. But without money everything is nothing. It's as simple as that. But money is nothing too. Especially when one has a lot of it. Was he still supposed to be especially horrified at having to thank a 10,000-mark check for that instant of loftiest and deepest harmony with his mother? But surely it was only natural that he and his mother should be able to achieve such harmony over something like a check. And if it had to be called horrifying he wouldn't object, since he didn't think he was qualified to judge, but he wanted to acknowledge emotionally that whatever was horrifying in this prerequisite for harmony gave to the intensity of that moment a well-nigh limitless dimension.

While the bellboy assigned to him by the head porter was escorting him to Mrs. Leistle's suite, it suddenly occurred to him that, of the five real estate agents she was seeing, he was probably the last. Whatever he achieved—supposing there was anything left to achieve—could not be eclipsed by anyone else. Why would she consent to see him if everything had already been settled? So.

He heard the *Eroica*. From one of the rooms the bellboy was escorting him past. Or was it already resounding in him? If he could speak perfect Italian, he would have whispered to the bellhop walking ahead of him: I'm as young as you are. But happiness is to feel young when you're young and to feel old when you're old. He had felt old when he was young. Now that he was close to fifty he felt young. He was never synchronized. Never at one with himself. Always at odds with the moment. This struggle is what makes a symphony, a novel. Gottlieb let himself be borne along by the *Eroica*. He enjoyed being gripped by that nervous tension of Fate. I shall never die, he thought. My death has been canceled because it is unimaginable. The boy knocked at the door. He approved of that. The boy was his herald. "Misterr Zirrn," the boy announced in an Italian boy soprano. Gottlieb had a five-mark tip ready. A sacrifice. The boy in turn looked at him as one relative looks at another relative who is facing an ordeal.

Mrs. Hortense Leistle stood up, put the *Neue Zürcher Zeitung* down on the desk, and offered Gottlieb a fragile hand. She had visibly reacted to the deterioration in the weather since yesterday. She now wore sand-colored slacks, cut in the latest style, thus with a rather bold effect: ballooning slightly just below the belt, narrowing toward the ankles, clinging tightly to foot and heel. Also a double-breasted, assuredly feather-light cashmere jacket in an ocher that just avoided being piercing, somewhere between camel and pumpkin. And nothing underneath. Nothing one could see. All she revealed was brown skin. And gold. At neck and wrists. She offered him a chair, some tea. Only now did he discover how absurdly he had gone astray in his attempts to visualize Hortense Leistle.

On the little table between them there was, apart from the tea things, a tape recorder, beside it a microphone. That also looked different from what he had expected. Her hair appeared to be carefully cultivated, the ends neatly turned under so that it rested on her neck like a gently rolling rampart of blond brass. She was forty-one or thirty-nine. For all he knew, forty-six or thirty-six. On his unverifiable scale she was older than he. She was sixteen. Whenever the conversation made him want to look her in the face, he immediately had to avert his eyes again; he was afraid that otherwise she might see what he was thinking, or what he wanted. Nor did he dare accept as true what he saw in her eyes. She was merely dressed like that and sitting like that and looking at him like that as if she too were thinking of something other than what they had to discuss, but actually she had a whole series of appointments and disposed of each as she had done yesterday with Paul Schatz and was now doing with him. What kind of offer could he make her, she asked in a low voice, as if she were scared of him. He stared ahead, then out of the windows: the lake was there, surely that made sense. He told her that on Friday night he had learned that his colleague Kaltammer was offering the Bansin villa, and that was why he hadn't gone to Stuttgart. What he really wanted to say was: Just before reaching your house I saw no further point in calling on you. And I didn't want to crawl. I still don't want to. I know you can give this listing to whoever you like. Anyone can sell that house of dreams which my virile colleague calls a temple of romance. So I'm very much *de trop* here and would appreciate your confirming that. By a nod, perhaps. Then I'll leave. It's all right to fight for a single-family-house listing. But not for a contract to sell the Swan Villa. That kind of a contract, if there is such a thing as justice, can only fall from Heaven, into the maw of some villain. So, I'll leave now. You can, of course, ask me to stay, if you like. . . .

But what he said was that he had carefully studied the house, which he had known since boyhood, where he had spent many a happy hour with his schoolmate, Eberhard, so that he felt justified in saying he was pretty familiar with both form and content of the house. In the case of a property worth well over two million, this was not without importance since every eligible buyer was going to bring along experts to examine the property from top to bottom; that might lead to endless wrangles if one couldn't immediately supply a concrete answer to every question. Anyone who could spend two and a half million marks or more was entitled to be taken seriously. He had gone through his list of clients. At first he had believed he knew of five clients who could be considered for a house worth somewhere between two or three million marks. He had begun with the former Greek naval attaché in London. Next was a financier from Düsseldorf who specialized in beauty farms. The third, now living in Ascona, had made his money—one must be fully aware of that—from brothels. It depended on whether one liked that or not, but he must, he felt, mention it. The fourth is the first one he could recommend: Arthur Thiele, Chemnitz Dentures, he's been looking for just this type of house for a long time. For the fifth, Baptist Rauh, a composer who lived in Hamburg like an exile, the house would mean the beginning of the realization of his true personality. At present he, Gottlieb Zürn, can mention such names only in passing. After all, the most important thing was the price. Three million might be aiming too high, yet at 2.5 he considered it almost a gift. She thanked him for coming. He got up immediately. If all went well she would let him know by Sunday. She pressed a button on the tape recorder. She hoped he wouldn't mind her using the tape if necessary to jog her memory. She had shaken hands with him, he was outside the door, remembered the prospectus he had prepared, wanted to knock again, show her the prospectus.

He waited in the hospital parking lot for Anna to come. He couldn't get out of the car and visit Regina. For the first time he felt how right it had been not to go and see this Leistle woman last Saturday. Anna arrived with a face crisscrossed with shadows. Regina has lost her appetite again. Has to take antibiotics. Until a bacteria culture shows which particular remedy is indicated. Anna has asked that Eusaprim be discontinued. The doctor: "The infection must be thoroughly cleared up. After all, one day Regina will want to have children, won't she?" Anna has prevailed upon them to let her take Regina home tomorrow. She has already called her cousin Leonhard from a phone booth. He'll be coming tomorrow from the

Allgäu to have a look at Regina. The fact that, in talking to
Gottlieb, she mentioned that Leonhard would be coming
tomorrow from the Allgäu while Gottlieb knew perfectly well
where Leonhard would be coming from—from Simmerberg,
to be precise—could only mean that her soul was crying out,
crying out for deliverance. To him? He shrugged his shoulders. In his present attire he felt like a carnival clown on Good
Friday. Quite likely he had already ruined all his chances at
Mrs. Leistle's with his getup. He must look like someone
hoping to get the attention of a Technicolor producer. The
only gleam of hope: that he had offered the lady prospects of
2.5 million. Apparently Paul Schatz wouldn't want to go
beyond 2.3. He was right, of course; Gottlieb couldn't imagine
anybody paying 2.5 million.

That evening Baptist Rauh phoned. Bruni was now more
than willing. They would be there on Saturday. Gottlieb
sweated. He was spending many hours every day, he said,
arguing with the other party over the price. The other side, led
astray by an irresponsible fellow realtor, had dug their heels in
at 2.5. Until he had them down to 2.1 he couldn't in all
conscience allow the Rauhs to come. Now he was utterly
confused, said Mr. Rauh. Hadn't Mr. Zürn said last week 1.6
or 1.7? *Perhaps*, he had said, Gottlieb cried almost imploringly into the phone, he had made a point of saying *perhaps*.
By this time the buzzing going on around this property was
like a beehive in June. New figures were shooting up every
day. Today's 2.5 meant no more than the 1.6 of last week.
Don't lose your nerve, Mr. Rauh. Mr. Rauh and he, the
proven combination on the local real estate front, would have
to keep their cool now that the battle for the core piece was
beginning. "You are the only one of my clients, Mr. Rauh, to

whom I have confided the basic formula of the real estate business: only the man who can afford to lose can win." Mr. Rauh breathed heavily. What a tragedy if this property were to slip through his fingers! For Bruni, all Hamburg was at the moment a dump, she couldn't wait to get away. In keeping with traditional Jewish advice, her money was fighting on three fronts and she didn't want to touch the one-third that was gold, but she would now be prepared to flip the one-third of industrial shares over to the real estate third. "A unique situation, Mr. Zürn," said Baptist Rauh in a weak voice. Gottlieb said he was almost as acutely aware of the gravity of the moment as Mr. Rauh was. To own this house amounted to owning a share in the finest that history had produced over the centuries in Europe. But one must be able to lose it, or one won't get it. "Yes," said Mr. Rauh and silently drew twice more on his cigarette, then hung up.

Gottlieb phoned the garage to say he was capitulating, which meant they could definitely book the order. It often amazed him that somehow things always worked out. From across the hall Anna was calling the family to supper, already convinced of the hopelessness of her attempt. By the time Gottlieb arrived they were all seated at the table. He fell heavily into his chair. But he had forgotten to bring up his evening bottle of wine from the basement. "Julia, would you mind getting it for me? I'm already sitting down," he said. "So am I," said Julia, as rudely as she could. He had to jump up from the table and yell and run off and slam the door and even yank open the door to his office and slam it and keep on yelling until he was sitting in his armchair. What he was yelling was extortionate accusations. She couldn't even get a bottle of wine for him. He was just about fed up with this family. . . . He had caught the sounds of Julia also jumping up from the table and running upstairs to her room, from which her music was now reverberating. He waited until Anna appeared at his door. She said nothing. This meant: Don't push me too far. . . . He understood immediately and followed her back as slowly as possible. He was aware of how ludicrous it was that, after his yelling fits, he should let himself be led back so meekly to the table. He would have been incapable of returning alone. His bottle of wine now stood beside his plate. It was obvious that Magda had brought it up. In a low, martyred voice he said: "Thank you." Then he asked Magda to go and bring Julia back. Magda immediately went upstairs, knocked at the door for a long time, but Julia refused to open up. So Anna also went upstairs. Julia refused to open up. Gottlieb went upstairs, sent Anna and Magda down again, made his presence known to Julia, asked her to open the door, just open it, that was all. After he had waited for a while in silence, she opened the door. He took her hand. When he held her hand and felt that she wasn't drawing it away, he walked with her to the door and down the stairs. He didn't pull her at all. He merely carried her hand beside her. Then they all sat silently around the table. The food was cold, they could start.

The news commentator announced—as he put on an expression of gloating satisfaction—that on the following day the bank rate was expected to rise to seven percent. Gottlieb thought: Of course. He turned over onto his side in bed.

Today he could understand Anna's desire to be left to herself. Knowing that she lay there thinking of Rosa, he had to think of Rosa too. If she hadn't applied for that job as an extra, that Stöckl fellow would have never laid eyes on her. And she had applied because she wanted to earn some money. And she wanted to earn some money because for twenty years he had cultivated the notion in the family that they were short of money. But they *were* short. Eighteen hundred marks a month just for interest and amortization. . . . Had there ever been a single occasion when they had really been short? Or is it in the inherent nature of money that a person must always feel he doesn't have enough? And the built-in normal state: fear that any day now one will have none at all. It was the fear of the man in the motorboat who, because of a leak in the bottom of the boat, had to always drive at top speed. The fear when driving an analogy boat. A fear he had brought with him. From home. These were the consequences of those years 1918 and 1929 that reached back into his childhood. It seems that, when one has experienced something unforgettable in childhood, one remains tied by that experience to one's childhood and to that extent still a child.

In the morning he could tell himself—and this was to be reckoned a success—that he had slept no more than Anna. Shortly after nine Mr. Fichte phoned. "He is asking," said Mrs. Ortwein, "whether he can have another peek at the downstairs Immenstaad apartment." Let that skinny Leistle woman shove her magic castle up whoever she likes; Gottlieb Zürn will carry on as he's expected to. He immediately had

Mrs. Ortwein get Mr. Ammon in Munich on the phone and suggested that he reduce his price for the Immenstaad apartments, at least for the lower one, by some 15,000 marks.

Mr. Ammon seemed to have been battling since crack of dawn with terrible news. It sounded now as if he were simply continuing in the same tone he had been driven into early that morning. So now Mr. Zürn was on his neck too! The way he was being badgered from all sides was beyond belief! And the Federal Bank was in on it too, of course. The bank rate at seven percent now, the prime rate at eight. And who gets hit? The developer! And the small developer, of course! The middle class, as usual. The union drives up the cost of construction steel, the government drives up interest rates. And who is being systematically pulverized, destroyed, between the two? Mr. Ammon. And what does Mr. Zürn do? He wants to reduce the price! And where, might he ask, does Mr. Zürn live? Not in Munich, that's for sure. On Mr. Ammon's construction sites, costs are rising every week by what Mr. Zürn wants him to throw away in Immenstaad! And Mr. Ammon has signed for firm prices. This very day he was going to phone Mr. Zürn to tell him that, in view of spiraling costs in the construction market, it was high time to increase the Immenstaad apartments by 10,000 marks each. But reduce, no way! Gottlieb said that, logically speaking, Mr. Ammon's conclusion was unassailable; the trouble was it couldn't be applied to the market. At least not to the real estate market. While everything else is still going up, real estate is already declining. Real estate always reacts with the greatest sensitivity. It is also the sector that will head up the rally later on. "It's the flagship of market trends, Mr. Ammon." It doesn't do a

damn thing for him, he won't reduce. More likely he'll have
no option but to let the exclusive listing expire in September.
Yes, yes, he receives the advertising copy regularly, but what
good to him are ads without sales? So there it was, Mr. Zürn
still had a couple of weeks' time. Not to give away, mind you,
but sell, right? He has another appointment to view this very
afternoon, said Gottlieb in a somewhat pained voice. Mr.
Ammon wished him luck.

Mrs. Ortwein, whom he would have preferred not to have
around today, said: "Did you have a bad night too?" Mrs.
Ortwein came from Ehingen. Today he was irritated by her
whining, flat-footed Swabian accent. Before the Kaltammer
effect could gain a foothold, he told himself: It isn't the dialect,
it's Mrs. Ortwein. Anna urged him at least once a week not to
have Mrs. Ortwein come anymore. She wanted to resume
writing all his letters herself. Hadn't she done so for years?
And the children had been much younger then! But as long as
Mrs. Ortwein wrote for him one half-day a week, he was a
company.

Anna had just driven off to pick up Regina when Railway
Delivery brought an enormous plastic sausage to the house:
the rug from Stuttgart. He cut open the sausage, laid the dark
blue Kashan in place of the pale Kirman in the living room;
the Kirman went into the office. Mrs. Ortwein's ponderous
cries of admiration over the new rug almost spoiled his pleasure in the beautiful object. Anna ushered Regina in as if she
were a corpse. Mrs. Ortwein cried—and now at last her
drawling whine seemed appropriate: "What a sight you are,
child!" Once again Gottlieb suspected that Regina was acting

out what she was suffering. She hadn't lost this power. Maybe in some people it increases with suffering. It was time to leave for Immenstaad.

"Let's have another go, Mudder," said Mr. Fichte. Once inside the apartment, they again forgot that Gottlieb Zürn was there too. They were in a different mood from Sunday. He proved to her on the floor plan that she had drawn in some things incorrectly. The Orinoco chest couldn't possibly be fitted into the living room. The rattan table and the chest in the same room, whatever was Mudder thinking of? She in turn fought all the more vigorously against the animal skins. It would mean constant brushing and vacuuming. He was annoyed by her lack of logic. If she wants the chest in the living room, she could say so without bringing up the skins again, couldn't she? Surely it should be possible to discuss the chest problem by itself. What drove him up the wall was the way she changed her mind. Well now, she cried, and who had maneuvered the Orinoco monster into the living room? He had, if she remembered correctly! All she had said was, the chest rather than the skins. And now all of a sudden *she's* the one who's supposed to want the chest in the living room! Well, if that was Erich's kind of logic he was welcome to accuse her of being illogical. Mr. Fichte said with a chuckle that they now had enough new impressions to discuss. He said "kick around."

"Buying an apartment isn't like changing hats, is it?" said she, who came from this area. "The problem is," he said, "that the apartment is too small and the price is too high." By at least 15,000 marks; he'd confirmed that when comparing it with other projects. Two months ago, Gottlieb replied, he would have said so too but, in view of the rapidly spiraling construction costs, the price was becoming more justified by the hour. Mr. Fichte exclaimed: "Listen, with money getting more expensive every day, who can afford to buy at all?" "Ask me another," said Gottlieb, and laughed with the Fichtes. The Fichtes said they were good and hungry now. Gottlieb watched them drive off. The worst ones were those who were on vacation here. As soon as the weather clouded over, they had the time and the inclination to look at houses. Till the sun shone again. This time he had at least made sure of their Mannheim address. As he watched the Fichtes leaving, he felt he knew this couple too now. They don't love each other, but they are terribly compatible.

Mrs. Ortwein had left the house, so he could lead Anna to the edge of the rug and ask her how she liked it. "Very nice," she said. Her tone implied that for the time being, because of Rosa and Regina, she could only experience everything in a very limited way.

He asked Magda and Julia how they liked the rug. Magda, who had been more approachable since Gottlieb's accident, said she didn't know why rugs were necessary. Yet she was obviously sorry not to be able to give any other answer. Julia said: "How much did it cost?" That was of no importance, said Gottlieb. Had it cost more than 2,000? Yes. More than 3,000? Yes. More than 4,000? Yes. "Oh that's terrible," she said, and left. Once again he stood alone before the blue background with the interlacing yellow-green tendrils: the small ovals in the dense arabesques of the border, which he had first taken for flower-filled vases, were neither flowers nor vases, any more than the tendrils were tendrils; all was color, convolution, pattern. Its own kind of nature. Pattern—nature. 8,811. Plus 21,000 equals 29,811. And the miniboom on the point of collapse. Probably already collapsed. Throttled. Perhaps no more sales till Easter. Or Whitsun. How accurately his children reacted. To buy something. Only with money. That is the sin. The consumer sin. That's how his mother would have reacted too. Whereas he, as he well knew, was still grinning. Does a guilty conscience stem from being able to afford the rug or from not being able to afford it? Both. While he had been standing there, a brimstone butterfly had strayed in through the window. Now it was bobbing about over the tendrils of the rug. As if forever. Then it found its way out again. To Gottlieb it seemed as if the butterfly had brought him a message of approval.

Anna didn't come down for lunch. She stayed with Regina in her room. Regina evidently wished to lapse into an unrestrained state of illness. She moaned, wept, uttered little cries. Discovered a pain in her back, her stomach, her ear. Internal, external. Like a sunburn, it feels, as if her face were enormously swollen. As if she were beginning to rot. No, that's not right. She doesn't know. Constant announcements, descriptions of pain, visions. Even when she's not crying she can't recover her normal voice but persists in that high, inarticulate, feeble wail.

The front doorbell rang. Cousin Leonhard from Simmerberg. In his fine, rock-hard voice, the kind often heard in mountainous regions, he cried words of greeting full into each person's face as they shook hands. Although he hadn't been here since Magda's terrible throat infection three years ago, he remembered each name. He was hardly taller than Anna. Not a hair was missing in the thick black mop, not one was gray. The shaved surfaces of his face shimmered whortleberry-blue. In the sculpted, protruding chin, his unvarying hallmark: the sharply chiseled, noticeably dark dimple. He eyed each child as if he wanted to take in everything that had happened to that child since he had last seen her; but, with his genius for keeping up with the family, he also looked back at the others while discussing the child whose hand he was holding. He was without doubt an eye person. Each feature as displayed by each child had to be traced to the reservoir of the physical characteristics of Anna's families, the Völkles and the Krezdorns, and thus become part of that same reservoir to be handed down to future generations. Height, build, color of hair, shape and color of eyes, nose, complexion. The names of aunts and uncles came jingling from his lips. There was apparently nothing in this family that Cousin Leonhard hadn't already noted in Auntie Resi or Uncle Alfons or other Völkles and Krezdorns between Stuttgart and Zürich. There was no evidence of the Zürns or the Unsicherers.

But now for the patient. Anna is about to tell him Regina's history. Cousin Leonhard doesn't want to hear it. He wants to look at Regina. He can never have enough of holding hands and looking. Regina lies there quietly. He takes his copper wand out of a linen bag. They knew he would. He always did. He approached Regina with it. The closer he comes, the greater his effort seems to be. His face is contorted. The lips are drawn wide apart. Then one hand lets go of the wand. Did they have any quartz rocks? He has to go down to the shore himself and collect quartz pebbles in his linen bag. Downstairs and upstairs, he places wet quartz pebbles in the corners of all the rooms. Against radiation from water. This house is positively floating on a water bubble. Probably some water-bearing strata were also intersecting below the house. Were they bothered by ants? And how! He wasn't surprised. He had already noticed the subterranean water conditions when he came in, from the watershoots of the shrubs and trees. He places a few extra pebbles directly under Regina's bed. These were all too small, he would bring proper ones. He tries once more.

Now the wand starts jerking. Each time it jerks, he flinches. After that he strokes the whole length of Regina's body with both hands. Then her neck. Then her head. Each time he shakes out his hands as if wanting to rid them of something that had clung to them as he stroked. Then from his rather new leather briefcase he takes out several little bottles containing different kinds of herbal teas, places a selection of the teas on Regina's stomach, tests them with his wand, then he's done. All right. Everyone downstairs now. Everyone. Above all, Regina. A bed is made up for her on the living-room sofa. He puts a few extra pebbles under the sofa.

When Regina is lying down and they are all sitting around her, he speaks. Regina must stay downstairs until she is well. Always in the bosom of her family. Only at night may she sleep upstairs. But then alone. He says she has an inflammation that the liver can't handle, so her liver has been affected too and now one kidney is threatened. Stop all medication immediately. Instead, an infusion of two tablespoons each of stinging nettles, goldenrod, marigolds, yarrow, one tablespoon Saint-John's-wort, one teaspoon juniper berries, half an onion, a clove of garlic, a sprig of parsley. Five cups of this to be drunk with milk. One tablespoon sunflower oil three times a day before meals. And three teaspoons of a mixture of calcium bromate and fuller's earth. And certainly no fresh fruit, nothing raw. Only vegetables cooked in plenty of oil, and mashed potatoes. Not even stewed fruit. The body was suffering from acute hyperacidity. He'd be back tomorrow. Today he hadn't been able to demagnetize her fully.

After Cousin Leonhard had gone, he left a bright spot around which everything revolved. Gottlieb admired Cousin Leonhard's boldness and confidence. That night Regina vomited only once. In the morning when Gottlieb asked her whether she still felt any pain, she replied that when she said it hurt, it hurt; when she said it wasn't too bad, then it wasn't too bad. This information showed him that Cousin Leonhard had succeeded in placing himself between Regina and her illness.

Gottlieb felt a sense of happiness suffusing him like a warm tide when he noted that this Saturday the Swan Villa was absent from the long column of the JFK ad. So the fellow had been bluffing again. That could mean that Mr. Gottlieb Zürn was in the lead. For the moment. Why shouldn't the lady give the contract to the person who had the oldest connection to the house *and* who had also made the highest offer! He could feel it in his bones, he had the listing. It so happened that that girl had normal feelings. Nothing against Paul Schatz. Paul Schatz is a wonderful man. Really he is. But this time he has outmaneuvered himself. If Schatz had his way, he would have raped that girl. That fragile thing, with the mouth that was always trying to pucker up as it spoke. Gottlieb yearned for the presence of Hortense Leistle. He was not the man to comment on what she thought or meant while she looked at him. In a situation like that it would be enough to be allowed to stroke each other a little. Preferably at a not entirely insensitive spot. Each would have conveyed something to the other. No words. For God's sake nothing that could be misconstrued. Just stroke one another for a moment. Then his yearning would have more to hold on to. But since what is most important is not usual and he is incapable of doing the unusual, here he is hoisting Hortense's almost piercing ocher in his memory and groping for the unassuming blond hair lying like a soft rampart around her neck.

This Saturday Paul Schatz's message offered some warning advice under the heading: *"May I? Should I?"* The question was whether, with interest rates on the rise, one should build or buy. In conclusion, the sage pronouncement: *To vexing questions there are only individual answers.* And it is of course he, *your honest broker*, who has them. Today the Schatz message arouses pure pleasure in Gottlieb. He doesn't even begrudge him the highlight of today's offer: *Haven't you been longing for years for a private lake in Wisconsin? 52 acres, surrounded by 128 acres of wooded shoreline, including two log cabins, four rooms each. Landing stage. Unlimited fish stocks. Complete seclusion. For $250,000.*

This was the first time an American property had appeared in the local paper. And of course it was Paul Schatz who ushered in the new era. The urge to buy in America had been growing for some time. It was due. Why should such fairy tales be dished up only in the *Frankfurter Allgemeine Zeitung*? He had been caught napping. Once again. Next week he would knock them over with: *Art nouveau jewel on Lake Constance.* To hell with Wisconsin. His jewel was no more necessary than the lake in Wisconsin was, so they'd compete for dreams. Fine, my good sir, let's compete: here the Swan

Villa, whose essence is romantic feeling, there a fairy tale—in other words wilderness. But what about the mosquitoes, Mr. Schatz? Gottlieb knows about the mosquitoes the buyer has to expect. Gnats one can live with. But mosquitoes. . . ?

In the living room the Schneiders were just paying their bill before leaving. He was always glad when he could avoid the money-taking procedure. Mrs. Schneider called out: "And now let's hope our little lambikins will soon feel better, eh?" Unfortunately Anna came over to say: "Gottlieb, the Schneiders would like to say good-bye." What he lacked was the back-and-forth formulas for leave-taking. Anna had as many of those as there were fish in the lake in Wisconsin. He was saved by a ring at the door. Gottlieb called out his good-bye and ran to the door. Rudi W. Eitel and Claims-Maier. Whenever they appeared together, these two looked like an adventure. Gottlieb said: "It's not winter yet!" Today they had apparently both agreed on long mufflers. Because Claims-Maier's head was directly attached to his rotund torso, the muffler covered his mouth. Gottlieb walked with them around the house to his office. Armin rubbed his whole length along Claims-Maier. "Sure!" cried Claims-Maier. "Dogs always like me, let the poor beastie have his feastie." Gottlieb was reminded of Kaltammer.

They had decided to tramp all the way here in windy weather, said Rudi W. Eitel, because there was something important to discuss. Rudi allowed Claims-Maier to speak first. Claims-Maier looked about him to see where the wineglasses were, but there were none around. Gottlieb brought glasses and wine, they raised their glasses, Claims-Maier tasted. He conveyed his judgment of the wine by his eyebrows, which shot up from a critical frown of concentration into high arcs of admiration. He had found out. . . . He broke off. He finds it quite odd for three friends to be sitting and chatting together and not playing Skat. He'd find it more pleasant to sit here in this snug little room if, in addition to the discussion and the wine, they could flip a few Skat cards too. Rudi nodded like a mute eager to express vigorous assent. Gottlieb brought the cards. Claims-Maier now had two roles: informant and Skat interlocutor. His martial voice and the vowels of his Swabian dialect, rounded almost to bursting point, plus a temperament always ready to exclaim, complain, berate, curse, moan and groan, hankered to be employed in this way. After a botched attempt to shuffle the cards like an American pro, he calls out in conspicuous High German: "Some of the queens must have lain down crossways again, what?" Rudi giggles shrilly. Gottlieb says there is a child lying in the next room who came back from the hospital only yesterday. Whereupon each of the two yelled at the other to lower his voice, damn it. That gave them a shock, and in a whisper they promised from now on only to whisper. But whenever Rudi bid a nullo—which he did often enough—and Gottlieb led a suit which, in Claims-Maier's superior judgment, was the wrong one, Claims-Maier would shout that Gottlieb must be God's own Skat player. Gottlieb asked Rudi to order Claims-Maier to go pianissimo. Claims-Maier's enormous eyeballs lay on their lower lids like two heavy full moons about to roll out. His name was Helmut, pretty please.

So: their reason for coming. To begin with, Kaltammer has never flown from Constance to Burgundy on a Friday; he has always flown to Geneva, where he has an apartment. He enters it as Kaltammer, leaves it as a woman with shoulder-length chestnut hair wearing a skin-tight leather suit and high-heeled boots. That's how he goes out. Into the city. He comes back with adventurous men. So now, what are we going to do about it? "Just a moment, just a moment," cried Rudi. "There's more to come!" "All right," said Helmut. "Paul Schatz has seen Mrs. Leistle. He's buying for himself. On Monday the deal goes through. On Tuesday demolition starts. He's going to build an apartment complex." Gottlieb said he was in constant touch with Mrs. Leistle and aware of every word that had passed between her and Schatz. Claims-Maier said, as if Gottlieb hadn't spoken: "How d'you like that! As a woman! In a leather suit! With heels that high! And that's the man who said to Anni, Helmut's youngest sister . . ." No, he wouldn't repeat that. Only a Kaltammer who roams the streets of Geneva dressed in leather like a woman from Milan could say such things to a young girl. Now the harm done by Kaltammer had been completed by a dentist, who had deadened Anni's two front teeth so that they were now black. "Black, my friends, that's what my youngest sister's front teeth are." When Gottlieb went to get another bottle of wine, Anna asked him how long the two men intended to stay. He didn't know. But not for lunch, she hoped. Leonhard was coming after lunch. "I know, I know," Gottlieb said in some distress, he hadn't invited them. She failed to understand him, Anna said and turned away.

When Gottlieb was back in his office, Rudi drew out the real estate page with the Schatz advertisement and cried: "Now that guy is trying to do me out of the New World, fellows. Wisconsin! Ridiculous! Forty below in winter and a hundred and five in summer, a real killer climate! And then that show-off spiel tailored for the benefit of the victims of low-cost housing. No, my friends, now we have him by the balls!"

Hold everything, said Helmut, first he wanted to play this hand in no trumps. . . . The phone rang. At last, thought Gottlieb. But it was Paul Schatz. Gottlieb immediately switched to his brightest vocal key but avoided mentioning Schatz's name. Paul Schatz asked after Anna, after Gottlieb, whether they had fully recovered from the shock, that long-overdue encounter, worthy of a different form, had given him an idea, as follows: he intended suggesting that their association's journal publish a series of articles entitled "Great Realtors," and he would like to write a profile of Dr. Enderle. Did Mr. Zürn still have any letters, documents, biographical material? Gottlieb said the widow had made off with every last scrap of paper. But he would look into it. On hanging up he was furious with the two men. But for them he could have spoken quite differently to Paul Schatz. There he actually phones and these two scarecrows have to be sitting around! He was in a sour mood. He refused to tell inquisitive old Claims-Maier who had called. "Now he's mad," Claims-Maier said to Rudi. Rudi said: "Your bid." "And what I'm about to bid, my lad, will make your ears ring like the trumpets of Jericho. . . ." After five minutes Anna phoned from the other room to say that the racket the two men were making was more than Regina could take. Gottlieb passed on the message. "Racket!" Claims-Maier exclaimed. "That's a word I don't like to hear applied to my pronouncements. Which means, Rudi, that the responsibility for that word rests on your shoulders." Anna phoned again.

They were going to have lunch now. He passed on the message. Personally, said Claims-Maier, he wasn't hungry. If Gottlieb would just pop in another couple of bottles, they might be prepared to dispense with his company for a few minutes. Gottlieb put a bottle on the table and went across to the family. When he saw Anna he knew she had come to the end of her tether. The Schneiders have left the apartment in such a condition that Anna will have to do a radical clean-up. And that's what those people call leaving it "in clean condition," Anna said. And they were from Stuttgart too! So what could one expect from others? And at four o'clock the Paffrath family were arriving from Remscheid. Gottlieb suggested she put Julia to work. Julia had to be at the dog-training center at three with Armin—this was the day of the test, didn't he remember? And Magda? "It's more work when she helps," said Anna. Gottlieb felt Anna had said that in order to provoke Magda into contradicting her, into proving the opposite. But Magda gave no indication as to whether she had even heard her mother's words. Anna said she wanted those two men to be out within half an hour, otherwise *she'd* leave. Gottlieb nodded.

Before the meal was over Leonhard arrived. The first thing he did was look into the teapot and express disapproval that Regina should still be drinking tea that had been made at six that morning. Stinging-nettle tea, if it stood for more than ten hours, could be used to kill aphids. Now did they understand? He looked at Regina again for a long time, as if he had never seen her before. With what deep interest that man could look at a person! Then he demagnetized again. He added bearberry leaves to the tea blend. Anna said that during the night Regina's pain had become more and more concentrated in the groin area. Leonhard nodded, as if this showed that the pain was following his instructions minutely. At that moment the office door opened and Claims-Maier appeared saying: "Good day, signore e signori, do not regard me, please, as an intruder. Prompted by a call of nature, I beg leave to be allowed to pass inconspicuously." Anna said to Gottlieb: "This simply can't go on, not with Regina so sick!" Claims-Maier stopped and asked how come they hadn't heard about this! His old pal Gottlieb had only told them that a child had returned from the hospital, but not whether it had recovered or not, Mrs. Zürn! "What have we come to, Mrs. Zürn, in terms of the intelligibility of human communication, et cetera? But if the child is ill, my friend Rudi and I will be the first to leave your house. Ruudi! Come here at once, there's a sick child here who's not well yet! Via, amigo, via!" Rudi W. Eitel appeared in the doorway, visibly pulling himself together. "Helmut," he said. "Enough of your fiddle-faddle." And turning to the Zürns: He regretted being unable to remain a little longer. They had talked so much they hadn't noticed the time. But now he had to leave. Good-bye, good-bye. He seized Claims-Maier like a rabbit by the scruff of the neck, or rather by his muffler, and dragged him outside. Anna sighed with relief.

Cousin Leonhard went out to his car and lugged in a quantity of bluish-gray, fist-sized quartz rocks which he proceeded to place in every corner. Gottlieb collected the pebbles. Then Gottlieb had to drive off to Meckenbeuren and Immenstaad to show the hop shed and the apartments. In Meckenbeuren it was a young cabinetmaker who wanted to start manufacturing windows. He laughed at the price. The laughter turned into abuse. Gottlieb had to listen to a diatribe. In Immenstaad a young Dornier engineer continued in the same vein. Today he could take abuse. On the way home it occurred to him that the most recent sale, in Kluftern, early in August, had also been due to Anna's efforts. As had the Baiten mill. He had been to the property twice with the Fichtes, result: zero. The suspicion that he was no longer capable of making a sale was becoming undeniable. An agent is only an agent as long as he can inspire his clients with the feeling that they can abandon themselves to the decision he has brought about because he is going to carry them through all difficulties to their final goal. If he no longer exuded this confidence, he might as well quit.

At home Magda was lying on the new rug, studying the job ads. Julia was slumped in the armchair. But Regina was propped up on pillows reading. Anna was talking outside with Mr. and Mrs. Paffrath and their five children. Armin had failed his watchdog test. By a long shot. That dummy, said Julia.

Gottlieb went to his room and started index cards for the parties to whom he had shown properties that day. Then he phoned Franz Horn to tell him some other time for sure but not tomorrow. There was a knock at the door. That must be Magda. First of all, she was the only one ever to knock, and secondly, she was the only one among billions of people who could reveal as much hesitation and diffidence in four barely audible taps. She stood by the door and asked how a person could learn to clean. She did not place the slightest emphasis on any one word. Why did she want to know? Magda: A cleaning woman must know how to clean, mustn't she? Where could she learn that? What does one have to know? What must one be able to do? It wasn't the first time Gottlieb felt that Magda's imagination was at its most vivid when it was imagining difficulties. Moreover, she apparently knew from experience that there was nothing she could do on her own.

First she must learn everything. To Magda, life appeared as something she would never master. He was familiar with this, but he had to pretend he was surprised. While trying to reassure her, he felt and saw that his attempts at making light of things were cutting no ice with her. At some point she broke into his discourse by saying: "So you don't know either." And left.

He opened all the windows and the door to the garden to get rid of the acrid stench of cigarettes left behind by his two visitors; carried out ashtrays and glasses; brought in the vacuum cleaner; started polishing the furniture until he was convinced that the very last whiff of the two adventurers had been obliterated. Then he sat in his chair and missed them.

He phoned Claims-Maier. Gerda, the older sister, answered the phone. She, too, had her brother's exclamatory manner of speech, but in her case it sounded shrill and hard. So sorry, he'd gone off early that morning. With Rudi. They always tried to make it look so important. Usually it turned into nothing but a pub crawl.

He realized that he was longing for Helmut and Rudi. He had to apologize to them. Besides, he hadn't paid his card debts. Helmut had kept score and taken along the score sheet. Now they were sitting around somewhere, pounding their fists on the table and calling on the moon to witness assertions whose level of boldness rose as swiftly as water in a tidal wave. He should never have allowed Anna to treat the two men like that. She had practically thrown them out of the house. He really had wanted to hear more about the long-haired woman from Milan in her purple leather suit. Everything to do with Kaltammer was fascinating. A Norwegian ballerina for a grandmother, next thing to a Latin American dance pro, an airplane every Friday, château broker in Burgundy, a dewy-eyed baroness, and masquerading in Geneva as a leather-clad woman from Milan. Kaltammer's latest status affected Gottlieb more than any previous one. Gottlieb's most private and secret—because no doubt most absurd or at least comical—inclination was to escape a little from the sexual camp to which he had been assigned. When someone called him a child, or scolded him for being a child—Anna's stereotype: You're worse than a child—his mind automatically added: But a girl.

Not that he wanted to acquire a different sex. Although he found girlishness more beautiful than any other "-ishness," his dreams either went beyond the division or stopped short of it. He hoped that what one really was had nothing to do with those sexual characteristics that prescribe the role one has to perform in procreation. Gottlieb did not want to stroll about as a leather-clad woman from Milan in the twilight of Geneva, but there were times when he would have liked to take his innermost self out into the open. To give that odd creature an airing once in a while. And perhaps it wouldn't quite match his outward appearance. On the other hand, it was through the necessity of concealment that he had developed the little bit of strength he did have. Oh Jarl Fritz Kaltammer, you stroll beside Lake Geneva, shunting your uninvolved gaze, watchful and feminine, and here Master Paul is demolishing my jewel. He couldn't do that. Gottlieb visualizes Schatz's eyes. Wit or pathos, but always involved. A dispenser of homilies. Concerned about flowing or standing water, inattentive train travelers, tottering medieval gables, unsuspecting meadows and accident-shocked married couples: such a man can't possibly tear down a house like that. He thought: It's easier for you to sink your teeth into a moonbeam than to believe anything that Eitel and Claims-Maier say.

Before falling asleep, Anna spoke straight up to the ceiling about Regina's pain, now centered in her legs, and about Rosa not having called, and about how Gottlieb was wrong to support Magda's evasion tactics. Was he doing that? Yes, because he hadn't categorically opposed her attempts to avoid taking her final exams. He felt like saying: Our kids don't happen to be made for passing exams. But Anna would say that was his fault. He said: "Our kids are embarrassed to show what they can do." Anna: "Bull." Then she added that the Paffraths were nice people, the husband was a masseur and intended to go on a three-week fast here; because he always had to eat so much in his job, he had decided on this as his vacation treat. She had put the six-year-old Paffrath twins into Rosa's room, the lower vacation apartment being really too small for seven people. Just so he knew, in case they ran all over the house during the night, looking for the toilet and calling out. Gottlieb looked at the place on the curtain behind which was the camera. He indulged in visions in which he took his revenge on Anna.

The following morning he was already out swimming by seven. How much more natural swimming is than walking! Even for a clumsy swimmer. Ludwig, of course, would have reached out quite differently into these waves, which today were driving in, green and crowned with spume, from the southwest. And because Gottlieb was swimming all alone under the lowering sky, he felt the scene to be heroic. Later he collected the flat cakes of waterweeds that had been thrown up by the storm onto the shore and laid them out, starting at the water's edge, that was receding day by day, to make a soft trail over the pebbles and across the path as far as his garden gate. And who was he doing this for? Also for the soles of Paffrath's feet, Paffrath the masseur from Remscheid, for soles that were becoming tender from fasting. But that feet could be so sensitive was something he had noticed with Ludwig. Throughout his childhood and youth, the soles of Ludwig's feet had been so sensitive that they had never become calloused. Every barefoot step on pebbles had drawn forth sounds of anguish from Ludwig. He had thrown up his hands, and as he staggered along his knees had given way. Whenever Gottlieb laid this soft waterweed trail over the pebbles, he thought of Ludwig. The idea that Ludwig might come and the trail would be ready for him gave him pleasure. From the next garden Gottlieb heard the rasping cries of a magpie. Hadn't he heard it once before this past week? One only hears it on hearing it for the second time. Mrs. Sonntag is now encased in an unrevealing blouse.

At breakfast they all sat surrounding Regina. Julia said it really bugged her that Regina should always be lying right in the middle of everything. When she, Julia, had been sick, they had shut her up in her room, that's why she had got well again so quickly too. If everyone kept dancing attendance on Regina, she would never get well. She wasn't that dumb! Before anyone could answer Julia, Regina said she had dreamed that night that Antje's dog could play the piano fantastically well and Antje had accompanied the dog on the clarinet till everybody had clapped like crazy. And Mr. Gerber, who had been the conductor, had pointed to Regina in the audience and called out: Now you see what can be done! The phone. Mrs. Leistle?! But luckily not Baptist Rauh either. Just Mr. Fichte. They would like to have another peek at the

upstairs apartment. Two-thirty at the building. He asked
Anna whether she could take over this viewing—an unneces-
sary and pointless viewing that had been requested merely
because the weather had turned bad—just in case Mrs. Leistle
hadn't phoned by then. Because it's Sunday, Cousin
Leonhard plans to be here at eleven, so Anna can manage it at
two-thirty.

He looked at Regina and felt misfortune ebbing away.
There would be no disaster. Not this time. At the last visit, the
specialist had threatened that, if the parents stopped giving the
antibiotics and failed to clear up the bladder infection, the girl
would suffer cirrhosis of the kidneys by the time she was thirty
and consequently develop abnormally high blood pressure,
fatal at the age of forty or fifty. The cousin from Simmerberg
took the bearberry leaves away again, added goldenrod. He'd
be back tomorrow evening. "Whatever you do, don't offer
him any money," Anna whispered hurriedly to Gottlieb.
When Leonhard has left she explains to Gottlieb that
Leonhard looks upon money as an insult. Gottlieb could
understand that in a way. On the other hand, Leonhard was
working full-time in Lindenberg as a bank teller.

By one o'clock Mrs. Leistle had not yet called, so Anna had to
take over the Fichte viewing. Gottlieb tiptoed past the peace-
fully sleeping Regina and sat down at his desk in his yielding
armchair. When Mrs. Leistle called she should see from the
promptness of his response that he had been waiting for her
call. If all went well she would phone, she had said. Was that a
riddle or uncertainty? Suddenly he was overcome once more
by the desire to crawl out of the house. Fortunately he felt just

as strongly that he must control himself. God knew he had already resisted other temptations! To get down on hands and knees and then wish to crawl outside through the door: that kind of impulse didn't necessarily have to be called a temptation. This desire to crawl out of the house was nothing more than a ridiculous notion. He knew he had to reckon with such things. If he hadn't been almost alone in the house—Anna had taken Julia and Magda along because she wanted to visit some Völkle relatives after the appointment with the Fichtes—the idea would never have occurred to him. But ideas that come to a person when he is alone in the house on a Sunday with a sleeping child must not be taken seriously. To be alone means getting silly ideas.

Having thought thus far, Gottlieb Zürn felt that it was all right now for him to get down on his hands and knees to crawl around a bit. Not out of the house. Never. But why not around his room? It always bothered him slightly that in Europe people tramped around in their walking shoes on these rugs and placed tables and chairs with sharp legs on them. He would rather have lived down there on the rugs. If that wasn't possible, he wanted at least to crawl around a bit on them. Seeing that he couldn't crawl outside. That was his true inclination, he was well aware. But since when did he give way to inclinations? And who does? He knew very well what his neighbors, the Jägers and the Paweks, would say to that. If they were at home. Most of the time they weren't. But the neighbors in the houses beyond. And all the people living between here and town. They would say how terribly surprised they were and—even worse—that on the other hand they weren't a bit surprised. Did he want to implore Mrs. Leistle in spirit to phone him immediately, otherwise she would be responsible for whatever he might do here? Black-mailing appealed to him. Now Mrs. Leistle, it's time you took a stand against the rumors entwining themselves around the Swan Villa like a threat.

He looked in on Regina. She was sleeping soundly. He took his poetry sheets out of the drawer. But after reading only a few lines he put everything back again. Today he would only be capable of crossing out, tearing up. It had been like this for quite a while. The illusion of being a poet could be summoned less and less often. What must he be prepared to face? He would have liked to put on his symphony-of-the-moment now. But he mustn't disturb Regina's convalescent sleep. So, while he simply watched the day growing stormier, he let the symphony, or what he remembered of it, run through his head. There can be no more beautiful beginning to anything. A young man who believes things that will be as he imagines them. The triumph of imagination over experience. The pre-vention of experience by imagination. The second movement admits that the first was too presumptuous. Thumb and forefinger spread into a noble fork on which the chin, wearied by the exertion of will, is laid in order to let the gaze wander over a downward-spreading expanse where all definable pain has ceased. A dark light emerges. Within. From within. Can the sky do otherwise than respond in kind? A chasm in the clouds allows sunlight to filter down. Brightness flows together. The world partakes of it. Within and without, a team. Time, an error. Phenomenon is all. As long as something is, every-thing is. The next two movements . . . The third movement he couldn't remember at all. But the fourth came to him. The way something that appears to be light becomes heavy. But because one nevertheless demands of oneself an attempt to rise to the challenge, the mood becomes heroic. His mood. Actually, he almost always seemed heroic to himself. Because danger never diminished. The spurning of new ideas. He liked that. Finiteness of material. Infinity of expression through impact from outside. So imagination does not remain inviolate. It is distorted by experience. Something can be learned. Something exquisite follows on something else, but without preening. Every note then goes all out. Result: history. Or: opportunity to dance. Gottlieb even saw himself joining in the dance. Everything is equally easy and equally difficult. But then he ends it all, that young man. The swiftly falling curtain means: it was all make-believe.

Anna came back into his room and, instead of remaining by the door as usual, walked right up to him and placed the interim contract before him on the desk. The Fichtes had signed it, thereby ensuring the commission payable by the purchaser. She played down her achievement. But Gottlieb wanted to know how she had managed it. She had merely pointed out the healthy environment, she said, how straight the trees grew on the property, signifying no underground streams, let alone any intersecting ones; brick walls, so no concrete cells. She had merely spoken as she felt in that environment; the apartment open to positive radiation from above with no negative radiation from below, so that she felt one could live a healthy life there. She had recommended to the Fichtes that they rip out the faded, worn synthetic fiber floor coverings and replace them with hardwood or travertine. The Fichtes had been delighted. And the skins, the Orinoco chest, the rattan table? Anna had distributed them. The skins on the walls, the chest in the study, the rattan table in the

living room. "So let's celebrate!" said Gottlieb. The look
Anna gave him said: Rosa!

At that moment the phone rang. Let it be Mrs. Leistle! But
once again Anna's wish was the stronger. It was Rosa. She
said she was not going to the clinic tomorrow. The people
there had treated her like a criminal. Gottlieb said: "Hey!"
And immediately handed Anna the receiver. He went outside
and ran up and down in the garden, groaning out loud. After
a while Anna came out and said: "Thank God." He failed to
understand her relief. If Rosa were to have this baby, they
would have five children. "So what?" said Anna. One could
actually see her renewed pleasure in movement, see her fea-
tures brightly reassemble. Gottlieb felt as if he had been under
a steamroller. While Kaltammer was walking into the twilight
of Geneva as a woman from Milan; while Paul Schatz is trying
to inveigle an eternal sixteen-year-old into a boat trip to
Romanshorn—perhaps he's managed it by this time, Schatz
isn't one to give up—while Helmut and Rudi, swathed in
superfluous mufflers, are on a carefree binge à deux—he has
to swallow the information that—the phone again. Hortense
Leistle? No. Dionys. To tell him he has just been ordered to
have all the animals ready to be moved by tomorrow evening.
He had to let Gottlieb know that, didn't he? Absolutely,
Dionys. Wouldn't it be best if Gottlieb could come over again
Tuesday morning in case anything happened at this end?
Gottlieb said: "I'll be over at nine."

Gottlieb stayed by the phone till midnight, then went to bed
totally unfatigued. He couldn't understand why Hortense
Leistle hadn't phoned. He recalled every word of their conversation, once again watched her teacup hands. Hadn't he told

himself then and there that those glances meant absolutely nothing? Lissi Reinhold: Hortense reacts only to figures. Not for a second could he reconcile this statement with his sixteen-year-old. That was just like him! Imagining he shared a feeling with others! For years he simply hadn't been able to understand why Ludwig never came to see him anymore. He was sure he visited the area twice a year. His mother was still alive. Gottlieb couldn't grasp that Ludwig had developed into a man who wanted neither to swim nor ski nor play chess nor shoot pistols nor go fishing nor hike nor play tennis nor lie in a field chewing blades of grass with Gottlieb Zürn. And if Hortense was sixteen and he was clearly a few years younger than she, then all the more reason why she wouldn't want to have anything to do with him. He had had more than one opportunity to learn that. When he looked at women the way he had looked at Hortense Leistle, they became older by the exact number of years that they then put between themselves and him. But he had offered 2.5 to 3 million! Well then, someone else had offered more. Even so she ought to prefer him. That is his innermost emotion. Simple enough: he would like to be preferred. Unilaterally. Everyone should want to be his parents. Everyone should scramble to be allowed to be his mother. And he would like to be allowed to watch this rivalry all the time. He could only hope that this urge was no more than a normal anomaly, a commonplace abnormality. Wanting to suck his thumb, i.e., smoke, was not enough. Wanting to fall into a rhythm like the one at his mother's breast as it breathed in and out. And that breast had been bigger than his head. And where, he would like to know, could it still be found? He'd be there with the speed of light. And the rhythm, too, the one he had been rocked to sleep with in her arms, where is it now? Yes, how can he be expected to fall asleep without the rhythm that he can still feel in every bone and nerve? And rocked to and fro in the baby carriage. How is he to manage without that?

The following day he avoided his office. He sat down in the recess of the patio and watched the storm. He loved the idling of the wind through the trees, that rustling for nothing. He was moved by the vanity of the clouds that command the moment as if forever yet are already dissolving. He couldn't drive to Herdwangen, where he should have been taking down the particulars of a farmhouse. Mrs. Leistle wouldn't phone. And if Baptist Rauh phoned, he would be "out." He couldn't get down to anything until he knew who had been given the Swan Villa. The decision had been made. Against him. But in whose favor? He had to know the name. Then life could go on. He didn't yet know how. It was raining.

Watching the torrents of rain pour down before him as if in glass rods, he saw the summer drown. Dr. Gramer phoned. He was ready to sign the papers. Gottlieb said he would arrange a time with the notary and get back to Dr. Gramer. He hung up and went outside again, sat down in the recess of the patio, and looked at the roses standing in the rain as if they knew. From inside the house he could hear Anna storming around as she did her chores. She seemed as fresh as if nothing had ever happened. Armin joined him. Else lay down beside him. For those two he still counted. They didn't know, would never know, that he hadn't been given the Swan Villa listing. He wanted to associate only with those who didn't know that he hadn't been given the listing. It could be managed. He could do without Lissi Reinhold et al. But the family? Suppose Anna were to ask! He had always kept his defeats a secret from Anna. This time he had shot off his mouth too soon. This time nothing could be kept secret. Of course there was nothing to stop him crawling through the grass down to the garden gate and out along the path toward town. It had stopped raining. The sun had even broken through. The edges of the clouds were glittering at the point of breakthrough. Gottlieb stared into the dazzling brightness that came streaming through the hole in the clouds. Whenever he saw something like that, he still had to think of God. A holdover from his childhood. That brightness breaking through a hole in the clouds comes from God. Behind that brightness dwells God. The brightness, which he now has to look away from because it hurts his eyes, is God. He could persuade himself, when he saw God in this brightness breaking through the clouds, that he was merely reverting to a notion that had taken root in him in his childhood; but that wasn't enough to drive away the feeling that the brightness from the clouds was God. That feeling can only be refuted. But refutation is useless.

The power of that childhood notion cannot be broken by refutation. You ought to have matured, thinks Gottlieb Zürn. It isn't that now you're regressing, you've simply failed to develop. You have remained what you were. Primitive. A child. That's why scientific information has never been able to make any impression on you. Go ahead, crawl around in the garden. Through the wet grass. It'll do you good. I see: so you don't want to compromise. Out of the front door, that's the way you want to go. All the way into town. Coward, I know you're not going to risk it. But who would? Obviously everyone would like to crawl to the center of town and linger on the Münster-Platz or the Hofstatt. But no one was doing it. So he had nothing to reproach himself with. One can really demand too much of oneself. He was no more of a coward than others. Even so, he was the very one who should have done it, he could feel that. Ambition. Fantastic ambition. His old failing. Wanting to impress people, be popular, that was his real motive for everything. Probably he was a politician. Someone who wore himself out in the service of the common good and wanted nothing in return but always to be reelected with 98.8 percent of the vote. And who probably would have lain awake at night till he had chased up the remaining 1.2 percent and persuaded them to change their minds about him. Woe betide him should he fail to find them. He would shiver at night with fear and uncertainty because there were still 1.2 percent who had voted against him. Anyone who was not for him was against him. And for someone to be against him was unbearable. No, he couldn't have stood it for a day, being a politician. To find out so exactly how many people were against one! It's no help at all to know that so-and-so many are *for* one. A negation can never be compensated for.

Now crawl around the room at least, you coward. No, he would prove to everybody by his public crawling into town that he didn't care what they thought of him. For far too long he had been trying to conform. But wasn't crawling just as beautiful when people didn't see it, when he didn't try to prove anything by it? Wasn't it in itself a demonstration of freedom to crawl around even if no one saw him? Wasn't that true freedom? Wasn't he much freer crawling around here alone than if he yielded to the compulsion to prove his freedom, his independence, to other people by crawling? Was there anything freer than this totally unobserved crawling around on his own home ground? Was there anything more meaningless? This much was clear: his crawling would have meaning only if it were seen, would provide proof of his courage and independence only if it took place in public. Since when did he feel he had to make his crawling a test of courage? He'd never intended such a thing. He had wanted to crawl, that was all. In public, though. Into town. But with no particular thought or motive. It had been purely an urge. Now everything was spoiled by thinking and supposing. There was no point in even kneeling down. The whole idea of crawling was ruined. Once again he had made the mistake of mentally presenting his desire to the public for their judgment. If this practice had always been followed, the best things in the world would have remained undone. But he wanted more than anything to run first to Lissi Reinhold, that personification of banality, to ask her what she would think of a person who wanted to crawl into the center of town. Off to the psychiatrist with him, she would say. So, if he should ever again feel this urge: don't strive for publicity, just get down there and start crawling. Even if the crawling is meaningless because no one is aware of it. As meaningless crawling around it is closest to being your crawling and no one else's.

Late that afternoon Magda stood in the doorway and said: "It's too bad, but I'm staying on in school," and her face contorted as if she had meant to smile. It wasn't quite a smile but rather a demonstration of goodwill. Gottlieb sprang up, walked over to her, and touched her on the shoulder. He would rather have given her a kiss.

In the evening Cousin Leonhard arrived. He was satisfied. Pain now only in the legs. Although Regina does look as if she hasn't quite made it yet. Not a trace of color in her face. But Leonhard knows the liver is working again, the gall is flowing, one kidney, he says, is still trying to clown around a bit, he says, but not for long. At supper Magda speaks unprompted. She eats what they all eat. She tells them what they are saying in school about the first Mrs. Terbohm. It seems she left some notes behind. Toward the end, when she was too weak to get up, she wrote on the wall. She stopped eating, she wrote, while her refrigerator was still full. She felt wonderful. It would be horrible not to be able to eat anymore because the refrigerator was empty. She was about to elude that horror forever. Toward the end she seems to have been in a cheerful mood. On the other hand, as always in such cases, carpet fuzz had been found under the fingernails of the dead woman. Magda couldn't stop talking about her. She ought to have gone to see her. After all, she'd been in the same class as Bernhard Terbohm. Now that Bernhard was away at Salem School she should have gone to see his mother. She should have offered to do that when she'd seen Bernhard. She couldn't understand why she hadn't asked him during vacation whether he would like her to visit his mother now and again. His sister is away too, spending a year in Connecticut.

Julia has something much more important to tell them. Stefan Schatz has triumphed over the principal. The complaint barrel will be set up. Only an experiment, but Stefan Schatz is already walking around the school as if he were the principal. Julia insisted it was high time her father grasped that Stefan Schatz is a brutal egocentric. Of course he always throws his weight behind the right kind of projects, fantastic projects always, but for him it's just an ego trip to show all the others what a great guy he is. For her, a person who can't stand being anything but Mr. Big is the lowest of the low. Gottlieb protested, his voice growing louder and louder. That was typically Julia, he said, typical of his children: flabby and limp and bone-lazy themselves, but always quick to rail against those who take on something, put their backs into it, who don't give in until they've achieved something terrific! Of course, if she would rather mooch around than get involved, if she prefers to be ordered about someday by people who've got ahead because she feels it's beneath her to order other people around, then she should simply accept her self-imposed wet-rag existence, but then she shouldn't pick on those who've worked their way up and are now on top forever, above the duds, the dummies, the washouts. . . .

Once again he couldn't control himself. He had to leave the table, go across to his office, and slam the door. As soon as he was seated and the spasm racing through his whole body had subsided, he took a sheet of paper and made a list of all the assets he had acquired. The house with the two vacation apartments, the little house in Immenstaad, mortgage investments, homeowner savings plans, savings accounts. Then he tried to divide these into four parts. He refused to rejoin the family at the table until he had figured out how each of the four children was to acquire some landed property of her own. Each was to have something over which she had sole control. He was seized by the notion of equipping his children to become small but self-sufficient battleships so that they would never be subjected to the will of outsiders. Or so that there would at least be a place where they would be unassailable. He calculated that, if he hung on and circumstances remained favorable, he would have to work another fifteen to twenty years before he had provided his children with enough property to protect them in today's society from the worst experiences. As a child he had loved to build tree houses. High up in the fir trees, he and Ludwig had plaited and patched together tiny huts where they would lie out of reach for days, smoking and playing cards. One's own home, one's own house, those are what used to be weapons. He expected the children to arrive at any moment to accuse him of bringing them into a world where there was no need for them, in which one was only noticed if one asserted oneself. They had developed—and he had no idea how it had happened—this luxurious kind of self-effacement. In school they were embarrassed if a student who had learned something raised his hand to show what he had learned. Only too often he had been summoned by teachers who were stymied because his children failed to take the slightest part in any classroom discussion. What would it be like later on in real life?

When he was thoroughly mired in those difficulties that flourish mainly at night, Claims-Maier phoned. Rudi W. Eitel has disappeared or been arrested: does Gottlieb know anything about it? Claims-Maier was calling from the hospital. All that was left of his steely voice was a croak. He has burst another blood vessel. That'll be the last time. He wished Gottlieb all the best. Gottlieb, the child, must give Rudi, the con man, regards from Helmut, the old soak. Claims-Maier hung up. Gottlieb decided to regard it all as an alcoholic fantasy and went to bed.

As he lay there, Anna's hand moved across. And she talked as though they were once again living in the profoundest peace and everything was turning out right. In a soft, vibrant voice she uttered that sighing tone which tried to sound casual, tried to sound cuddly, that provocative tone which, according to their art of interrelating, should have elicited a responsive tone from Gottlieb. He could only use what he heard in the same way that an astronomer only uses light from a star to measure distance. This distance seemed to him infinite. Obviously Anna no longer had the slightest idea where he was at this particular time. And he felt incapable of telling her. He had no authority over himself. He was not his own master. Full of embarrassment and shame, he must wait for Anna to fall asleep: only then could he return to the scene that was haunted by the unbanishable ghost of the Swan Villa. In this atmosphere of seething hostility, the figures representing his debts flared up; what he saw became a threat; the miniboom writhed, suffocated. Gottlieb grinned. Everything was as unfavorable as it could possibly be. But what did that have to do with him? He was aware that his concern was a pretense. It was, of course, possible to believe that there was nothing *but* this pretense. Yet perhaps there was something else after all. His unconcern. How, if disaster were all there was, could he be grinning?

By nine next morning he was in Mitten. In detective fashion, he again parked a few hundred yards away from the entrance to the driveway. Outside and inside the entrance, and farther along between the gate and the two lime trees that formed the true gateway—lime trees that today for the first time he recognized for what they were, two Royal Highnesses—between the stone gate and the lime-tree Royal Highnesses, then, a whole contingent of vehicles had assembled, most of them yellow in color, miliary in effect. Trucks, power shovels, cranes, fire trucks. And soldiers, as it were. And camp followers. Involuntarily Gottlieb thought: Good Friday. He walked straight to the coachhouse, ran up the steep, narrow staircase, knocked at the kitchen door. Dionys called: "Come in!"

Gottlieb placed the two bottles of wine on the table. Dionys shook his head, waved them away, then gestured toward the villa. At ten they'll start blasting. Gottlieb sat down. Beside Dionys. They both looked out. Dionys pointed to the center of the action. A van. In it three men sat at a table, one of them wearing a yellow hard hat. The demolition foreman. Another is Mr. von Reventlow, an architect. The third one he didn't know. Gottlieb knew him. "His name's Kaltammer," said Gottlieb. The demolition foreman seemed to be explaining his preparations for the blasting with the help of a floor plan. A few workmen were still emerging from the house to report to the van. From time to time the demolition foreman spoke into his walkie-talkie. Dionys had heard that some company had bought the building, was having it blown up and torn down, and was going to build an apartment complex of fifty or a hundred apartments that would cover the entire ground up to where the lime trees now stood. They were going to be removed too. From the buckets of their giraffe-trucks two men were already at work in the treetops with their power saws. "Those trees are under environmental protection, I know that for sure," said Dionys. "Once they're gone," said Gottlieb, "the owner gains an extra ten thousand square feet, which are worth a hundred and fifty thousand marks here, so, even if he's reported, he won't mind paying a ten-thousand-mark fine. That's the way things are done, Dionys."

Yesterday evening, when they came to take away the animals, they had had to shoot the injured swan, whereupon the other swan had turned so ferocious again that they had no choice but to shoot that one too. Then they had expected him to take away the corpses. He had refused. Then they had said that, since the place was going to be blown up anyway, the two carcasses might as well be left in there. That was how he had found out they were going to blast. They've drilled a hundred and fifty blasting holes in the foundations. They got going at five this morning. Everything was going lickety-split because of the pile of money invested in it. Bubi had been missing since yesterday evening. Gottlieb said: "Look!" Kaltammer, the foreman, and the architect had emerged from the van. Lightly built, Kaltammer was a head taller than the other two. His yellow hair rivaled the foreman's hard hat in brightness. Kaltammer always stood with his hands propped over the back of his waist so that his arms stuck out like jug handles. And he always bent his head slightly as if to show people how easy it was to talk to him. Today he was wearing a voluminous beige scarf with his shot-silk raincoat.

At ten o'clock sharp the horn sounded, curious onlookers were pushed back into the area between the lime trees and the gate; the workmen removing the branches of the lime trees were brought down. The demolition foreman pointed out that each person was here at his own risk. Then he pressed. A dull, muffled roar mingled with the shrill tinkle of broken glass. And instantly, shooting out of every cellar window, a dirty cloud of dust in which the house disappeared, the trees disappeared, and the vehicles and the people. Gottlieb coughed. He lost all sense of time. When the dense seething clouds subsided, when the house gradually became visible again, it seemed more like an eternity that had passed rather than an instant. The Swan Villa had apparently survived the assault. Only the ridge of the roof sagged a bit in the middle. The flagpole terrace had tipped sideways. Kaltammer and the architect were not satisfied with the result. They remonstrated with the foreman, who then turned away as if to say there was no point in arguing with laymen. He beckoned to four of his men, and they carried four packages into the house. Kaltammer could only shake his head. The architect tried to reassure him. Kaltammer wouldn't be reassured. He pointed to his wristwatch, spread his fingers in the air, counting them off. The workmen who had to trim the lime trees were hoisted up again. The foreman had followed his men into the house. On their return, one of the workmen walked over to the coach house, opened the door downstairs, and called out: "Dionys, your dog's had it." Bubi was lying in the hall, tied to the hall staircase, which had been left intact by the blasting. The dog didn't seem to be injured either. Maybe it was a heart attack. Brought on by terror. "Leave him there," said Dionys, and placed two glasses on the table and filled them. Gottlieb and he raised their glasses to each other and drank. Dionys closed his eyes as he drank. Because he was doubled up, it looked as if drinking must be the most strenuous thing in the world for him. He remarked that, throughout his life, wines had continued to improve. The tiny gold ring in his ear shone in the dim kitchen.

As soon as the foreman and his assistants came back out of the house, the workmen were lowered from the tops of the lime trees and all the spectators were told to leave the grounds. One more warning, then the second blasting was set off. This time there was hardly any dust cloud at all. The walls could be seen to tremble from the shock. Although the house still stood, it did so only like a man tied to a stake after he has been shot. At once the wrecking crane drove up to the doorway, swung back its arm, and slammed the steel ball against the doorway. The swan relief with the motto was smashed. The ball swung back, struck again: the gable with its melancholy curves did not budge. Dionys said the ball weighed a ton. Engines roared. A bulldozer drove up, two mighty hooks were fastened right and left into the doorway, the bulldozer reversed, the steel cables rose, tightened, the bulldozer halted, reversed again with even more power, reared: a loud crack, the steel cables snapped, the doorway stood. Kaltammer spun around twice on one leg in a kind of pirouette. The foreman personally inserted new charges into the doorway only. After this blast, the gable collapsed under the blow of the steel ball. From two hoses, firemen shot water into the point of collapse. Kaltammer forgave the foreman. He seemed to be congratulating him.

Then Kaltammer and Mr. von Reventlow walked away from the grounds chatting. Dionys mimicked: "Mission accomplished—good show!" And then: "Look, the workmen are happy enough." He pointed to a group of men laughing. He hoped his wife wouldn't be coming right away with Lydia for a visit. He'd already told his wife he might not be able to see Bubi safely through her absence, but he'd been thinking more of the dog's food and exercise. And now he's leaving him in there. Great God in heaven. He must have had quite a fright. But he had been spared a lot of suffering. Who knows how much? Gottlieb got up to leave. How long did Dionys intend to stay here? Until the first, said Dionys, then off to the old people's home. Gottlieb said he would drop by and look in on Dionys. Gottlieb had better things to do than visit him at the old people's home, said Dionys. "Don't be silly," said Gottlieb. "You'll see, I'll be there." He wasn't going to let Dionys die of thirst. "Whatever you say," said Dionys. By the time Gottlieb was outside, the lime trees already looked like cripples. Workmen were in process of erecting a billboard over the fragments of the demolished hedge. Gottlieb read: LUXURY APARTMENTS UNDER CONSTRUCTION. At the sight of the barber shop across the street, he knew where he had to go.

He drove very slowly. At the site of the car crash he took a deep breath. At the barber's he had to wait an hour. But he didn't want a newspaper. When Gottlieb sat wrapped in the sheet, the barber said: "The usual?" And as usual Gottlieb said: "The usual." After that—as was usual too—only the barber spoke. Whenever Gottlieb goes out the door after the procedure, a shiver runs through him. Even in summer. If he could, he would always turn around, hurry back, and ask if he might sit down under the barber's sheet again. Not that he felt especially happy under those wrappings. Rather he sat there as if suffering from tetanus. Every few seconds he had to command himself to loosen his legs, to release his feet from clenching the foot support like a bird clinging to its perch. He had to keep telling himself: There was absolutely no risk that the barber would cut his scalp. This fear went back to the days of that first barber, whose shop is across from the gate to the Swan Villa. That barber had instructions from Gottlieb's mother to crop his hair as close as possible. To do this he had used an implement that probably corresponded to the modern ones powered by electricity. In those days he wasn't going to waste any current on kids paying thirty pfennigs. So when he nicked the scalp with his clippers and the child gave a little shriek he would shout, Couldn't they sit still for a few minutes? One accepted the blame foisted upon one in this way in the hope of not having to put up with intentional nicks plus those unavoidable ones caused by the hand clippers. Looking back, nowhere had it ever again been as pleasant as under the blue-and-white checked sheet of that first barber. Nowhere since then had the anticipated injuries ever been as harmless. Now, again, Gottlieb would have gladly remained longer than necessary under the sheet. He imagined that the longer he sat under the sheet the smaller he became. Eventually he would become so small that the barber could completely comb him away. After that he would find himself in the brush the barber used to clean his comb. He had never yet seen what the barber used to clean the brush, so there was no way of knowing where he would finally end up.

Back in the car he realized he couldn't possibly drive home. He phoned Anna. The Swan Villa had been blown up, he said, and went on talking before she could make any comment. He had to drive right now to Herdwangen to take particulars of a farmhouse. He brightened his voice as much as he could. He hoped Anna and the kids were feeling as fine as he did. She knew that taking particulars of farmhouses was his favorite pastime since after two semesters of church architecture and graduating from law school he had become a real estate agent in the hope of being able to specialize in farmhouses. He spoke rapidly, impetuously, forestalling any comment. And please, Anna, send a telegram to Baptist Rauh: Swan Villa blown up, stop. Construction company outbid everyone. Regards Zürn. Then he drove slowly away toward the hills. Oh damn, he should have told Anna that Paul Schatz didn't get the Swan Villa either. Kaltammer did. Neither Schatz nor Zürn, but Kaltammer. Claims-Maier is the real genius. He recognizes the law, the system. You don't have the Swan Villa on your conscience. It's all very simple. That's why you can grin while the car slowly eats up the rises and dips gently through the hollows. You are a person who at this moment is driving to a job he likes doing. Thrusting your nose into the smells of a centuries-old farmhouse, smells that change sharply from room to room, letting your fingers run sensitively over old wood, discovering skills developed to cope with needs, a lovely afternoon.

He delayed driving home until he could be sure the girls would be asleep. Anna was already in bed too. But she was still reading a book about earth radiations. He lay down as closely as possible beside her. On noticing that he wanted to lie beside her she had stretched out her arm. She went on reading but gently pressed him to her. Anyone who came in the door now would have thought she was protecting him. Hadn't everything he had ever heard from his father conveyed that he had to be protected by his wife? He looked at the place on the curtain behind which was the camera. Tomorrow he'd move it into his office. The family will be told that it was acquired so that prospective clients could take home instant pictures of properties they had been shown; occasional use by the family was a possibility. At some future time he could still take his revenge on Anna with the camera. How feeble the notions of revenge he had recently been harboring against Anna now seemed! She went on reading because last night he hadn't listened to her. She would go on reading for centuries if he didn't show that he was sorry about his failure to respond last night. According to the code of their art of interrelating, it was up to him to appeal to her. He would appeal to her as soon as he could. His smashing up of the car had been harmoniously matched by his debacle with Mrs. Leistle. All he could say at the moment would be: Anna, Schatz didn't get the Swan Villa either. Not even Schatz. But Kaltammer. Of course Kaltammer. But even Kaltammer . . .

Gottlieb realized that he had actually put something behind him. Hadn't all his hostile notions toward somebody always seemed artificial? It was just that he hadn't admitted it. He had believed he must be able to see himself as an adversary. But as soon as he had felt hostile toward a person, hadn't he lost the ground from under his feet? And as soon as he felt or spoke *for* a person, he sensed how true that was. Moreover, a warmth immediately emanated from whatever he said in favor of another person. After saying something against Schatz or Kaltammer he always felt troubled, as if he had wounded himself. Did he really? Or was he dragging that idea out of his hothouse of illusions so that he could finally fall asleep? He could still grin, couldn't he? Inwardly at least. Had he ever before felt so clearly that Kaltammer and Schatz could fade within him? Even if it were life itself that had to fade in order for those two to become less important to him, he wouldn't mind. Perhaps, now that the Swan Villa was in heaven, it was true that an era had passed.

He snuggled up to Anna like the nesting blackbird that snuggles to make its materials pliant. Maybe he should try sending a final message to Mrs. Leistle, saying it would have been almost incredible had she strayed so far from her inherent nature that she would have entrusted the Swan Villa to him. Things being what they were, that had always been impossible. His friend Helmut had told him so. He and she had nothing in common. Not a word, not a gesture. The *Eroica* again. Through shimmering doors. And, as a farewell, with its ending. An ending must be impersonal. Bring on the rush of the finale, the thunder of the ending, no rhyme or reason. Opus 55, if you please. E-flat, if you please. So what are you looking for! The same age as the composer's when he made that music: that's how old he felt now too. The triumph of experience over imagination.

He turned toward Anna. She had fallen asleep. He removed her book from the quilt, switched off the light, and withdrew carefully to his own side. Grin, can't you. And blow your nose. Then you can fall asleep too. At the moment his only breaths were those he took consciously. He groped for his handkerchief, withdrew with the handkerchief under his quilt, closed himself off on all sides, and began to blow his nose; but, out of consideration for Anna's sleep, he blew it slowly and softly. Suddenly the quilt was pulled back from his head, and Anna asked in a voice of alarm: "Gottlieb, what's the matter?" Now he blew his nose loud and strong. She asked why he wasn't asleep. He asked why she wasn't asleep. She said, because he wasn't asleep. "So now I have to sleep so you can sleep," he said. "Yes," she said, "go to sleep now." That was not just a selfish wish, it was also the conferring of the strength needed to fall asleep. Gottlieb wanted to say Thank you! to Anna, but for that he already felt too heavy.